I0563053

Under the Dragon's Shadow

by

D.G. Schulman

Flying Dragons: A Martial Arts Saga

Cover Art by *Lisa Dawn MacDonald*

The Wild Rose Press, Inc.
PO Box 708
Adams Basin, NY 14410-0708
Visit us at www.thewildrosepress.com

Publishing History
First Edition, 2025
Trade Paperback ISBN 978-1-5092-6308-0
Digital ISBN 978-1-5092-6309-7

Flying Dragons: A Martial Arts Saga
Published in the United States of America

Dedication

To Master Tadashi Yamashita,
With deepest respect and gratitude for your
unparalleled dedication to the martial arts and the
wisdom you have imparted to so many, including my
husband, whose journey as a black belt under your
guidance has been a cornerstone of our family's life.
This book, born from years immersed in the principles
and stories of martial arts, is a tribute to the discipline,
resilience, and honor that your teachings exemplify.
Thank you for inspiring a legacy that reaches far
beyond the dojo.

Part One 1978

Chapter 1

Payoff
Jon
New York, New York

The sound of barking stopped Jon cold.

He froze on the crowded street, his breath caught in his throat, his hand tightening around the strap of the blue duffel bag slung across his chest. The black pit bull emerged from the alley, teeth bared, eyes steely with lethal intent. It charged straight for him, its growl rising above the honking horns and shuffle of pedestrians.

Jon's instincts kicked in. The dog leaped. Jon moved. His hand shot out, gripping the beast by the throat. With a sharp, practiced twist, he flung the dog to the ground. The animal let out a pitiful yelp before lying motionless, blood pooling on the pavement.

He stared, his heart pounding as the reality of what he'd done hit him. The pit bull hadn't chosen this life— it had been shaped for violence. Just like him.

The smell of garbage and hot pretzels clung to the air, mixing with the faint tang of iron from the dog's blood, now streaking his jacket. Around him, the crowd barely reacted. New York didn't ask questions.

Jon crouched over the lifeless animal, the weight of

regret settling heavily on his chest. Just weeks ago, his sister, Kim, had asked him, "Do you ever regret the choices you make?" Her eyes had searched his face as if she already knew the answer.

Of course, he regretted it. The choices, the life, the people he'd trusted—all of it. But he couldn't tell her that. Not then. Not now.

He took a shuddering breath, forcing himself to his feet. The cab driver he'd hailed only moments ago was staring wide-eyed at the scene. Jon reached for the cab door, desperate to leave, but the driver shook his head, threw the car into gear, and sped off. Jon's bloodied fingers scraped against the yellow paint, leaving streaks behind as the vehicle disappeared into traffic. He stood frozen on the crowded sidewalk, stranded and exposed.

The duffel bag hung impossibly heavy, its contents—bundles of hundred-dollar bills—pressing against him like the weight of a death sentence. He had less than two hours to get to the docks and vanish aboard a cargo ship, but every minute on the streets put him closer to his demise.

He ducked into the crowd. Any of these strangers could be the one to end him. The prostitute on the corner. The blind magazine vendor. Even the hot dog vendor. His picture was everywhere by now. They'd be looking for the short, solid American with the coarse black hair, the wide almond-shaped eyes, and the high forehead they'd once laughed at. The "half-Chinese courier," they'd called him, but the price on his head was full-sized. He kept his head down and tried to blend in to the crowd. Impossible.

No one left the Flying Dragons. Not alive, anyway.

The weight of Daniel Wu's words echoed in his

mind. "The only way out is in a box." As a retired New York City police officer, Wu would know.

Wu's warning had haunted Jon since Friday. Three days ago, he'd been preparing for a routine drop—his last errand as a courier for Sifu Qiu and the Flying Dragons. But when Jon overheard plans for his assassination, his whole world shattered.

"The American is expendable," Sifu had said. "We use him. Then we bury him."

Sifu Qiu wasn't content with controlling Pell Street and Doyle Street anymore. His appetite for power and wealth had grown, and Jon had become a pawn in Sifu's latest game—international drug trafficking. The duffel bag he now carried had been intended for the Chinese Triad's Golden Triangle heroin—a million dollars in cash, the final piece of a deal Sifu had struck to expand his empire.

But Jon knew too much. And the Flying Dragons couldn't afford to leave loose ends.

"You half Chinese, I half teach you kung fu," Sifu's voice taunted him in his head. The insult burned as much now as it had the day it was said. Six years of training, and he'd been nothing but a tool to them. A courier, a pawn.

Chung, Sifu's eldest son and heir to the Flying Dragons, had been his enforcer. Jon had sparred with him before, but it was never a fair fight. Chung was faster, stronger, and deadlier—a ruthless extension of his father's ambition.

Jon's fingers brushed the star-shaped darts hidden in his jacket pocket. Sifu's mocking laugh echoed in his mind.

"Kung fu too hard. I teach you something simpler."

The memory flashed sharp and vivid—the day Sifu had tossed the weapon onto the training mat, calling it a *mei hua dart*. Back then, it had seemed like a curiosity, too small to matter. But Jon had trained relentlessly, mastering its lethal accuracy. Now its sharp edges gleamed, ready to strike.

Jon had adapted quickly, learning to control the throwing stars with exacting skill. A properly thrown dart, Sifu had said, could pierce the retina and penetrate the brain. He'd demonstrated once, striking a wooden board with enough force to make the weapon quiver on impact. "Simple," Sifu had said, "but deadly. If you miss, no second chance."

Jon's chest tightened as he glanced at his watch. Ninety minutes.

He turned a corner and nearly ran straight into a man emerging from a convenience store. The man muttered a curse, but Jon barely heard it. His senses prickled with the unmistakable feeling of being watched.

They were here.

It started with shadows—figures slipping out of doorways, rounding the corners of buildings. Five of them, dressed inconspicuously in dark jackets and jeans, but their intent was unmistakable. They weren't only after the money in his duffel bag. They were after him.

Jon's breath quickened as they fanned out, cutting off his escape. His gaze darted to the alley behind him, then back to the brotherhood closing in. He couldn't outrun them. The code of the warrior was engraved in his bones. *First, you hurt. If necessary, you maim. Without alternative, you kill.*

The first attacker lunged. Jon sidestepped, his palm slamming into the man's nose with a brutal shatter of cartilage. The man dropped, blood pouring from his face.

Another rushed in—a boy, no older than eighteen. Jon recognized him as one of Sifu's younger students. His spin kick was flashy but poorly executed. Jon punished the mistake with a sharp sidekick to his knee, and the joint collapsed with a grotesque crack.

Two more attackers came at him simultaneously. One overcommitted, slipping on the blood-streaked pavement and landing awkwardly. The other struck a glancing blow to Jon's ribs, but Jon countered with a gouge to the man's eyes. The scream that followed was guttural, raw.

The last assailant stood fifteen feet away, reaching into his jacket. Jon's hand was already in his pocket. The dart flew before the man's gun cleared the holster. The blade hit its mark, embedding itself into the man's eye.

Silence fell. He stood amid broken bodies, blood spattered across his leather jacket. He scanned the street, searching for more attackers, but the pedestrians around him hurried past, stepping over the fallen as though nothing had happened.

He wiped the sweat from his face, his head pounding from the exertion. His watch read seventy-five minutes. He adjusted the duffel bag, adrenaline keeping him moving. He spotted an alley leading toward the river and took off at a sprint.

He didn't hear the cars until it was too late.

A gray sedan screeched to a stop in front of him, blocking the alley. Behind him, a burgundy van idled at the mouth of the street.

The sedan's door opened, and a figure emerged—a tall, broad-shouldered warrior with a deep crimson headband tied around his forehead. The gold embroidery glinted in the afternoon light—the coiled dragon and sword of the Flying Dragons.

Chung.

Jon steadied his breathing, forcing his focus. He'd faced three, even four opponents before—but Chung was different. His technique was razor-sharp, his strikes unforgiving. He wasn't just strong—he was the heir. Sifu's successor.

Chung didn't waste time. He closed the distance with the speed of a coiled spring, snapping a low kick toward Jon's knee. Jon deflected it, but Chung was relentless. His elbow slammed into Jon's ribs, and a backfist to the temple sent Jon staggering.

"Come on, American," Chung sneered, his Cantonese-accented English dripping with disdain. "Show me what Sifu taught you. Or is this all you've got?"

Jon gritted his teeth and launched a desperate front kick aimed at Chung's chest. But Chung sidestepped smoothly, grabbed Jon's ankle mid-air, and swept his supporting leg out from under him.

Jon slammed into the pavement, the duffel bag cushioning the impact but sending a sharp jolt though his body. Pain exploded across his back, but he didn't have time to think. He tried to roll away, but Chung was already there, driving his knee into Jon's sternum and pinning him in place.

"This is why you'll never be one of us," Chung said, his face inches from Jon's. His hand clamped around Jon's throat like a vice. "You don't belong. You never did."

Jon clawed at Chung's arm, lungs burning. A dart was in his pocket—his fingers fumbled for it. But before he could draw the weapon, Chung's fist crashed into the side of his head.

Pain erupted in his skull and sent shards of red glass across his vision. The world tilted violently. His grip on the dart loosened as darkness began to creep into the edges of his vision.

Chung's cold, satisfied smile was the last thing he saw before everything went black.

When Jon came to, he was slumped in the back seat of the sedan, his head throbbing. The taste of blood filled his mouth, and his vision swam. He reached for the duffel bag. It was still there, shoved onto the floor near his feet.

Chung sat in the front seat, one hand on the wheel, the other holding the bulky bag phone to his ear. He spoke calmly, smugly.

"Fuqin Shifu," Chung said with a quiet chuckle, glancing in the rearview mirror. "The American gave us some trouble, but he's done now. We'll clean up and deliver the money."

Jon forced his breathing to stay shallow and even, his eyelids half-closed. Chung appeared confident he was still unconscious—*helpless.* But Jon's mind sharpened, pulling focus from the pounding in his skull to what was in his pocket.

His fingers brushed the familiar weight of the *mei hua biao*—the dart hidden in his jacket. Small. Lethal. Exact. Though his hands trembled, Jon gripped the weapon tighter. The blades were cold, unforgiving. It was not meant for close quarters—but it would have to do.

His vision blurred, but his mind sharpened as his fingers brushed the chain around his neck—the medical alert tag. It dangled loosely from his collar, its cool metal pressing into his skin.

A sharp pang stabbed his chest. His mother had given it to him when he was six, engraving his name, address, and *penicillin allergy* on the back. He'd worn it ever since. It was a part of him.

The cold, star-shaped weapon was as familiar to him as his own hands. Its four razor-sharp blades gleamed faintly in the dim light. It was meant to fly, to strike from a distance—but right now, Jon had no other choice.

He gripped the weapon tightly at its center, his knuckles white.

The sedan slowed as it approached an intersection. Chung cursed at a driver, barking something in Cantonese.

Jon struck.

With a sudden lunge, he drove the dart into the side of Chung's temple. The blades hit with a wet snap. Blood sprayed across the front seat as Chung lurched forward, his face locked in shock. The sedan jerked violently, slammed a curb, and Jon was thrown sideways against the back door.

He didn't wait. He kicked the door open and hurled himself onto the pavement. Pain shot up his side as he hit hard and rolled, the world spinning in a blur.

Behind him, the car careened through the intersection, slammed into a parked delivery truck, and flipped onto its roof. Screams erupted as pedestrians scattered.

Only Jon ran toward the wreck.

He crouched beside the crumpled driver's window. Chung was already dead. Jon's hands shook as he unclasped his medical alert chain and draped it loosely around Chung's neck.

A sharp scent hit him—gasoline. A dark river snaked from the ruptured tank, pooling beneath the car. He reached into his pocket for a lighter, then froze—his duffel bag. It was wedged behind the headrest.

Jon snatched it, made sure no one was watching, and flicked the lighter to life. He dropped it into the spreading fuel and bolted.

The explosion came a second later, a deafening roar that tore through the intersection. Heat seared Jon's back as a fireball engulfed the car. The blast's force sent him sprawling, his arms instinctively shielding his head as shards of glass and metal rained down around him. For a moment, he lay there, gasping for air, his chest heaving. The ringing in his ears faded as his mind caught up to what had just happened.

They'll find it.

The necklace, wrapped around what remained of Chung's body. They'd believe Jon had been in the front seat. They'd believe the explosion had claimed him.

It wasn't perfect—nothing ever was—but it would buy him time. Time to disappear.

He forced himself to his feet, every muscle screaming in protest. The duffel bag was still clutched in his hands, its weight dragging him forward.

The docks loomed ahead. He stumbled toward them, every step an act of will. His family's faces flashed in his mind. His mother and father. His sister, Kim. His best friend, Ethan.

He wouldn't see them again—not anytime soon.

Survival demanded everything now.

And Jon had nothing left.

Chapter 2

Borings
Kim
Zilwaukee, Michigan

Kim knelt in the dirt, taking borings and soil samples near the Zilwaukee Bridge. A memory from last Tuesday night seared her mind, the night when Officer Gonsky had arrived with life-altering news.

"Jon Fenton appears to have died in a car fire yesterday in New York City." Gonsky's voice was grave, just delivering the facts.

"No! Not my Jonny, he can't be—" her mother cried in shock and disbelief, tears cascading down her cheeks.

"Officer, we'll need proof of my son's death," Dad had said, his voice tight as he held Mom.

They had few details, only a scorched medical alert tag.

Adjusting a red bandana over her thick, black hair, she pulled another one up just below her eyes, both to shield from the dust of the relentless traffic and to catch the tears she blinked away. Kim, a civil and environmental engineer, was investigating soil composition and grade for a proposed Michigan Department of Transportation project to construct new on- and off-ramps in the M13 interchange.

She rose, brushing dirt off her worn jeans, gazing at

the calm and shining Saginaw River. The sun glittered on the surface, disguising the industrial contamination beneath. Rob, the newest hire, was gone, fueling her frustration after she'd learned his starting salary significantly surpassed hers, despite her two years on the job. This coupled with the revelation of her brother Jon's mysterious death had her emotions oscillating between grief, anger, and disbelief.

On the deserted sandy stretch near the river, a foreign blue compact sedan pulled up. The setting sun cast long shadows as a lone man, dressed in black denim and a tight-fitted black T-shirt, approached her. His Asian features looked out of place in this remote area.

"Excuse me," he said, his voice cool. "Do you know how to get to St. Mary's Medical Center?"

His question was ordinary, but the intensity of his gaze was not. Kim hesitated, sensing something amiss, but responded, "M13 south, along the Saginaw Bay, straight to downtown Saginaw."

His eyes never leaving hers, he murmured a thank you. But just as Kim began to feel relief, he added, "One more thing. Where's your brother?"

"My who?" A chill raced down her spine.

"Your brother, Jon. Where is he?" His eyes narrowed, and his voice turned cold.

Trying to keep her voice steady, she said, "He died in a car fire last week. Who are you? How do you know my brother?"

A dark smile played on his lips. "So, really, where is he now? And where is the money?"

She hurriedly climbed into the driver's seat of the red pickup truck, started the engine, and hit the accelerator. Her heart raced. Her mind buzzed with questions. Was Jon still alive? What did this man know about her brother? The last thing she knew, Jon was in NYC, engrossed in his studies and his passion for kung fu in a club in Chinatown. The police thought her brother was dead. This man was convinced he was alive. What the hell had her brother gotten himself into?

Chapter 3

Homecoming
Ethan
Grand Rapids, Michigan

"I caught an earlier flight, Dad," Ethan murmured, hugging his father tightly. As a boy, he had always seen his father as strong and invincible. But now, at sixty-three, he appeared diminished and vulnerable. Ethan's concerns deepened, especially about the impending coronary bypass surgery.

"You didn't need to come. I'm fine." His father's smile was weak.

"Traveling on Thanksgiving Day is a dream. The flight was nearly empty; guess everyone else made it home yesterday." Guilt probed at his edges. He'd been away too long. He needed to be here, supporting his father.

"First Thanksgiving without your mother," his father said, his eyes misting. "It's been hard."

"I know, Dad. I miss her too. It doesn't feel the same without her."

"There's something else, Ethan. Martha and Robert Fenton invited us for dinner. They insisted. Said it wouldn't be right without you. Kim will be there too."

"That's good to hear. It'll be nice to see them." Ethan smiled at the thought of Kim.

"But there's more. Something you need to know. Jon is missing, Ethan. They think he's dead."

"What? What happened?" A lead weight dropped in his stomach.

"The police found Jon's medical alert tag in a car fire in New York last month. The chief medical examiner is investigating, but they believe he died in the fire."

"I didn't know. I've had three postcards from Jon in as many years. He kept his distance…wouldn't let me in." Ethan was stunned.

"Martha and Robert are devastated. They're hoping you might know something."

"I wish I did. This is the first I've heard of it." Ethan shook his head, still reeling from the shock.

As the sun began to set, Ethan and Will stood on the Fentons' wide front porch, both dressed neatly for the holiday. Ethan reached over and adjusted the knot in his father's tie, giving it a gentle tug into place. He needed to be here.

When Martha Fenton answered the door, Ethan handed her a large basket of flowers in rich autumn hues.

Martha gasped and threw her arms around him in joy. "Welcome back, Ethan! Good to have one of my boys back for Thanksgiving! Robert, look who's here."

Robert gripped Dad's hand in a two-handed shake and led them into the living room where a football game blared on the television. "Now let's get down to business and relax. Help yourself to snacks on the sideboard. The fridge and the bar are stocked with drinks. What can I get you?"

"A beer is good for me," Dad said.

"Have they scheduled your surgery yet, Will?" Robert reached into the fridge, screwed the cap off a longneck amber bottle, and handed it to Dad.

"The bypass is booked for four weeks from Monday. I'm told a drink a day can prevent stiff arteries." Dad winked and raised his bottle. "Cheers to good health!"

The Fentons' home, warm and welcoming, seemed unchanged. But Kim, she was unrecognizable. The fifteen-year-old girl he remembered was now a stunning woman. He didn't anticipate how glad he would be to see her.

Kim's almond eyes widened slightly as she set down her magazine, a wistful smile crossing her lips as she gazed at him. The feeling was mutual.

"So you finished that eastern medicine thing at UCLA?" Robert's voice broke through the silence.

"Yes, I was at the American College of Traditional Chinese Medicine." Ethan sank into the worn tan sofa beside Kim.

"What the devil was that all about?" Robert cracked open two more amber bottles of beer, the hiss filling the room. He handed one to Ethan and kept the other for himself. Before setting it on the table, he took a long pull.

Ethan delved into discussions about his studies in acupuncture and Chinese medicine, sensing a mixture of curiosity and defiance from Robert.

Dad interjected, "He could have been a real doctor." He lifted his bottle to his lips and took a deliberate swallow.

Robert's eyes narrowed. "Isn't that where they stick you with needles?"

"Yeah, very fine needles. Most people don't feel it at all, and there are plenty of health benefits. Are you game to try it?" Ethan leaned forward, excited to share his passion.

"No, sir! After the army, I swore off needles. Being shot at was nothing compared to those needles…" Robert's voice trailed off as he gave a visible shudder.

Ethan caught the flicker of something distant and dark in Robert's eyes.

Silence settled over the room for a moment, thick with hidden thoughts.

Finally, Robert cleared his throat and looked directly at Ethan. "Have you kept up with your martial arts training?"

"Absolutely. My commitment has only deepened over the years. I went through a series of local instructors in San Francisco, and then I got lucky. I was referred to the renowned Sifu Hin in San Luis Obispo."

Robert's eyebrows shot up. "Sifu Hin? That's impressive."

"Yeah, he took me under his wing. I met with him weekly, and it took everything to the next level—opened up a whole new world for me."

Robert nodded approvingly. "I'm glad to hear that. You and Jon always had such potential. It's good to know you stuck with it."

"Jon and I used to talk about those tournaments you took us to," Ethan said, smiling. "Those were some of the best times of our lives."

"I remember." Robert's eyes softened. "You were like a second son to me. It's good to see you've grown into the man I always knew you could be."

Martha burst into the living room, apron-clad and indignant. "Robert, for God's sake, how can you hear the boy with that box blaring?" She turned down the volume, the room suddenly quieter. "Ethan, you must tell me, when was the last time you heard anything from Jon?"

"Martha, we were just—"

"Oh, there'll be time for that," she interrupted, her voice anxious. "Police found Jon's medical alert tag in a car fire last month. He's disappeared, Ethan. They think he's dead!"

Ethan's mind was still reeling with the news his father had shared, a storm of thoughts he couldn't untangle. Every face was suddenly marked with worry. "I can't believe this is happening." The words tumbled out before he could stop them. "In the last few years, Jon pulled away from me. No calls, no visits, just silence. I thought he wanted it that way, that he didn't need us. But now…" He paused, his throat tightening, unable to finish his thought. His gut churned. Had he missed the signs? Could he have done more?

Martha's voice cracked as she continued, "The New York City Chief Medical Examiner is investigating." Her voice faltered, her hands wringing her apron. "Oh, that turkey's going to dry right out if we don't eat it. Let's all come to the table."

Ethan tried to shake off the gloom with casual talk over dinner, but the weight of Jon's disappearance hung heavily in the air. As Kim passed the mashed potatoes, she casually mentioned her encounter with an Asian man at the Zilwaukee Bridge site who had been asking about Jon's whereabouts.

"Oh my God!" Martha's hands flew to cover her mouth. "This happened at your work site?"

Robert's eyes were clouded with concern as he ran his hand over his thinning hair. "Someone believes Jon is still alive and is banking on him contacting his family."

Ethan pushed back his chair. "But they don't have

any proof."

"My heart tells me Jon is alive." Kim's face was pale, but her voice was steady. "Until I see proof otherwise, I have to believe that. But it seems like Jon was mixed up in something shady. I thought that was the case when I visited him in New York last fall and he took me to his kung fu club in Chinatown."

"That might explain Jon's disappearance." Ethan spoke in a low deliberate voice. "Martial arts isn't just about balance and self-control. It has a dark side too—triads, Chinese-American gangs—they've turned it into a tool for power and violence. But that's just a small corner of the larger martial arts world."

Robert interrupted. "I never thought I'd see the day when I'd worry about my children being unsafe because of some martial arts gang."

Kim's gaze locked on Ethan. "But there has to be something we can do."

"What I do know is that Jon is smart and skilled. He loves his family and friends. He wouldn't do anything to put those he loves at risk. If he's alive, as others suspect, contacting us would only put everyone in jeopardy. And he would never do that. We have to trust that he will reach out to us when it's safe." Ethan held Kim's gaze, steady and unwavering, and silently hoped she'd understand.

"Someone is watching and believes we might lead them to Jon," Will said, his voice firm with quiet resolve.

The quiet murmurs around the table were punctuated by the sound of utensils clinking against the plates. Ethan's words hung in the air. A sense of dread coiled deep inside him. He hoped Jon was still alive, but the silence from the others only deepened his doubt.

"Ethan's right. We need to be careful and watchful. And…we need to believe in Jon. He's strong and determined. No one is to speak to the police. That will only put Jon in further trouble once he comes home, not to mention that we don't know if the criminal group has informants in the police. Even with the little we know, it is obvious Jon was involved in some questionable activities, likely illegal. We just don't know the extent." Robert exhaled slowly, then squared his shoulders, his tone leaving no room for argument.

Kim lifted her chin and drew in a long breath as she started to clear the table. Ethan helped, their movements almost mechanical.

"Stop that, you two," Martha said, her eyes brimming with love. "Get out and take a walk. It's a beautiful evening. The young shouldn't be holed up here with us old folks. Fresh air will do you good."

With a heavy silence, they stepped out of the warm, glowing house and into the crisp autumn air. The chill bit at Ethan's skin, and the rustling leaves amplified the quiet tension between them. The soft luminescence of the moon cast faint shadows across the yard, and the crunch of fallen leaves punctuated each step as they moved deeper into the night. His breath clouded in the cold air, mingling with the foreboding pressing against his chest.

Kim stopped suddenly, turning to him. Her brows drawn tight, worry etched into every line of her face. "Ethan, do you really believe Jon is alive?"

Her question hit him harder than he expected. He held her gaze, the mix of hope and fear twisting inside him. "It's likely," he said at last, his voice low. "But there's another side to Jon we haven't talked about. Your brother has a fire in him—an obsession that can blind him to everything else. And in his pursuit, I don't know what he'd sacrifice to get what he wants." He paused, the words catching. "That intensity…it's always scared me. But it's also what makes him remarkable."

She shivered beside him, her arm slipping through his as they walked, her movements hesitant but deliberate. The weight of his words hung between them. "Ethan, I don't feel safe. Can you teach me to protect myself? Can you teach me kung fu?" Her voice was barely more than a whisper in the darkness.

His mind was a battlefield, torn between the life he'd left behind and the uncertain path ahead. *I can't go back to California. Not now, maybe not ever.*

California was impossibly far now, its pull dimmed by everything churning inside him. He was drawn to Kim—her quiet strength, the way she saw through chaos and saw what mattered. Being near her steadied him, like she filled a space in him he hadn't realized was empty.

The autumn landscape around him, bathed in the soft silver glow, echoed that pull—maybe this was a chance to rebuild. Home. Family. A place to put down roots and pass on what he knew to those who needed it.

But Jon's disappearance still hung over everything. His father's fragility, Kim's safety, the questions no one could answer—it was all tangled up in something he hadn't expected but couldn't walk away from anymore.

Ethan turned to Kim, resting his hand on her arm, his eyes meeting hers. "Yes," he said. "I'll teach you kung fu."

Something shifted between them. This wasn't just about Jon anymore. It was about what came next.

Chapter 4

Passage
Jon
New York to Sweden

Jon barely noticed the synchronized ballet of cranes moving gigantic colored containers onto the massive cargo ships, each destined for foreign shores. Among these vessels was the SS *Liberty*, his escape route. For this plan to work, he had to pass as the man in the forged passport, the fair-haired "John Smith."

He spotted a nearby restroom, hurried inside, and locked the rusted door behind him. The air was thick and stale, carrying faint traces of industrial cleaners mixed with the reek of urine. He didn't have a second to waste. He pulled baking soda, hydrogen peroxide, and protective gloves from his bag and swiftly combined the ingredients to form a gritty paste. Gingerly, he applied it to his dark hair and eyebrows, ensuring even coverage to prevent any conspicuous patches. He covered his head with a shower cap, hoping the trapped heat would accelerate the bleaching process.

Daniel Wu's words echoed in his mind. *No one ever leaves the Flying Dragons alive.* But Jon was determined to prove him wrong. He would feign his death, disappear into the shadows, and safeguard his family from afar. Wu had promised to keep tabs on them, send reports and photos. Jon trusted him, the retired Chinese cop turned PI who had warned him of Sifu's true nature. Learning Sifu was not the master he'd imagined was a bitter pill. The errands Jon had run for Sifu were surely illegal, drug-related. This final errand, a trap meant to kill him, had failed. But Jon had survived.

He slipped his hand into his pocket and touched the key to his family home. He knew he might never see them again, but this small piece of his past would always remind him of his love and connection to them. His poor judgment had led him here, but his love for his family would guide him forward. He would find a new path, far from the reach of the Flying Dragons.

Twenty agonizing minutes later, the dark hue of his eyebrows had transitioned to a golden brown. The fear of his hair turning an awkward shade of orange ebbed away. At the half hour mark, he rinsed away the paste, revealing hair that, while not perfectly matching the passport, was close enough.

As Jon boarded the SS *Liberty*, the scrutiny of the crew was unmistakable. Officer Lopez, the second-in-command, approached and introduced himself, his sharp gaze studying every detail, comparing the man before him with the image on the passport.

Jon's tension tightened across his shoulders, but his composure remained steady as he locked eyes with Lopez. When the officer finally smiled and handed back the passport, relief surged through Jon, though he gave no outward sign.

"Your accommodations are ready." Lopez tapped a finger against the manifest. "We were starting to wonder if you were going to make it. Once we're launched, I'll show you to your room and give you a tour of the ship."

As the ship's engines rumbled to life, Jon stood on the forward deck, watching the shoreline recede. The air carried the tang of salt and fuel, a stark contrast to the heavy, stale scent of the city he was leaving behind. A strange calm settled over him. He was free. He was alive. And he would find his way, no matter where it led.

The ship's horn cut through the night, a low resonant sound that seemed to echo his decision to let go of the past. He turned to the horizon, a vast moonlit expanse of the sea opening before him, bound for Sweden. A new beginning awaited, yet the weight of regret settled heavily in his heart.

In the city, he'd once been a man full of dreams, seeking mastery under Sifu Qiu. To earn a place in the academy, he had crafted a story of lineage, training harder than anyone else to prove himself. But betrayal had met him there—a humiliation he couldn't erase.

The memory rose unbidden. The tournament had been the culmination of months of training, every movement of his kata sharp, controlled. But the judges gave him the lowest scores. Laughter erupted. The jeers of his peers cut deeper than any blow.

"What went wrong?" Jon asked Sifu, his voice trembling with disbelief.

"The duck walk kata is from Islamic kung fu and not taken seriously here. You think you half Chinese, I half teach you," Sifu replied, his words cold and dismissive. The sting of that rejection had followed Jon ever since.

Now, standing beneath a canopy of stars, Jon understood. Sifu had been right. He had only gone halfway, never fully committing to his path. His mastery remained ahead of him, waiting for him to claim it.

Alone on the forward deck, Jon began to move.

Under the moonlight, his body flowed with the elements: metal, water, wood, fire, and earth. The rhythm steadied his thoughts, sharpening his focus. He would start again, forge his own way.

Memories of Ethan surfaced, unbidden and bittersweet. Ethan had been his closest friend, the only one who knew about his dreams. Their friendship had been rare, transcendent, forged in shared passion and trust. But after Jon left for New York, he'd kept his distance, knowing Ethan wouldn't approve of his new path. That distance was a loss he could never reclaim.

The ache for that lost bond lingered, but Jon let it settle beside his growing determination. The ship sliced through the dark, rolling waves, its steady rhythm mirroring the resolve building within him. He turned to the open sea, the vast expanse stretching endlessly beneath the star-studded sky. A new chapter was beginning. He had survived the Flying Dragons. Now he would find a new way to soar.

Chapter 5

Fika
Jon
Stockholm, Sweden

Jon cleared a circle in the steamy bathroom mirror using the white terry-cloth towel around his shoulders. The face reflecting back was unfamiliar, making him feel as if he were staring at a stranger beside him. The military-style buzz cut had shorn any remnants of the bleach job and complemented the chiseled jawline and pronounced cheekbones. The surgery had broadened his slender nose, transformed his almond eyes to a rounder shape, and reconstructed his prominent forehead. The results, though startling, were handsome in their own right, and he believed he'd come to embrace them with time.

Memories of his arrival in Sweden seemed like a distant dream. The impressive express train from the Gothenburg port to Stockholm Medicus had been a revelation—spacious, clean, modern. The medical facility, lauded for its groundbreaking reconstructive surgeries and stringent patient confidentiality, was rumored to serve not only A-list celebrities, but also disgraced politicians, elusive fugitives, and those seeking a fresh start from the shadows of their past. Jon's procedure was an anomaly—drastic, elective, and uninsured. Yet the exorbitant cash payment guaranteed discretion. After an intense surgery, he spent two weeks in close post-operative observation followed by two more weeks in a rehab clinic to gain full jaw movement. The surgeon was visibly proud of the transformation—from distinctly American to authentically Chinese.

Once medically cleared, Jon relocated to a chic two-bedroom apartment, courtesy of a nurse's globe-trotting friend. The original plan was solitude, but loneliness proved far more suffocating than anticipated. Eager to see more of Sweden, Jon decided to visit Helsingborg, a coastal city known for its medieval fortress and vibrant cultural scene. The trip provided a much-needed respite and a chance to experience the country's rich history and picturesque landscapes.

He met Lise on the train from Helsingborg. Their conversation was an easy mix of fact and fiction, as Jon artfully wove a life story that portrayed him as an American-born child of Chinese immigrants. Lise, a law student with aspirations in the arts, exuded a vivacity that contrasted with Stockholm's crisp September air.

Their stroll from the train station after arriving from Helsingborg was filled with laughter and shared stories. Jon didn't want their time together to end. "Can I walk you home?" he asked.

"I'd like that. Want to go for a fika?"

"A fika?"

"You truly are a newcomer to Sweden! Fika is a tradition here—sipping coffee or tea, enjoying pastries, and engaging in leisurely conversation. It's our way of pausing and connecting. So are you in?" she said, her eyes shimmering with mischief as they paused outside her go-to café.

"Absolutely." The rich scent of cardamom beckoned them in.

It had been past midnight when they reached Lise's doorstep, their hands clutching a bag filled with fragrant cardamom rolls.

"This was a delightful evening. Thanks," she said, only to find the apartment door bolted from the inside. Her repeated knocks went unanswered. "I think my roommate misunderstood my return date," she commented, visibly puzzled.

"You can crash at my place. I have an extra bedroom," Jon offered, though second-guessing his impromptu invitation.

He quickly discerned that compared to Americans, Swedes had an open-minded perspective on intimacy, evident in their legal age for relationships and the absence of societal judgment. The soft morning glow illuminated the bathroom. Lise's voice pulled Jon from his thoughts. He handed her a towel as she stepped from behind the curtain, her sculpted form stirring something deep within him.

"What's your plan for today?" he asked, toweling off his newly dark hair.

"Classes till nine. Don't wait for me."

"Did you always know you wanted to be a lawyer?"

"Not even close. When I was a child, I thought I would be an artist, a painter. Not exactly a practical way to make a living." She chuckled, her tone tinged with a hint of melancholy.

Jon, always curious and keen to learn more about Lise, responded, "Maybe not crafting unique masterpieces straight off the bat, but there's merit and livelihood in creating decorative and commercial art. Do

27

you still paint?"

She sighed, a shadow crossing her face. "My parents believe studying art at university is frivolous and see painting merely as a hobby."

"What a waste," he said, shaking his head. "The world needs more people chasing their passions."

"You really mean that, don't you?" She stepped onto the cool tile, water droplets cascading from her hair.

He leaned against the sink, his lips quirking into a faint smile. "I don't say things I don't mean."

"Hmm," she mused, running the towel over her arms. "You're an enigma, Jon."

"And you're an artist, whether your parents like it or not."

She chuckled softly. "Careful, or I might start to believe you."

Jon, as an American, was permitted a three-month stay in Sweden without a visa. But with a mere fortnight left, time was pressing against him. As each day passed, he and Lise settled deeper into a comforting routine. He was acutely aware that the longer he lingered, the harder it would be to say goodbye. A sudden restlessness gripped him—a yearning to leave for China. He had taken care of the necessary smallpox and cholera vaccinations during his clinic recovery. Now only the entry visa stood in his way. He clung to the belief that the visa and passport would soon be in his hands.

Every afternoon, with Lise occupied with classes, Jon retreated to the American Center Library, immersing himself in everything related to China. Donning the headset in the language lab, he diligently practiced Mandarin. But today, he had a strict deadline, needing to leave by two for an important appointment.

His concentration wavered. The magnetic pull toward Lise was unrelenting. He pondered, trying to recall if he'd ever been this infatuated before. He'd had moments of vulnerability when he relaxed and nearly exposed his true backstory—his authentic family ties, memories of Kim and Ethan. He wished to confide that his family most surely thought he was dead, and the crushing loneliness threatened to consume him. Lise's comforting embrace would help him momentarily forget the mask he wore and the internal battles it ignited, providing a transient sanctuary.

Lise had been his anchor during his most vulnerable moments, but his feelings went deeper than mere gratitude. Their bond had intensified with every interaction, tempting him to envision a future beside her. A disconcerting fear gripped him, though he couldn't determine whether it was the idea of staying or the challenge of leaving.

He hadn't rigorously trained since the surgery. He was growing too accustomed to the comforts of Sweden. He needed to act.

Navigating through the bustling pedestrian pathways, Jon finally spotted Strandvägen Street. The journey to the US Embassy had taken longer than anticipated. The sight of the towering US flag fluttering brought relief. Glancing at his watch, he noted the time was two twenty-five p.m. He'd make his two-thirty appointment after all.

He was to wait on the fifth step from the bottom, umbrella in hand, reading the Paris edition of the *International Herald Tribune*. He double-checked his breast pocket—the money was there, five thousand dollars now, the other five on delivery. Inside the sealed envelope were two passport-size photos, taken just yesterday. The first since the surgery. He'd stared at them a long time before sealing the flap—studying the face that was now his.

He climbed the white steps to the embassy, counting each one. At the fifth step, he turned, sat, and looked out over the stream of hurried pedestrians. Holding the *Herald Trib* visibly in front of him, he placed the umbrella beside him on the step. But his eyes were scanning the crowd—for someone carrying a copy of *TIME* in one hand and an umbrella in the other.

For a week, he'd wrestled with the right alias. Back in New York, he could only hope they assumed Jon Fenton was dead—but there was no way to be sure. He wanted a name that felt authentic, poring over a list of Chinese names, mixing and matching, until something clicked. His visa and passport would get him into China—leaving was another matter. Reentering the United States was a challenge for another day. Even as "Li Chi" flowed from his pen, doubt gnawed at him. He folded the paper and slipped it into the envelope with the money and photographs. Because deep down, he knew no alias could define a man without ancestors. A name bore witness to lineage, and Li Chi had none.

A blonde woman in a classic brown trench coat appeared at the edge of Jon's vision, her purposeful stride slowing as she approached the embassy. Clutched in her hand were a copy of *TIME* magazine and an umbrella—details he'd been told to watch for. His stomach tightened. He hadn't expected her to be a woman.

Jon's instructions were clear—wait on the fifth step from the bottom, hold the Paris edition of the

International Herald Tribune, and let the contact initiate. He kept his expression neutral, but his thoughts spun out of control. Could she be trusted? Had something changed in the plan?

Their eyes met—briefly, but deliberately. She stopped in front of him, her body language calm but intentional.

"Excuse me, is that the *Herald Trib*?" she asked, her voice measured as she adjusted the *TIME* magazine on her knee, the movement too intentional to be casual.

His rehearsed response dissolved in the heat of the moment, panic flickering at the edges of his mind. "Uh, no, it isn't. Do you know where I could get one?" The words tumbled out before he could stop them—his voice steadier than he was.

"By the Gothenburg Consulate," she replied smoothly.

Jon's pulse steadied as recognition clicked. His hand moved on instinct, retrieving an envelope from his inner pocket. He slipped it smoothly into the *Tribune*, the motion crisp and practiced, then passed it to her. "When?"

Her gaze flickered in acknowledgment, her hand brushing his briefly as she accepted the package. "A week from Thursday, the twenty-fourth." She slipped the *International Herald Tribune* into her bag and handed him her copy of *TIME*, the exchange seamless and unremarkable to any passerby.

"Understood. I'll be sure to grab one," Jon replied, his voice steady despite the tension coiling in his chest. He weighed the magazine in his hand, trying not to grip it too tightly. By the time he glanced up, she had already vanished into the sidewalk crowd, her trench coat blending with the flow of pedestrians.

Jon rose quickly, his movements sharp with purpose, then stepped away from the embassy steps without a backward glance. He headed in the opposite direction from where he'd come, his pulse pounding in his ears. Sweat dampened his hairline as his mind reeled. A week from Thursday at the consulate. Or was it the embassy? They'd just departed the embassy—it had to be the embassy.

He slowed his pace, forcing himself to take deep breaths. The details came back in fragments. Gothenburg Consulate. The twenty-fourth. He repeated it silently like a mantra, anchoring himself as his racing thoughts began to settle.

Relief washed over him as he turned a corner and merged into a quieter street. The rendezvous had gone without a hitch. In his possession was the *TIME* magazine, unassuming but key to his impending departure. The photos, his new identity, and the money had been handed over. Soon he'd possess a passport and visa that would serve as his ticket to China. As he passed a trash can, he tossed in the empty glass soda bottle—its curved, ridged shape unmistakable—though he didn't remember picking it up. The act punctuated the moment. A strange mix of finality and anticipation swept over him. Jon Fenton was already fading—a shadow he'd soon leave behind. The new identity would make him untouchable, untraceable, and one step closer to a destiny he couldn't fully grasp yet but was determined to face.

Lost in thought, he barely noticed as he wandered into a secluded alleyway. The weight of the recent meeting and the impending journey had clouded his focus, his feet carrying him without direction. Suddenly, a firm grip on his shoulder yanked him back to the present.

"Where are you off to, Chinaman?"

Chapter 6

Emperor of Sovereign Fire
Ethan
Grand Rapids, Michigan

Ethan moved through the tiger form, his muscles taut as he sank into a low stance, the familiar burn steadying his focus. The basement was his sanctuary—a makeshift studio where memories of training sessions with Jon lingered in the scuffed floor and echoes of laughter. Here, his friend was still close, a constant presence just beyond reach.

The sound of the basement door creaking open broke his rhythm, followed by the familiar thump of footsteps on the stairs. He exhaled, finishing a strike, and glanced toward the stairwell.

"Ethan, I found it!" his dad called, his voice carrying over the muted hum of the furnace.

Ethan straightened and bowed, concluding the snake form he'd just finished. "Found what?"

Waving a rolled-up newspaper in one hand, Dad stepped carefully onto the basement floor, a grin lighting up his face. "The ideal office space! I did a walkthrough this morning and even had a chat about lease terms with the owner over a cup of coffee."

Ethan grabbed a towel to wipe the sweat from his brow, hesitating. "Dad, I appreciate it, but I'm not sure

I'm ready for this leap."

"I get it. It feels rushed," Dad admitted, his voice carrying a newfound vigor. "But my years in the business world have taught me to recognize an opportunity. Accessibility is key. This location? Right off a main road with a bus stop right across the street. Plus, the landlord's willing to work with someone just starting off."

Ethan hesitated, mulling it over. "Where is it?"

"Parkside and Sylvan intersection." Dad handed Ethan his jacket, his movements gentle but insistent as he guided him toward the stairs.

Ethan hesitated again. "I should check how close other acupuncture clinics and kung fu studios are, first."

"Already on it." Dad grinned. "The nearest competition is nine miles out, in East Grand Rapids."

Despite himself, Ethan couldn't suppress the spark of excitement he was starting to feel. Relenting, he let his father help him with his jacket. Slipping his leather messenger bag over his shoulder—always prepared with his ID, checkbook, or any other essentials—he trailed Dad into the garage where their old full-size sedan sat waiting—an American-made beast. The broad chrome-plated bumpers reflected the fluorescent garage light, and its squared-off hood stretched long in front of them, hinting at the power beneath. The vinyl bench seats let out a quiet creak as they slid across, the faint scent of aged upholstery and gasoline clinging to the air. It wasn't flashy, but it was solid—built for the kind of man who valued dependability over frills.

"The landlord's suggesting a ten-year lease." Dad started the car, the engine purring softly.

"That sounds like a huge commitment," Ethan remarked, narrowing his eyes in contemplation.

"Wait till you see it. The potential will blow you away." Dad's eyes sparkled. "We're talking two hundred fifty a month for the first year, escalating fifty dollars a month until year five, topping out at five hundred a month through year ten. Plus, an option to buy. And the best part? They're offering renovations. It used to be a video arcade, but they're bringing in a contractor to revamp it—lower the ceilings, four treatment rooms, a reception, and a waiting area."

Ethan swept his gaze over the building, a jittery thrill running through him. The owner's voice hummed in the background, listing planned renovations, but Ethan's mind was already ahead. He pictured patients lying in serene treatment rooms, the soft chime of the door as someone entered the reception. In the untouched back room, his vision expanded—hardwood floors catching the glow of warm lights, mirrors along the walls, and lockers neatly tucked into the corners. His pulse quickened. The place was alive with possibility. "Can we have a moment alone?"

"Of course. Take all the time you need—I'll be waiting in the office when you're finished," the owner said with a courteous nod before stepping away.

Once they were alone, Ethan turned to his father. "This place...it's got potential, doesn't it? It could be both an incredible clinic and a kung fu academy." He measured the space with his steps. "Do you think I'm making the right move by signing the lease?" he asked, mapping out the layout in his mind.

Dad smiled, though Ethan noticed him pressing his hand briefly to his lower chest as he leaned against the wall.

"If it was me? I'd jump at the chance."

An hour later, in the rental office, Ethan hesitated for a brief second before putting pen to paper. As he signed the lease and wrote out a check for the down payment, a wave of exhilaration crashed over him. Beside him, Dad beamed, wiping away sweat with a cloth handkerchief. With the paperwork completed, they shook hands with the owner, sealing the deal.

"Dad, I can't thank you enough for nudging me in the right direction," Ethan said, his arm comfortably slung around his father's shoulders. Ethan's breath caught as his father flinched. "Dad, what's wrong?" He barely had time to catch him as he crumpled.

Panic surged through Ethan, but his training kicked in. He eased his father to the ground and slipped off his jacket to cushion his head. "Hold on, Dad."

The building's owner rushed out, alarm evident on his face.

"Call an ambulance! He's having a heart attack," Ethan commanded. He recognized the telltale signs: labored breathing, a cold sweat, sharp pain in the shoulder. "Dad, do you have your nitroglycerin on you?"

His father managed a feeble shake of his head, indicating "no." Without missing a beat, Ethan pulled out his acupuncture kit, his hands steady despite the chaos. He pushed up the sleeve of his father's right arm, traced the familiar line of the heart meridian, and inserted the slender needles with practiced care—just enough to stimulate the flow of qi. "Heart 4 to 7," he murmured to himself, activating the points carefully.

Ethan held his father's hand, his gaze steady even as the rising wail of sirens filled the air. The color in Dad's face improved.

"Hold on, Dad," Ethan said, watching his father's

breathing ease ever so slightly. "Feel any relief?"

Dad took a moment, then whispered, "The stabbing pain is subsiding. What did you do?"

"Temporary relief," Ethan said, his grip firm. "Help's almost here, Dad. Just hang on."

The paramedics rushed in, quickly assessing the situation.

"Why the needles?" one of the paramedics asked, confusion flickering across his face.

"I'm a doctor," Ethan said. "This is my father. I used acupuncture to relieve his pain and improve circulation. Those needles are stabilizing the heart meridian, known as the 'Emperor of Sovereign Fire,' in traditional Chinese medicine."

"We'll need to remove them," the paramedic said, reaching out.

Ethan intercepted his hand, applying subtle pressure to a nerve point, just enough to make the paramedic wince and freeze. "Those needles are there for a reason. They stay."

The paramedic pulled his hand back, blinking. A flicker of uncertainty crossed his face before he nodded stiffly. "All right…we'll work around them," he muttered, his tone clipped, not meeting Ethan's eyes as he turned his focus back to the patient.

Chapter 7

Territory
Ethan
Grand Rapids, Michigan

Ethan unlocked the door to the Wolf Acupuncture &
Kung Fu Vitality Center, his pulse quickening as he
stepped into the freshly renovated space. Sunlight spilled
through the etched glass window bearing his name and
the clinic's hours, the words *Walk-In Appointments
Available* gleaming proudly. It was everything he had
envisioned—and more.

He paused at the reception area, running his hand
over the smooth, newly installed counter. Hardwood
floors stretched into treatment rooms, and the faint scent
of fresh paint lingered in the air. His father had seen the
potential when Ethan couldn't, nudging him to take the
leap. Now, as he stood there, the clinic was more than a
business—it was a turning point.

Ethan surveyed the room, anticipating the chime of
the door opening and patients waiting for treatment in
quiet comfort. For years, people had challenged him,
dismissing acupuncture as pseudoscience. He
remembered the skeptics, the looks that questioned his
choices, but the results spoke louder than words—relief
from pain, anxiety, migraines—evidence that couldn't
be ignored. Even his father, whose skepticism had once

cut deep, had begun to look at him differently since the heart attack.

The weight of those moments hit him—eight grueling hours in the family waiting room, his father's life hanging in the balance. "What you did probably saved your father's life," the surgeon had said afterward, words Ethan replayed more times than he cared to admit.

Pushing those thoughts aside, he moved deeper into the clinic, checking outlets and phone jacks. The electrician had done good work. In the corner, a boom box sat plugged in, a sign the crew had been here late. Curious, Ethan pressed the power button, and the Beach Boys' "Kokomo" burst out, startling him. He laughed, shaking his head as he unplugged it to test another socket.

The shatter of glass froze him mid-motion.

He darted to the reception area where shards littered the gray and mauve carpet. A gaping hole remained where the front window had shattered. Three men stood inside—two tearing at the freshly painted walls while the third, an older man in a silk suit, watched with an unsettling calm.

Ethan's blood surged. Without hesitation, he intercepted one vandal mid-swing, catching his leg and delivering a sharp sidekick to the knee. The man hit the floor, screaming in pain.

The older man raised a hand, shouting commands in Chinese, and the second vandal backed off, retreating to his side.

Ethan glared at the intruders, trying to place their faces. Strangers. "Explain yourselves," he demanded, his voice cutting through the chaos.

The older man stepped forward, adjusting his cuffs.

"You see, Dr. Wolf. I am Dr. Gong. I too practice acupuncture, not far from here. Perhaps you'd consider relocating?" His voice dripped with condescension, a thin smile playing at the corners of his mouth.

Ethan squared his shoulders, his hands flexing at his sides. "Your office is in East Grand Rapids, a good nine miles out. Our clinics can both be successful and flourish. I will honor your practice if you respect mine. But let me be clear. This is my neighborhood."

"A mere oversight on your part, I believe. This, after all, is my territory. I was here first." Dr. Gong snapped his fingers. The second vandal lunged at the freshly constructed wall and punched his fists through drywall.

Fury lit through Ethan. "No," he growled, advancing with swift, measured steps. "I think *you're* the one who's mistaken."

The second man barely had time to react before Ethan dropped him with an explosive kick to the ribs. He crumpled to the ground, groaning.

Dr. Gong watched, amusement gleaming in his eyes as if this were a game. "You're well versed in kung fu, Dr. Wolf. A hobby, perhaps?"

Ethan didn't take the bait. "Take your thugs and leave. You've overstayed your welcome."

"Not quite," Dr. Gong replied. He shed his silk tie and jacket with practiced grace and draped them neatly over the chair. "You may have bested my students, but you won't best me."

Ethan dropped into a ready stance, his breath steady, his muscles coiled. Dr. Gong moved first, lunging with surprising speed. His strikes were calculated, flowing seamlessly between punches and sharp kicks. Ethan deflected each blow, responding automatically, his

41

movements efficient and controlled.

For his age, Gong was fast—surprisingly fast. Ethan narrowly dodged a hook aimed for his ribs, but the speed didn't rattle him. He focused on Dr. Gong's patterns, discerning the rhythm of his attacks.

Dr. Gong transitioned to a series of linear strikes, the deliberate, undulating force unmistakable—hsing-i. Ethan recognized it immediately, matching the style. Rise, drill, fall, overturn. Each of his counters hit its mark, sharp and explosive at the moment of impact. The older man's confidence flickered as Ethan struck back with a perfectly timed palm strike into his chest, the force sending Dr. Gong stumbling back, his feet skidding across the floor.

"You've trained in hsing-i," Dr. Gong observed, his breathing audible now, though his tone remained steady. He adjusted his stance, his eyes narrowing.

Ethan said nothing, holding his ground, his gaze locked on his opponent. Dr. Gong shifted again, his form becoming circular, fluid. Ethan recognized the transition to pa-kua—the movements were deceptively graceful, and the strikes were deadly.

Dr. Gong advanced, weaving and circling, his open palms lashing out. Ethan adapted, meeting fluidity with fluidity, his own form transitioning to mirror pa-kua's open-palmed style. He kept his breaths deep and his body coiled, spring-loaded for defense and counterattack.

"Do you know the pa-kua?" Dr. Gong challenged mid-strike, his voice strained as he pressed forward.

In answer, Ethan's hands and feet fanned in arcs to attack and defend. "Enough to keep up," he replied coolly, deflecting two rapid strikes before snapping a counterpunch to Dr. Gong's chest, staggering him again.

The two men circled each other, locked in a silent dialogue of skill and experience. Frustration crept into Dr. Gong's movements—each frenzied punch and kick growing more forceful. The aggression turned sloppy, exposing a crack in the armor. Ethan's focus sharpened.

Dr. Gong lunged, his strike overextended—just the opening Ethan needed. He pivoted, coiling his body before unleashing a powerful jump-spin kick. His heel smashed into Dr. Gong's jaw, the impact cracking through the air like a whip.

A sickening *pop* accompanied the blow. Dr. Gong staggered back, his hand flying to his face, his eyes wide in shock. His mouth hung awkwardly, blood trickling from the corner of his lips. The jaw was broken—its unnatural angle and the muffled groan escaping between clenched teeth left no doubt.

Ethan closed the gap between them, his stance unwavering, his voice calm and steely. "That kick," he said, eyes fixed on Dr. Gong, "could've targeted your temple. It would've been fatal." He let the warning hang in the air before adding, "Always guard your face."

Dr. Gong's eyes narrowed, confusion and pain mingling behind his gaze, but he said nothing. His reply came as a faint, garbled hiss, betraying his injury. Slowly, he retrieved his jacket and tie, movements stiff and deliberate, his dignity fraying with each strained breath.

"Gather your students and leave," Ethan continued, glancing at the two men still writhing on the floor. "This is my clinic. My neighborhood. I won't warn you again."

Dr. Gong shot Ethan a final look of resignation before motioning for his students to follow. They limped out of the shattered office, the sound of glass crunching beneath their feet lingering in the silence.

Ethan exhaled, the adrenaline slowly ebbing from his system. He uncurled his fists, and his shoulders relaxed as he took stock of the damage. The waiting room was in ruins—broken windows, shattered drywall, scuffed floors—but the foundation held strong. *Like me*, he thought, rolling his shoulders and steadying his breath.

This wasn't over. Men like Dr. Gong didn't walk away quietly. But for now, Ethan had sent a message. This was his territory.

Chapter 8

Reparation
Ethan
Grand Rapids, Michigan

Ethan drove another nail into the plywood covering a portion of the shattered window, the late afternoon air biting at his skin. The rhythmic pounding of the hammer echoed in his head, a distraction from the lingering tension.

"What happened? Are you okay?" Kim's voice cut through the chill as she stepped onto the sidewalk. Her wide eyes flicked over the wreckage, lingering on the broken glass and the boarded-up entryway.

Ethan offered a faint smile, brushing the dust from his hands. "Just someone trying to scare me off. I'm fine, though." He picked up another board and positioned it over the window. "Here—hold this in place."

Kim stepped closer, pressing the plywood against the frame as he reached for another nail. "This isn't a joke, Ethan. Look at this mess! They've destroyed everything you've worked for."

Her grip on the board tightened, her knuckles whitening as frustration simmered beneath her words.

Ethan met her gaze briefly before lifting the hammer again. "It's just the waiting room." He drove another nail into the frame.

He straightened with a stretch and set the hammer gently against the wall. "Dr. Gong dropped by yesterday with two of his finest," he said. "I invited them in for tea."

"You what?" Kim blinked.

He grinned. "They declined. Instead, they trashed the place."

"And you just let them?" Her voice sharpened.

"I wouldn't say that." He rolled his shoulder with a wince. "I didn't stand aside, either. Three against one, but they limped away worse off than I did."

"We need to call the police."

Ethan shook his head. "That's not how this community works."

"Why not?" she pressed, arms crossed now.

"Because calling the police sends a message—that I don't belong here. It'll escalate things, mark me as an outsider, and Gong would use that to tighten his grip. In this world, respect is earned face-to-face, not through a badge or report."

She studied him in silence, her brow furrowed with concern. "You've dealt with him before?" she asked.

"I've looked into him," he admitted. "When I was scouting locations for the clinic, I made sure there wasn't another acupuncture practice nearby. His clinic's on the far side of East Grand Rapids—well outside any reasonable competition zone. But Gong doesn't play by standard rules. He thinks he owns the entire city."

She exhaled sharply, glancing at the boarded-up window. "And you're just going to let him get away with this?"

His gaze locked with hers. "I'm not letting him get away with anything. I've already shown him I won't back down. Bullies like him prey on those they think are weak. I'm not weak, and I'm not leaving."

"What can I do to help?" Kim's hand touched his.

"Have dinner with me. I'm starving." A small smile tugged at the corners of his lips.

"Are you sure you're up for it after today?"

"I just worked up an appetite."

****

Morning light filtered through the windshield. The drive to the clinic was quiet—the kind of silence that didn't need filling. Ethan's hand rested casually on the gearshift, his fingers brushing hers, a subtle echo of the night before. The faint scent of her lingered in the air, warm and familiar.

"You didn't have to come with me." He glanced at her.

"I didn't want our time together to end," she said, almost hesitant—enough to make him glance at her again.

As the clinic came into view, the warmth between them thinned. The shattered window was no longer covered with plywood. Ethan tightened his grip on the wheel, his instincts sharpening.

"Stay in the car," he said as he parked.

"Be careful," she whispered, but he was already out the door.

Inside, the scene was not what he expected. Instead of destruction, the clinic hummed with measured purpose. Eight Asian men moved through the space with practiced efficiency—sweeping up glass, patching drywall, replacing fixtures.

Ethan halted, tension rising. One of the men—on crutches—limped toward him. Recognition struck. He

47

was one of the attackers from the day before.

The young man bowed deeply. "Master Wolf, we are here to repair the damage."

Dr. Wolf," Ethan corrected.

The man straightened slightly. "You defeated Master Gong. He has lost face and left. You are now our master."

Ethan's pulse ticked. Master Gong. The name landed with weight. He hadn't been a random confrontation—Gong was a martial arts master, and these were his students. It all made sense now. This wasn't just a show of force. It was a ritual of succession. Whether he wanted it or not, he had a responsibility to them.

From the doorway, Kim hovered, visibly confused.

Ethan crossed to her and whispered, "Can you get us all some lunch?" He handed her the car keys and a few bills.

After seeing her off, he turned to the steady rhythm of restoration unfolding in his clinic. Two of the men worked with noticeable limps.

He gestured for the injured students to follow him into an exam room. One settled carefully onto a chair, and the other stretched out on the table.

"You've dislocated your hip," Ethan said as he assessed the damage. "What's your name?"

"Jen," the man said through clenched teeth. "It was a good move, Master."

Ethan sighed. "Let's get this fixed."

He worked quickly, hands steady. With a sharp adjustment, the hip snapped back into place.

Jen groaned, then flexed his leg, a tentative smile breaking through the pain. "Better," he murmured.

"Good," Ethan said. "Come back tomorrow for follow-up." He turned to the second man and motioned for him to take his place.

By the end of the day, the waiting room had been fully restored. Near the door, the group gathered in a line. One by one, they bowed deeply.

Jen stepped forward, speaking for them. "Thank you, Master Wolf."

"You'll make follow-up appointments for your injuries."

Jen hesitated. "And…you will be our instructor?"

Ethan studied their faces—open, eager, expectant. If not him, they would seek out someone like Gong.

He nodded. "Come back tomorrow at seven p.m. We'll begin your training."

Chapter 9

Dreams
Jon
Stockholm, Sweden

Jon meandered into an unknown section of the city. His footsteps echoed softly against the cobblestones, the distant hum of city life a muted backdrop to his wandering thoughts. The narrow alleyways of Stockholm twisted like a labyrinth, each turn unfamiliar and cloaked in shadow. A tall fair adolescent swinging a chain blocked his way. He quickly brought himself to alertness and looked over his shoulder. Another slightly broader kid sneered at him from behind.

"Me and my friends are a little short this week, bloke, and we hoped you might help us out with some cash." The blond punk with the chain spoke with a British accent.

Ever since he absconded with the payoff in New York, paranoia had been a close companion. Carrying the entire sum was impossible, but he'd kept enough with him for emergencies. Now eighteen thousand US dollars pressed against his chest, tucked safely inside the pocket of his jacket. It was just a fraction of what remained, but it was enough to secure his travel documents, book a flight to China, and sustain him if he needed to run. His recent liaisons only deepened his unease. Was this apparent mugging just a twist of fate, or had someone tipped them off about the fortune he'd left behind?

Ahead, the lanky youth began swinging his chain more assertively. Jon caught sight of another similarly dressed figure crossing the street. Assessing the situation, he knew that if handing over the cash would spare him from the imminent violence he envisioned, he would've done so. But the yearning in their eyes was not merely for money. He read their longing for danger in the swagger of their walk. This was about achieving status and belonging, something money would not satisfy. He remembered his early kung fu training, the lessons on using an opponent's momentum against them. Calculating his moves, he saw the weak points in their stances and planned his strikes accordingly.

With a calculated casualness, Jon remarked, "Seems I've taken a wrong turn." Observing the rhythm of the swinging chain, he continued with a disarming grin, "I'm looking for the American Center Library. Know where it is?" Swiftly, he stunned the chain-wielder with a reverse punch, seized the chain, and simultaneously incapacitated his companion with a hook kick that placed Jon's heel squarely on the bloke's throat.

Two onlookers lunged at him without warning. Jon deflected the first, twisting the attacker's limb to the brink of breaking. With the chain in hand, he fended off the fourth, each swing controlled and deliberate, a testament to his early kung fu training. Alert to every potential threat, he kept his distance, the chain's rapid motion creating an intimidating barrier.

Resuming his earlier tone, he reiterated, "Like I was saying, lost my way. Can one of you chaps guide me to the American Center Library?"

One of the blokes, wincing as he cradled his assaulted elbow, glared up at Jon. The hesitation in the man's eyes was unmistakable—he seemed to realize that Jon could inflict far more damage if desired. "All right, all right!" he spat out through gritted teeth, the words laced with pain and begrudging respect. "Take the next left, then head straight down till you see a bloody big building with flags—can't miss it. Now back off, mate!"

He shuffled back cautiously, eyeing the chain in Jon's hand with apprehension, nursing his injured elbow, and giving Jon a wide berth to pass. The others, too, seemed keen to avoid further confrontation, parting to create a pathway after witnessing their comrade's swift defeat.

As Jon navigated Stockholm's streets, his senses remained heightened, every shadow and noise making him glance over his shoulder. The library was no longer an option; it was too late, and he was too exposed. He examined his beefy hands, noticing the rawness on his knuckles. Stockholm had become too perilous. He needed to depart. Gothenburg was the logical choice, from where, come Thursday, as Li Chi, he could finally journey to China.

The aroma of roast chicken greeted Jon as he entered the apartment. It was only six, and Lise typically wasn't home from university until half past.

"Hey, what's all this?" he mused, throwing his jacket on the sofa and pulling Lise close. The surprise warmed him.

"My afternoon class got canceled," she murmured against him, her frame melding into his. "Thought we could have a cozy night in. I made a capon and picked up wine and dessert." She gestured toward the dining room where a chilled bottle of wine sat alongside a chocolate cake roll.

"I think you might've persuaded me. Though it's not just the meal I'm looking forward to," he whispered. His lips brushed against her neck.

As they sat down to eat, he caught a fleeting emotion in her eyes. "Are we celebrating something particular tonight?"

"Just making the most of now." Instead of avoiding his gaze, she met it with a warm expression that intensified the mood, inviting a shared, silent connection between them. Somehow, she knew of his impending departure. Did he wear his intentions so transparently?

Wanting to shift the focus back to her, he probed, "Tell me more about your studies. Are you enjoying your course?"

"Law? It's...fine." She reached for the plates, her movements quick and deliberate as she refilled their wineglasses. "But what I'd truly love..."

"Yes?"

"I'd like to paint your portrait tonight. Would you mind?"

He pondered her unexpected request, then grinned. "Sure, as long as it isn't an all-night affair."

She chuckled. "Promise." Lise gathered the art supplies he'd purchased for her and moved to the living room to set them up.

Jon recognized the familiar backdrop she'd painted on the canvas—the Café Albert, where their relationship had begun over fika. He smiled, remembering the first time he and Lise had met on the train, her laughter a bright spark that had drawn him in. "You've always had a knack for capturing moments," he said, watching her work with admiration and melancholy.

With practiced ease, Lise began mapping his face on the canvas—bold strokes defining the contours, subtle lines capturing the finer details. The room was thick with concentration, the only sound the rhythmic swish of her brush. As she painted his eyes, it was as if she were looking straight into his soul.

"Do I have to be still?" He tried to find a comfortable position.

"Not entirely. You can speak if you wish." Her eyes fixed on her canvas, fingers delicately gripping her brush.

"Where did you learn to paint?" His eyes shifted subtly, but he held his head stationary.

Her eyes softened. "It was my grandmother's gift to me. She was a perceptive soul, always keen on the finer nuances of life. She studied at Les Beaux Arts, an eminent art institute in Paris. She passed down the classical techniques to me." Her voice had a touch of nostalgia, her gaze distant for a fleeting moment.

"Ever been to Paris?"

"Only in my mind. As a child, inspired by my grandmother's tales, I aspired to study art in Paris. She once gifted me a watercolor pallet, and I would paint endlessly, announcing to everyone to preserve my art, confidently stating its future worth. It seems foolish now." She chuckled. Her cheeks had taken on the hue of wild cherries.

As she danced her brush across the canvas, Jon was drawn into the spell of her eyes, a clear blue that seemed to sing stories. "You know, I've always thought our childhood dreams were whispers of who we really are. Pure, unspoiled. But life, it somehow turns up the noise, and we can't hear them anymore," he shared, a softness in his voice as he held her gaze.

"You've stirred awake those long-asleep dreams in me, though I'm not sure how," she responded, her focus alternating between his features and the hues she mixed on her palette.

He watched her, the soft curves of her face making him momentarily forget everything he wanted to say.

She paused, revealing the canvas. Her eyes held storms and stories, pulling him in deeper. Before he could voice the whirlwind of thoughts inside him, Lise's fingers tenderly hushed him, pressing against his lips. "Let's savor tonight, without any regrets."

****

As tendrils of morning light spilled through the window, Jon watched Lise's figure disappear through the doorway, her daily pilgrimage to class beginning. In the quiet that followed, he turned his attention to the blue duffel bag stashed on the closet shelf. With measured precision, he divided the cash. Two thirds he kept for himself, and the remaining third he stuffed into an oversized envelope.

He positioned it prominently on the table, alongside his apartment key. He scrawled a quick note, his handwriting imperfect in his haste. It conveyed a simple, poignant message. *Use this money to make your Paris dreams a reality while I chase mine. P.S. The rent is paid until the end of the month—Jon.*

He folded the envelope with a pang of regret. Leaving Lise was like abandoning a life raft, but Sweden was only a way station on his journey. He glanced around the apartment one last time, the memories shared within these walls almost palpable. "This is for the best," he whispered.

Jon slung the duffel bag over his shoulder and headed for the door. The cool morning air met him as he stepped outside—crisp with the weight of goodbye, charged with the pull of what lay ahead. He was leaving behind another piece of his life, but the promise of what waited in Gothenburg—and beyond in China—kept his steps steady. His dream was finally within reach.

Taking a deep breath, he reached into his pocket and pulled out a small, tarnished key attached to a simple leather cord. It was the key to his family home, a tangible link to his past. He ran his thumb over the worn edges, recalling the times he had spent there—Thanksgiving gatherings with friends, the sound of his mother's laughter, and hot summer evenings on the porch with Dad and Kim watching thunderstorms. For a moment, he was transported back, the weight of the key anchoring him to those cherished memories.

He placed the key back into his pocket, feeling its comforting presence against his leg. The reminder of his family gave him strength, knowing that no matter how far he traveled, a part of him would always be connected to the home he once knew.

Jon walked away, the sound of his footsteps fading into the rhythm of the city's pulse, the key to his family home a silent witness to his journey.

Chapter 10

Exchange
Jon
Gothenburg, Sweden

Gothenburg's vast harbor bustled with activity, its reputation as Scandinavia's largest port affirmed with every ship that docked or set sail. Almost three months earlier, Jon, the American from New York, had set foot in the city from one such ship. But in a matter of days, Li Chi would be the one setting out on a journey home.

In the consular district, Jon settled into a modest hotel room. The murmur of American voices on the streets below offered a thread of familiarity in this foreign city. Beyond the urban sprawl, gentle hills hugged the city. Jon often found solace meandering through the woods and tracing the serene riverside. Nearby, a park with a spacious pavilion became his sanctuary. In the tranquil dawn, with Gothenburg still wrapped in slumber, he practiced kung fu there. Occasionally, an elderly onlooker would silently watch from a bench. The morning chill from the consistent salty breeze off the ocean kept him cool. He relished the anonymity of his surroundings.

His mind frequently wandered to Lise, only a train ride away. Their shared moments, their routines—he missed it all. Throughout the day, he'd steal glances at his watch, picturing her movements and activities. Seeking distraction, he immersed himself in Gothenburg's cultural life. He indulged in local cuisine and then, seeking further escape, discovered the Grand Theater. The ballet, alien in language but universal in emotion, captivated him. The dancers' grace left him spellbound. He yearned for Lise's company, her whispered commentary, the warmth of her shoulder against his.

As he exited the theater, a freshly blanketed city greeted him. Snowflakes shimmered under the lamplight, casting an enchanted spell. Leaving Lise compounded an anguish that was deeply buried, an echo of past goodbyes—Ethan, Kim, his parents, reminding him of the cost of his double life. Snow crunched beneath his steps as he trudged back to his hotel, the world around him aglow with ethereal beauty, untouched by his heartache.

Jon awoke on Thursday, the twenty-fourth, full of energy. The appointed day had finally arrived, after a stretch of waiting that felt endless. Sunlight streaked gold across the horizon as he pulled himself from bed and made his way to the pavilion, content in the familiar comfort of routine.

The chill of Gothenburg's October mornings invigorated Jon, urging him to quicken his pace as he practiced the fluid yet forceful movements of Lethwei. The Burmese boxing art cultivated endurance and fearlessness and embodied the qualities he would need to survive. With each deliberate motion, he welcomed not just physical warmth but also a sense of renewal, as the first rays of dawn marked a new chapter. The discipline of the form helped him channel his focus toward his dreams, distancing himself from past connections.

As the rising sun cast the world in a soft, golden hue, he transitioned from the deliberate art of Lethwei to a vigorous jog, energy surging as the wooded trails welcomed him. His feet struck the earth in steady rhythm, matching the quickening beat of his heart—a vibrant pulse echoing through every limb. Sunlight danced through the branches above, and with each breath, a surge of optimism rose within him, bright with visions of a future rich in possibility and adventure. He ran not to escape, but to meet the horizon—wide open, waiting.

By one forty-five, Jon found himself outside the consulate. He gripped the rolled *TIME* magazine securely in his hand, the pages of which hid five thousand dollars, his lifeline to a new identity. Nervous excitement bubbled within him. He had meticulously planned every detail of this rendezvous. The moments seemed to stretch, each second a drawn-out eternity. The omission of one seemingly trivial detail suddenly became a gaping hole in his plan. The umbrella.

He cursed aloud, drawing disapproving glances from a nearby woman who quickly covered a young girl's ears. He'd left the umbrella on the steps of the embassy in Stockholm. Desperately, he scanned the throng of people for anyone holding an umbrella, even as the blue sky mocked his predicament. Had he unconsciously sabotaged his own escape? He quickly dismissed that thought. Time was running out. In front of the consulate, he saw two men and one woman holding newspapers. The blonde woman in the trench coat was the same woman he had met in front of the US

Embassy in Stockholm—the one who'd given him the *TIME* magazine. She looked at her watch. Certainly, she knew it was him, but she wouldn't approach without the umbrella. The missing umbrella might be some sort of sign.

Suddenly, across the street, a beacon—a woman walked with a young girl clutching a white eyelet parasol. Without thinking, Jon sprinted toward them, narrowly avoiding an oncoming cab. Dropping to one knee before the child, he gestured urgently, trying to convey his need. The girl shook her head, clutching the parasol tighter, her defiance unmistakable. Before he could try again, the woman began swatting him with her purse, her blows landing with surprising force.

He raised his hands defensively, backing away as he dug into his jacket pocket. He pulled out a roll of hundred-dollar bills, peeled off three, and offered them to the woman. She snatched them from his hand, stuffed the bills into her ample bosom, and pried the parasol from the white knuckles of the screaming child. His last glimpse as he turned was of the fleshy woman struggling to lead the child away.

In front of the consulate, the blonde woman watched Jon with an expression of disbelief. She appeared unable to decide whether to approach him or disappear into the crowd. When she glanced toward him, he locked eyes with her, standing beneath the white eyelet parasol. He was drawing more attention to himself with every passing moment, desperate to seal the most critical deal of his life. Perhaps for that reason, she approached him, and they made the exchange. He gave her the *TIME* magazine, and she gave him the folded Paris edition of the *Herald Tribune*. He clutched the newspaper concealing the passport and visa within.

The exchange was swift. Before she turned to disappear into the crowd, she looked back at him, shaking her head. "How unfortunate you couldn't find a frock to match," she said, her words dripping with sarcasm.

Jon dropped the parasol into the first trash receptacle he passed and merged with the throng of pedestrians. A rush of freedom surged through him. With every step, the weight of his past lifted, and he moved confidently toward his dreams.

****

Jon awoke with a start, his heart pounding furiously against the cage of his ribs. For a long, breathless moment, he remained perched on the edge of the bed, the cold sweat clinging to his skin. Outside his window, the world was a silent expanse of white, the moon a luminous disc in the sky, casting an ethereal glow on the fresh snow. It was a stark contrast to the darkness of his nightmare, the haunting vision of being buried alive.

His flight to Beijing was scheduled for the evening, a reality that prompted him to glance at the nightstand. Inside the drawer lay his new passport, freshly issued, promising a future under the identity of Li Chi. But as he stared at the small booklet, his eyes drifted to the other objects beside it, a collection of passports and various IDs from a life he was supposed to leave behind. With a sudden, decisive movement, Jon stood and began to dress. He filled his pockets with these remnants of his past identities and left the hotel room.

The streets of Gothenburg were deserted, the city wrapped in the hush of the early hour. He found himself walking toward the nearby park, drawn to the isolation of its pavilion. There, under the pale wash of moonlight, he fed his old passports and IDs to the flames of a small fire he'd kindled. Each piece that curled and blackened in the fire marked the erasure of a chapter of his life, yet as he prepared to throw away his key ring, his hand paused.

The key to his childhood home was small, unassuming, yet heavy with memories. The scent of coffee, the warmth of toast, and the laughter shared over breakfasts flooded his mind. Despite the distance he put between himself and his past, these memories clung to him, stubborn and pervasive. His tight clutch pressed the key's jagged edges into his palm, a tangible link to a world he still held dear. Reluctantly, he pocketed the key and watched the last of the flames die down.

As dawn approached, Jon practiced kung fu on the pavilion's wooden deck, a meditation of sorts. The physical exertion was a balm, helping him organize his thoughts and steel himself for the next step.

He returned to his hotel room and sat down at the small writing desk. From his duffle bag he pulled a thick envelope containing a cashier's check—a substantial retainer he had prepared earlier, ensuring Daniel Wu, retired New York cop turned private investigator, would have no reservations about the task ahead. He laid the check on the desk and began to write a letter. The instructions were concise, dictating surveillance of his family, threat alerts, and annual reports including a photograph that could capture the essence of his family's current life. Upon arrival in China, he would set up a China Post postal box to receive communications and advise Daniel Wu of the necessary details to ensure proper delivery. His words were measured, betraying none of the hardship that accompanied each stroke of the pen.

Carefully, Jon folded the letter around the cashier's check, put it in the envelope, and sealed it. He addressed it with meticulous attention to detail, ensuring every line was perfect, every digit correct. As soon as the post office opened, he was there, handing over the envelope with a brief word and a nod to the clerk.

With the letter sent, Jon walked away from the post office. The early morning light was now stretching across Gothenburg, the city waking up around him. He moved through the streets with a lighter step, a man unburdened yet tethered still to the shadows of his past, carried forward by the hope that the threads he left behind would keep his family safe, even as he ventured into the unknown.

Chapter 11

Customs
Jon
Beijing, China

Jon navigated through the bustling Beijing International Airport, weaving around a sea of Chinese in navy and gray tunics. Overhead, gate signage indicated flights arriving from Hong Kong, Tokyo, Europe, and the United States. Women hurried toward the arrival gates, gripping the hands of only children, a stark reflection of the country's one-child policy, as they scanned the crowd for familiar faces. Among the steady stream of passengers, men in crisp three-piece suits emerged, their Western attire a stark contrast to the more modest, traditional clothing worn by the women waiting in the terminal.

Caught in the human current, Jon moved along, his carry-on bag slung nonchalantly over his shoulder. He absorbed the cacophony of Mandarin dialects that bubbled around him. His understanding was patchy, but he caught snippets of the northern dialect predominant among the Han Chinese.

Upon reaching customs, Jon received a baggage declaration form. The official, in a crisp uniform, examined his visa, sternly reminding him of the hefty fine should he exceed his thirty-day welcome in the

People's Republic of China. The form inquired meticulously about personal belongings, ranging from cameras to electric fans, requiring the quantities of each. With a benign expression, he declared only a wristwatch, despite the small fortune discreetly concealed in his luggage.

His declaration of foreign currency, a mere fraction of what lay hidden in stitched compartments, didn't raise an eyebrow. The customs official, a woman with a procedural air, rummaged briefly through his belongings before waving him through. Jon reorganized his bag quickly, aware of the growing line behind him.

Exiting customs, he moved toward the terminal's expansive murals, seeking the next checkpoint on his meticulously planned trajectory. He discovered an array of shiny, aqua-colored lockers, and after a quick detour to the restroom, extracted a hefty sum of cash from his duffel bag. He concealed the bills inside a T-shirt, creating an inconspicuous package, and stowed it in locker number 1027. The number held significance—it was both today's date and Ethan's birthday, a quiet nod to his friend during this pivotal step in his journey. He put the key into the duffel bag's inside zipper pocket.

After securing his cash, Jon headed straight to the China Post office in the airport. He was intent on setting up a postal box for receiving communications from Daniel Wu. He navigated through the labyrinth of counters and kiosks and finally found the China Post section. The green-and-white signage was a beacon of bureaucracy, promising to link him to news of his family.

The clerk, a middle-aged man with glasses perched on the end of his nose, processed Jon's request with mechanical efficiency. Jon filled out the necessary forms quickly but carefully, double-checking each detail. When the clerk handed him the keys to his new postal box, a wave of relief and anticipation stirred in his chest. He slipped them into the duffel bag's inner zipper pocket.

Before leaving the post office, Jon found a secluded corner and scrawled a short note to Daniel Wu, detailing the address of his new postal box. This step was crucial—Wu's reply would establish the critical connection. The urgency of this communication weighed heavily on him.

Exiting the airport, Jon was greeted by a line of taxis, their drivers energetically haggling over fares with a multitude of travelers. He located his bus connection, confirmed his destination in the business district, and settled into a window seat. His companion for the journey, a jovial freckled man wielding a tennis racket alongside his business attire, seemed pleasantly American.

"Did I hear y'all speak English?" the stranger inquired with a smile displaying big white teeth, his southern drawl unmistakable.

"Seems we're headed the same way." Jon returned the smile.

The man, Nathan Roberts from South Carolina, was a representative of the Frigidaire Corporation, on a mission to understand the domestic needs of Chinese households. Their conversation meandered from refrigeration to tourist attractions, with Nathan's enthusiasm barely contained.

As the bus trundled along, Jon's gaze drifted over the urban landscape. Nathan continued his animated commentary on the sights awaiting them, from the historical grandeur of the Forbidden City to the utilitarian culture surrounding bicycles in China. Jon, however, was only half-listening.

"My personal favorite, the Huadu Hotel. Well furnished, telephone, color TV, private bath, air conditioning, and fire warning system—you have to check that out with the recent rise in hotel fires. Not to mention Chinese and Western menu restaurants. You never know what the food is going to be when you travel. Do you have a refrigerator in your home?"

"What?" Jon was perplexed by the abrupt question.

"Sorry, son. I thought you lived here. It seems there's a big demand for refrigerators, but the models available don't quite fit the typical Chinese kitchen."

"I'm just visiting." Jon exhaled, the exhaustion of the long journey settling into his bones.

"Well, this is my second trip here. They say autumn is the best time of year. Warm, clear days like today. Reminds me of home," Nathan continued, seemingly undeterred by Jon's fatigue. "Have you had a chance to see the Forbidden City?"

The bus made its way through the thoroughfare, thronged with pedestrians and a multitude of bicycles. The landscape changed as they traveled, with traditional gray roofs and their distinctive upturned eaves giving way to more modern residential blocks.

"This is my first visit." Jon pulled himself back to the conversation at hand as he observed the bicyclists navigating the city's arteries, fascinated by Beijing's geographical contrasts—the merging of ancient history with modern necessity.

"I didn't get to do much sightseeing during my first trip, but this time, I'm hoping to visit the Great Wall and

Tiananmen Square. And the Palace Museum in the Forbidden City is a must—almost two million works of art, or so I've heard," Nathan recounted enthusiastically.

The bus now traveled along roads lined with willows, past orchards and makeshift rural dwellings. The countryside's raw beauty struck Jon, but what fascinated him most were the locals on their bicycles, each carrying improbable loads.

"They're a lifeline here, bicycles. Look at that guy," Nathan remarked, pointing to a man balancing a sizable pig tied over his bike's rear wheel. "You know, you need a license to ride a bike here, unless you're a foreigner. They even issue fines for maintenance neglect or cycling under the influence. Can you imagine? And there's a ration on them—often, it's one bike for life."

Jon's attention was momentarily caught by a scene in a nearby park where an elderly man was gracefully moving through tai chi forms. Then a teenager in dark glasses on roller skates darted in front of the bus, narrowly avoiding collision. He reminded Jon of the characters who were after him in New York.

"You need a license for a bicycle?" Jon interjected, finding the concept both foreign and intriguing.

"Absolutely, and it's not just that," Nathan continued, warming to the topic. "The Chinese have an array of IDs and permits—swimming licenses, bicycle licenses, work cards, travel authorizations. And then there's the bureaucracy—declarations, vouchers, health certifications, visas, travel permits. They have a kind of reverence for official paperwork—business cards, student IDs, anything with a seal or laminate."

The conversation meandered through the peculiarities of Chinese bureaucracy and the stark contrasts that Jon observed. The landscape, the people, their customs—like he had stepped into an entirely different world. Amid his eagerness to explore, there nagged an edge of nervousness about how he would navigate these foreign waters and manage to make this place home.

The bus rolled to a stop in the grand circular driveway of a first-class hotel, its facade promising comfort and luxury. Jon found himself caught in a mental tug-of-war between hunger and exhaustion, unsure which desire was stronger. As he prepared to disembark, a familiar voice reached him.

"Hey, I noticed you're on your own, and so am I. How about we grab dinner together in the Western restaurant here at seven? We'll have just enough time to check in and freshen up. I'm starving!" Nathan Roberts, the man from South Carolina, called out with an inviting smile.

"Thanks, I'd like that," Jon replied, shaking Nathan's hand.

Nathan's smile widened, his white teeth contrasting with his tanned skin. "Do you speak any Chinese?"

"Just a smattering," Jon confessed.

"Great, maybe we can help each other navigate," Nathan suggested with a chuckle. As they stepped off the bus, he paused. "I didn't catch your name."

Jon's mind went unexpectedly blank, the fatigue momentarily taking over.

Nathan laughed, breaking the tension. "Don't worry, it's not a trick question."

Rubbing his forehead in embarrassment and trying to recall, Jon apologized, "Sorry, I'm just really tired from the flight. My name is…" He paused, searching his memory for the alias on his passport. Then it hit him. "Li Chi."

Riding a wave of relief, he approached the front desk to check in. He appreciated the efficiency and luxury that a first-class hotel afforded. He even found a clothing store onsite where he purchased some sharp-looking khakis and a button-down shirt, noting mentally that everyone seemed to wear only navy, gray, and khaki.

At seven, Jon found Nathan in the Western restaurant, casually dressed in black slacks and a gray polo shirt, his hair still damp from showering.

The man looked up from the menu and announced, "I'm in the mood for a hearty steak, a loaded baked potato, and a crisp salad." He seemed entirely at home, despite being thousands of miles away from South Carolina.

Jon noticed a group of young Chinese girls at a nearby table giggling and pointing in their direction. He self-consciously checked his attire, wondering if he'd made a fashion misstep, but Nathan just grinned. "Having red hair in China is an experience, let me tell you." He chuckled with good humor.

As they settled into their meal, Nathan shifted the conversation. "Did you manage to exchange your currency yet?"

"No, I'm planning to head to the Bank of China tomorrow."

"Well, if you're considering stepping off the tourist track, I know a guy who can get you a two-for-one exchange on your FECs for RMB. Makes your budget go a bit further." Nathan sipped his espresso.

Jon furrowed his brows. "Is RMB necessary?"

"Here's the deal," Nathan began, leaning in. "China

operates on a two-tier currency system. Foreigners use foreign exchange certificates, or FECs. It's actually illegal for us to have yuan renminbi, the RMB. In most places catering to tourists, FECs and RMB have a one-to-one value. But I'd be cautious about straying too far from the usual spots. Last time I was here, I ended up in a remote mining town—no power, no running water. It was surreal. The people there didn't even know their ages; there were no birth or death records. If you're adventurous with food, you might handle it, but it's not for everyone."

Jon, now fully engaged, listened to Nathan's stories, finding himself increasingly absorbed in the details of this complex country he had landed in. The earlier weariness faded as his curiosity grew, the unexpected camaraderie proving to be exactly what he needed.

Chapter 12

Flying Dragons
Jon
Shanxi, China

The train jostled and screeched its way from Beijing to Datong, Shanxi, and Jon mused over his ticket class— hard seat. "Hard-to-endure" seemed more accurate. The extensive rail infrastructure to neighboring provinces meant the train departed Beijing packed, like a milk run they stopped in every city, and the density of passengers thinned as they reached the more remote regions of North China.

Throughout the sleepless night, the harsh glare of overhead lights remained unyielding. The stiff upright seat offered no rest, the challenge worsened by the periodic sound of nearby passengers spitting. An endless stream of announcements—a cacophony of news, weather forecasts, music, and public information— flowed from the carriage speakers, creating a background murmur that he couldn't quite tune out.

Jon noticed the way Chinese passengers glanced at the American tourists, their expressions flickering with curiosity. The foreigners wrestled with bulky luggage in the cramped space, pausing at well-marked stops, likely in pursuit of sights and stories to take home. But Jon stayed on, traveling farther into the inland depths of the country, where the air grew heavier, and the passengers fewer. He wasn't just an observer anymore. In Datong, he had become part of a rhythm that was both timeless and precarious, like the mines themselves, where even a small shift could send everything tumbling down.

Adapting to the rhythm of life in Datong, Jon found an unexpected sense of belonging. The city, with its unique culinary flavors and rugged landscape, offered a stark contrast to everything he had previously known. It was a place that survived on the fringes, its pulse intimately tied to the dark, underground world that shaped the city's identity.

In this remote corner of China, far from the glittering technological hubs, life was unpretentious and grounded in a different kind of reality. Here in a community where he was an anomaly, Jon discovered an accepting home. The miners, men shaped by the earth they worked, neither questioned his past nor pried into his plans. They carried their own silence, as dense and heavy as the coal they dug each day. Jon had seen their faces in the dim glow of the tunnels—stoic, resigned. The work wasn't what broke them, but the knowledge that the earth could take them back at any moment, and no one would know until the dust cleared.

He was growing accustomed to the routine and the food—mostly salty, oily noodles and smoked bean curd—but he had a special fondness for Datong's famous boiled lamb, dipped in aromatic sauce. For his daily lunch, he ate crisp fried yellow cake, made from millet flour and finished with intensely sweet preserved apricots for dessert.

He'd chosen Datong, Shanxi, which was south of inner Mongolia and located on a plateau surrounded on three sides by the Taihang and Luliang Mountains, because it was both the leading producer of coal in China and the most remote northern region. Outsiders didn't come often to Datong City, a small city by Chinese standards, in the Pingcheng District. Few sons stayed to work below ground in the dark, damp caves. They went to Shanghai or Beijing, where technology was rising and peasants were allowed to become rich. And so they accepted Jon, he assumed they assessed him to be strong, and allowed him to live as one of them. Although the rural mining community in the polluted old city was almost in ruins, the aging plumbing and electrical service sometimes worked. Nathan Roberts was right about the rest.

The majority of the mining community were Han Chinese, communicating in Mandarin, and following traditional folk religions with a reverence for natural spirits, as far as Jon understood. He was partnered with Li Wei, a fellow loner without family ties. Li Wei had welcomed Jon into his modest, hostel-style living space without hesitation, offering a quiet companionship that Jon found comforting. Their mornings began with shared meals of sliced noodles and mutton. Li Wei, Jon estimated, was about his age and had shared that he was orphaned recently, though he omitted the circumstances. Raised in Datong City, Li Wei was a reservoir of local knowledge, invaluable to Jon.

Despite grasping just fragments of Li Wei's words, Jon listened intently, storing away the bits he understood. Li Wei, undemanding of social chatter and skilled in the kitchen, was an uncomplicated roommate. As days passed, Jon found himself gradually tuning in to the language. His shifts at the mine stretched from two in the afternoon to the stroke of midnight, six days a week. He donned coveralls and a dented hard hat, equipped with a battery-powered lamp—a relic from Li Wei's father.

The talk in the mining camp had shifted after the cave-in at the neighboring shaft. No one had died, but it had taken hours to dig out the trapped men, and the black dust still clung to their faces like a warning. "Our shaft is stable," Li Wei said when Jon asked about it, though he didn't quite meet Jon's eyes as he spoke.

One breakfast, amid the soft morning light, Li Wei reached under his stack of neatly folded clothes and pulled out a worn paper wallet. He approached Jon, who was settled at the aged wooden table, still engaged with his meal.

"I once traveled to Shanghai, the big city," Li Wei began, a hint of pride in his tone, "and I got many important things." He presented Jon with a thick, yellowed square of paper.

Though the Chinese characters danced before Jon's eyes, unrecognizable but for a few, he discerned it was a form of license.

"This is my name—it's my bicycle permit." Next he offered Jon a laminated card. "In the grand cities, one must prove his skills to earn this swimming permit." His face lit up as he showcased his array of official papers.

Before Jon could fully digest the contents, Li Wei delicately reclaimed them, stowing them back in their resting place. "Do you cycle?" he inquired, a new note of curiosity in his voice.

Jon nodded, the mutton in his mouth altering his reply into a thoughtful chew as memories of bicycling slowly filled his mind.

"Do you possess a permit?"

A shake of the head was Jon's response. "I should venture into the city, acquire one like yours."

"Tomorrow is your day off while I work. You can borrow my bicycle," Li Wei suggested, his gaze locking with Jon's in a moment of genuine connection before he diverted his attention back to his noodles. "The officials here don't care much about permits, not like in the big cities. Just don't ride too close to the station, or you might run into someone looking to make trouble." He said it casually, but Jon caught the slight furrow in his brow before Li Wei turned back to his food.

Li Wei had entrusted Jon with more than camaraderie. The next morning, after breakfast and with Li Wei off at the mines, Jon pedaled to his sanctuary in Datong—the Nine-Dragon Screen Wall near the Confucius Temple. A 600-year-old Ming Dynasty masterpiece, it stretched nearly 150 feet long and rose twenty-six feet high. Glazed in vivid mosaics of green, blue, and purple, the wall depicted nine soaring creatures, the largest and oldest of its kind in China, built to ward off evil spirits at the temple's gates.

In the vast plaza—usually empty at this hour—Jon trained beneath the dragons. Under the piercing gaze of the central behemoth, something stirred in him. As if he, too, might rise.

That morning, to his surprise, he wasn't alone. Another individual was there, engaging in a practice of kung fu. Since his arrival in Datong, Jon had observed many practicing tai chi, the softer art endorsed by the People's Republic of China for its health-enhancing benefits, such as muscle strength, flexibility, and balance. While tai chi harbored lethal potential, few would master it to such an extent. Tai chi held a national reverence and was embedded in Chinese cultural practice. Witnessing villagers exercising more aggressive martial arts, characterized by sharp, rapid movements, was rare.

Jon was captivated by a solitary figure in the plaza, a man with weathered hands and sun-darkened skin moving through a kata unfamiliar to him. His simple, earth-toned clothing and sturdy, calloused bare feet suggested a life spent working the land. Jon settled onto a nearby concrete bench, studying the fluid grace of the man's movements—each step light, like a crane gliding over water. He suspected he was witnessing a form of northern Shaolin.

"Before his marriage, he devoted ten years learning from a master near the Buddhist caves in Gansu," an unexpected, gravelly voice commented. "And before taking on his wife's farm, he honed his skills in the mountains."

Jon started slightly, his usual awareness faltering. He hadn't noticed the elderly man who had slipped into a seat beside him—an occurrence he would typically detect. His alertness always extended to his surroundings, yet somehow, this stranger had slipped past it.

"His kung fu, he believes, is proficient, but I could best him easily," the old villager remarked, his focus unwavering from the performing farmer, his expression stoic.

Jon echoed, "Gansu," ensuring he'd understood.

The elder nodded slowly, a flicker of reminiscence in his eyes. "One hundred eighty-three caves. Within, a Maitreya of twenty-seven meters awaits, the prophesied Buddha destined for earthly descent." His gaze remained fixed on the plaza, now populating with others. "In the fourth century AD, Yue Zun's journey led him there, greeted by visions of a thousand golden Buddhas."

Jon's interest wasn't piqued by tales of caves or mystical figures. Instead, he took comfort in his improving linguistic abilities, now grasping more intricate details and undertones. When the elder shifted the conversation to discuss the "*tiān*," Jon initially froze, certain he'd misheard. Was the man talking about licking something? The word sounded identical to *tiǎn*, a term Jon had embarrassingly learned while watching locals feed their dogs. It wasn't until the elder gestured upward, his gnarled hand pointing to the pale sky above, that Jon's confusion lifted. He chuckled to himself, grateful for his progress but reminded of how easily the language could trip him up. Emboldened, Jon ventured, "Who is the master in Gansu?"

"Master Shen, famed for his kung fu prowess, descends from an esteemed line of martial artists. Initiated into wushu by his grandfather at eight, he journeyed across China, gleaning wisdom from various masters. His skills were refined under a thirty-fourth generation Shaolin monk in the Song Mountains for ten years. Yet despite his stature, Master Shen chose to anchor himself in Gansu, perfecting his kung fu," narrated the elder.

A hushed reverence fell among the growing audience as someone inquired, "Does he continue to mentor students?"

"Master Shen is selective, rarely accepting pupils," the old man responded, a cunning smile playing on his lips. "I, however, train under the esteemed Master Tong, a fortieth-generation Shaolin descendant, mastering the internal styles. Hence, I consistently best him." His chuckle faded as he melded with the dispersing crowd.

"Where might I locate Master Tong's school?" Jon called out.

"In the bustling heart of Shanghai," came the reply, punctuated by a knowing nod before the elder vanished into the throng.

Chapter 13

Crickets
Jon
Shanxi, China

Jon pedaled down the middle of the dirt road, the chill of late fall on his damp perspiring skin. An acrid burning smell was in the air. Most of the buildings were dilapidated and slummy, but from a westerner's perspective they were somewhat picturesque. He turned right at the temple and then right again at the next intersection and found himself in the middle of a jam-packed street market. Live pigs snorted in tube-shaped bamboo cages, and an array of local delicacies hung from stands. He looked for the cart stacked with cans of American drinks, cola and orange soda. A pedal rickshaw sideswiped Jon on the crowded street and took off the rear fender of Li Wei's bike. Crap. Jon circled back and reclaimed the separated piece. He would have to make this right. Live ducks and chickens ran into the road, and other animals, less fortunate, hung from their feet at the meat and poultry stands. He bought mutton and a pear that he ate as he wove between rickshaws and loud bargaining women.

He rode near a young boy sitting on the ground holding a stick that was top heavy with a small bamboo cricket cage. Another boy danced around him, taunting and teasing, periodically poking the boy with a stick. As he rode past, Jon snatched the prod from the fist of the taunting boy, and the sneer on his face was replaced with surprise, quickly merging into anger. The sight of the boy being taunted struck a nerve, dredging up memories Jon thought he'd left behind. He clenched his fists, his father's voice echoing in his mind. "You have to stand up for yourself—and for others."

Jon had been the target of relentless bullying in third grade. On the school bus, the older boys mocked his weight, calling him "chunky monkey," and cornered him before they got off, howling like wolves and punching his head while he shielded his face. The bus driver and other kids only laughed. Jon never told his parents, ashamed he couldn't stand up for himself and fearing telling would only make things worse.

One afternoon, tear-streaked and furious, he arrived home to find his dad in the driveway.

"Jon, what happened to you?" his father asked, pulling him onto the porch. The story spilled out. His dad listened, then demanded, "Why don't you defend yourself?"

That evening, his father took him into the garage, slipped boxing gloves onto his small hands, and taught him to punch. Hours later, they drove to Michael Abbott's house. Jon didn't want to go.

When Michael's father opened the door, Jon's dad shook his hand. "Our sons have a score to settle—right here on your front lawn."

Jon faced Michael under a naked maple tree, trembling as he put up his gloved fists.

Michael, taller and red-faced with embarrassment, hesitated. "I didn't mean anything by it. We were just kidding around."

Jon's heart raced, anger and fear colliding. Tears stung his eyes as he stepped forward. Then, without thinking, he threw a punch, hitting Michael square in the nose. Blood gushed as Michael howled in pain, clutching his face. The bullies never bothered Jon again.

Afterward, his dad had enrolled him in a martial arts class where he met Ethan. The lesson had stayed with him—he'd never let anyone hurt him again.

Farther down the street, Jon found the boy with the cart of cold cans of soda. He bought a cola for himself and another for Li Wei and pedaled back through the market to the mining community. He enjoyed the open-air market and the conversations with the local farmers. He wanted to know more about them. Horse-drawn rickshaws and woven baskets were their subways and grocery carts. He listened to them laugh and savored the thought that he was one of them.

As he approached his temporary residence, Jon stopped his bike and took a moment to catch his breath. He reached into his pocket and pulled out the small, tarnished key to his family home, attached to a simple leather cord. He ran his thumb over its worn edges, and his thoughts drifted back to his father's lessons in the garage.

He could still hear his father's voice, feel the weight of the boxing gloves, and remember the sense of empowerment that came from knowing he could defend himself. The memory of his father's unwavering support and belief in him had carried Jon through many difficult times. The key reminded him of his family. He tucked it back into his pocket, its reassuring weight grounding him.

Jon gripped the handlebars tighter, a renewed sense of purpose driving him forward. He wasn't just escaping his past—he was forging a future. As he neared the settlement, the usual rhythm of daily life had been disrupted. Women rushed in all directions, abandoning their tasks. Small children, tied to their mothers' backs, bounced with each hurried step, while older children stood frozen, watching the chaos unfold. Some began to cry, their voices carrying up into the mountains like a warning on the wind. Jon watched the activity and wondered what had happened.

In answer to his question, a woman running by shouted to another coming out of her hut with her baby, "The mine has collapsed." They ran toward the cave, and Jon followed.

All the women gathered in a group. The men were at the gaping mouth of the cave, talking wildly. Jon stood a few feet from the other men. As far as he could understand, there had been an explosion and fourteen men had been buried beneath the rock. One of the men was trying to organize the others to go in and dig them out. They shook their heads and argued that it was futile and dangerous. No telling how many more they would lose. Several insisted they could not have possibly survived the cave-in. The rock had entirely closed off the opening to the cave, and if any had survived, shortly they would suffocate. Jon looked for Li Wei. He was not in the group. His heart sank. He was in there.

While the men argued, Jon went into the mouth of the cave and started pulling large rocks from the wall formed by the violent explosion. His hands were callused, so he did not feel the jagged edges of rock cut into his skin. At the same time he was calling Li Wei's name. Every few minutes he stopped to listen for an answer. Several of the men from outside came in after him. They tried to drag him from the cave, but he yanked away from them and continued to pull rocks almost boulder sized from the wall. One of the men helped Jon tear down the wall while the others tried to drag them both away from the mine.

The cave began to tremble, and Jon froze. He had just pried a boulder from between the roof of the cave and the wall of rubble. At first small rocks fell from the ceiling, and dust stirred. Then the ceiling violently collapsed, and the wall tumbled toward them. Jon called to Li Wei, but his voice was smothered in the reverberation of falling bedrock. The men pulled Jon back and held his arms. Soot smoldered from the mouth of the cave.

As the earth settled, Jon relaxed and the men loosened their grip on him. They stood in front of the mine for a long silent moment. Jon walked past a cluster of women trying to comfort the wives of the lost men. Their wailing pierced the sky and carried back to the village and up to the thin mountain air.

That evening Jon sat alone at supper in the community hall.

One of the women spoke to him when she served his meal. "You are Li Wei's only family. You will take his possessions and distribute what you do not need."

He stared into his bowl of noodles, eyes unfocused. No one else mourned Li Wei. Would anyone mourn him? Even one?

The grief sat heavy in his chest—undeniable, intimate. In Li Wei's loss, he saw his own. In so many ways, they were the same.

Nothing held Jon here any longer. Li Wei's clothes were a good fit; he changed into them. As he sifted through Li Wei's few belongings, his fingers found the worn paper wallet and a personal diary. Nathan Roberts' words echoed in his mind. He'd once been in a coal-mining town without electricity or plumbing, where no one knew their age because no one recorded births or deaths.

Jon's visa had long expired. Now wearing Li Wei's clothes, he was different, as if he'd stepped into a new skin. He packed the wallet and diary and left the room that had been his haven. Li Wei had given him something unexpected—a chance to move forward.

Leaving the village behind, Jon thought about the kung fu masters the elders spoke of at the Nine-Dragon Wall. Their skills described with a reverence that made them seem almost mythical. One was in the northwest, not far from the mystical Buddhist Caves in Gansu. Master Shen, he recalled, was discerning, rarely accepting students. But then there was Master Tong in the vibrant heart of Shanghai, his teachings accessible. Instantly, he chose the path promising swift immersion into kung fu training—the kwoon in Shanghai. Yet before going to Shanghai, he would make the journey to Beijing to check his postal box, hoping for communication from Daniel Wu about his family. He drank the second can of cola and pedaled away from the village.

****

With a trembling hand, Jon retrieved the mailer from his postal box in Beijing, anticipation coursing through him. He hurried to a nearby teahouse, its modest wooden beams and dim lighting offering a refuge from the bustling streets. Settling into an empty table in the back, he ordered a pot of jasmine tea, though his focus was entirely on the envelope in his hand.

He tore it open, and several eight-by-ten black-and-white photos slid out. The first image made his chest tighten. Kim and Ethan stood before a shattered window, sunlight glinting off jagged glass. The etching on the door read *Wolf Acupuncture & Kung Fu Vitality Center*. Ethan was nailing a plywood board over the damage, while Kim held it in place, standing close—too close for Jon to ignore.

A swirl of emotions churned within him. Relief at seeing his sister and best friend alive warred with foreboding. What had happened? And why had someone targeted Ethan's clinic? His eyes flicked to the sign. *Wolf Acupuncture & Kung Fu Vitality Center*. Had Ethan brought their shared vision to life?

As he flipped through the photos, a smaller card fell into his lap. *Grand Opening Announcement—Wolf Acupuncture & Kung Fu Vitality Center*. Mystery solved—Ethan had settled in their hometown. Scrawled on the back in Daniel Wu's blocky handwriting was a grim note. *Ethan's clinic vandalized. Intimidation failed.*

Jon's grip tightened on the photo, his mind filling with Ethan's calm resolute voice. Ethan had stood his ground, just as Jon had always known he would. But guilt gnawed at him. Had the Flying Dragons been behind the destruction? Was their connection to him putting Ethan and Kim at risk?

He set the photos down, his tea forgotten, and stared out the teahouse window. Despite Jon's trust in Daniel Wu's vigilance, the threat of danger lingered like a shadow. He pushed the photos back into the mailer, seeking a shred of peace—until something else tumbled out.

A newspaper clipping fell to the table, its bold headline searing into Jon's mind. *Cargo Ship Officer's Body Identified.*

Jon's breath hitched. The article detailed the discovery of Officer Lopez, his body battered and broken, found off the coast of Norway. Signs of torture. Blunt-force trauma. A cold, watery grave. Jon clenched the edge of the table as memories flooded back. Lopez had known something was off when Jon boarded the SS *Liberty*. Maybe he'd reported it. Now Lopez was dead— a message from the Flying Dragons that they were still hunting him.

Panic clawed at Jon, but he forced himself to think clearly. He had vanished into the most remote region of China, altered his appearance, and covered his tracks meticulously. Yet, they had traced him to the SS *Liberty*. How? Had he overlooked a breadcrumb?

Jon tucked the clipping into the mailer, his heart pounding. The past he had fought so hard to escape wasn't done with him. The Flying Dragons were relentless, and as long as they were out there, neither he nor the people he cared about would ever be safe. Slinging his bag over his shoulder, Jon left the teahouse, his steps heavy with the weight of the threat tightening around him like a noose.

Part Two 1979

Chapter 14

Patience
Ethan
Grand Rapids, Michigan

The clinic's opening day had arrived, and light snow fell softly as Ethan and Kim approached the building. A crowd had already gathered outside, their breath forming faint clouds in the cold air. Now what? A crease formed between Ethan's brows as he took in the sea of faces, a kaleidoscope of anticipation and curiosity. Who were they? Patients? Passersby drawn by the buzz of the new clinic?

As he and Kim wove through the crowd, memories surfaced unbidden: the crash of breaking glass, Master Gong's challenge, and the silent determination in the eyes of his unexpected students. A heaviness settled in his chest, the weight of it pressing against him.

Kim's grip on his hand brought him back to the present. She looked up at him, her eyes brimming with unasked questions. Noticing her concern, Ethan took a steadying breath and managed a reassuring smile.

The crowd was a mix of ages, each person bundled in layers against the cold. Some wore modern, western clothes, while others stuck to traditional Chinese tunics and pants. All of them had an air of anticipation as they gathered near the entrance.

Ethan swept his gaze over the assembled crowd. A stocky woman in a red sweater comforted her child, her arms protectively wrapped around the little one. An elderly man in an olive-green Mao suit—baggy pants with a tunic-style button-down jacket—was absorbed in a newspaper. Nearby, groups engaged in animated conversation, while others stood silent and still, their expressions distant, as though waiting for something.

"You Dr. Wolf?"

The voice drew his attention to a slender woman standing in front of him. She wore a faded Western Michigan University sweatshirt, her stance assertive despite her modest height. Her sharp eyes locked on his, commanding attention.

"I am," Ethan replied evenly. "How can I help you today?"

Without a word, she thrust a postcard toward him— the grand opening announcement for Wolf Acupuncture & Kung Fu Vitality Center. His pulse quickened as he studied the card in her outstretched hand.

"Dr. Gong was my doctor," she said, her tone flat but tinged with something implied. "But he's gone back to China. Now I'm here to see you."

"Are you all patients?" Ethan asked incredulously.

The woman in the sweatshirt, tucking a lock of loose dark hair behind her ear, scrutinized a slip of paper before responding in cautiously articulated English, "You practice acupuncture?"

"I do," he confirmed, his voice steady. "Please, come in from the cold. I didn't expect a crowd this early. Let's get you all inside."

As he turned toward the door, he met Kim's gaze, and she flashed him an encouraging smile.

"Welcome to our grand opening!" Her voice rang out, clear and bright in the crisp winter air, drawing the crowd's attention.

A surge of resolve straightened Ethan's spine. This was real. His patients were waiting, trusting him to help. Overwhelming as it was, their need outweighed his doubts. He was determined to meet them where they stood, starting now.

The waiting room was cramped, with not nearly enough chairs for everyone. Ethan noticed younger people standing, gesturing for the elderly to take the available seats. The steady hum of conversation surrounded him, Mandarin flowing in quick melodic bursts—unfamiliar, indecipherable.

He glanced at Kim, who met his eyes. No words were needed; the implicit understanding passed between them—they would need help navigating this.

Kim stepped forward and smiled warmly. "Please help yourselves to tea, coffee, and a few sweets," she said, gesturing to the small tray on the side table. "The almond cookies are especially delicious."

A few of the older women exchanged approving murmurs and made their way toward the refreshments, while others smiled politely or nodded in gratitude.

Then Kim made her way to the young woman in the sweatshirt. "My name is Kim. I work with Dr. Wolf. What's your name?"

"Yan Guo," the woman replied.

"Yan, do you have a job right now?" Kim asked, her tone warm but direct.

Yan stiffened. "Not yet. I studied information

technology, but I can pay for my treatment."

Kim shook her head quickly. "Oh, that's not what I meant. Dr. Wolf doesn't speak Mandarin, and he could really use someone to help translate for his patients today. Could you help? He'll make sure you're compensated for your time."

Understanding dawned on Yan's face, followed by a tentative smile. She bowed slightly, hands pressed together in acceptance. Relief washed over Ethan, mirrored by Kim's subtle fist pump. Kim grasped Yan's hands and guided her to the reception desk.

Yan moved confidently through the crowded room, clipboard in hand, her presence bringing a sense of order to the chaos. She guided patients through their intake forms, bridging the language gap with ease and reassuring the growing crowd. "Dr. Wolf will see each of you as soon as he can," she promised, her calm demeanor settling anxious murmurs.

Ethan stood momentarily rooted to the spot, his gaze scanning the packed waiting room. He spotted familiar faces—Jen and several of the young men who'd helped rebuild the clinic after Gong's wreckage. Only now, they hadn't come for treatment. They stood near the wall, hands clasped behind their backs, eyes scanning the space with the composed discipline of students awaiting instruction.

Pushing through the crowd, Ethan approached them. "What's going on?" he asked, keeping his voice low.

Jen stepped forward, his posture respectful but unyielding. "We're here to learn kung fu, Master."

Ethan studied their determined expressions—some faces bruised, others still stiff from healing—and knew they weren't here on a whim.

Without a word, he motioned for them to follow.

He led them through the side corridor of the clinic, past storage shelves and stacked cartons, until they reached a metal door at the rear of the building. With a firm pull, he slid it open, revealing a large unfinished space: concrete floor, exposed beams, walls bare except for insulation and electrical conduit. A wide loading dock opened to the alley, the metal shutter currently rolled up.

Ethan gestured around them. "This is what will become the training room—the kwoon."

Jen and the others stepped inside, their footsteps echoing in the emptiness.

Ethan crossed to a corner where supplies were stacked—rolls of hardwood flooring, mirrored panels leaning against the wall, and a pallet stacked with bricks. He pulled down the metal shutter and rested a hand on the nearest stack of bricks. "One day, these bricks will seal up that loading dock. The hardwood will cover the floor. Those mirrors will line that wall."

Jen ran a hand along the brick's rough surface and gave a single nod. "Yes, Master. I understand."

The others followed his lead, walking the perimeter of the room, their gazes sharp with interest, even reverence.

Ethan stood rooted for a beat, absorbing the moment. He hadn't invited students. He hadn't advertised a school. But here they were, showing up anyway, expecting to be taught. Trusting him.

"I have patients to see," he said. "We'll talk again later."

Jen bowed. "We'll be ready."

Ethan turned and walked back toward the hum of

voices in the waiting room, his mind already shifting back to the work ahead. But the weight of what had just begun pressed lightly on his shoulders—not unwelcome, but unmistakable.

Focusing on his immediate challenge, Ethan turned to Yan. She introduced him to his first patient, and together they moved to Treatment Room One.

The day blurred by—twenty-seven patients treated, a dozen more booked for tomorrow. Ethan worked nonstop, needles, manual therapy, cupping, and careful reassessments. Yan moved between reception and treatment rooms with tireless grace, keeping the chaos from overtaking them both.

It was well past eight by the time they emerged from the final session. Ethan slumped into a chair, his stomach growling with hunger. Charts were stacked like fallen dominoes across the counter. The last of the patients had trickled out, the waiting room now empty.

Then the door opened.

Kim stepped inside, arms stacked high with pizza boxes. Ten of them. The scent of garlic and warm crust filled the space, and Ethan blinked at her like she'd descended from heaven.

"I brought reinforcements," she said, breathless but grinning. "There are more in the car."

"What's with all the pizza?" he asked, rising with a tired grin.

Kim tilted her head toward the back of the clinic. "Haven't you seen what's going on?"

Ethan followed her down the corridor. Kim pushed open the side door to the former storage space—and stopped just inside to let him take it in.

He stepped through the threshold and froze.

The space was unrecognizable.

Where the open loading dock had been, a wall of freshly laid bricks stood, expertly mortared and still faintly damp. The concrete floor now gleamed with new hardwood, perfectly installed. Drywall had been hung across the beams, giving the room definition and warmth. Full-length mirrors lined the far wall.

A crew of thirty men swept sawdust and wiped down equipment. Jen, his shirt dark with sweat, was on his knees buffing the floor with a towel.

Ethan blinked, stunned. "How—"

"They've been working all day," Kim said. "Ten hours straight. You started something, Ethan. They just finished it."

He walked farther into the room, absorbing the transformation in silence. His hand brushed the new wall. Solid. Permanent.

Near the front of the room, someone had laid a wide sheet of plywood across two sawhorses, creating a makeshift table. Kim began setting down the boxes of pizza, and as soon as she did, the workers drifted toward her, grinning and wide-eyed.

Then someone called out, "Master Wolf! Pizza?"

He turned to find Kim opening boxes and handing slices to the volunteers laughing and elbowing one another like brothers at a reunion.

"Tell them there's more in the car," she said to Ethan as she wiped her hands on a napkin.

The smell pulled everyone in. They sat along the edges of the new hardwood floor, pizza boxes between them. Someone cranked on a radio. Mandarin, Cantonese, English—conversations blended together like the patchwork of this place. The beginning of something.

Ethan sat beside Jen, taking a slice and a bottle of water. "I didn't mean for you to do all this," Ethan said.

Jen looked around the room. "We wanted to. This is our place now too."

When the last box was empty and the final crumbs brushed away, Ethan stood.

The music cut.

He stepped to the center of the new floor, the group rising and facing him in loose formation.

"We begin your training now," Ethan said, his voice carrying across the open space. "Prepare for your first class."

The men lined up quickly—two uneven rows, still wearing jeans or work pants. But their faces were focused, eyes lit with purpose.

Ethan nodded. He moved through the first form—a powerful kata for building foundational strength. Low stances, driving fists, transitions sharp as a blade.

Once.

Twice.

Then he paused and looked down the line. "Volunteer."

Jen stepped forward without hesitation.

Ethan smiled faintly and demonstrated the first movement of the kata—then its application. A wrist trap, hip turn, a throw, and a clean palm strike to the chest.

Jen landed with a thud but rolled quickly to his feet, grinning. "Again?"

Laughter rippled through the group.

Ethan nodded. "Again."

And so it began.

Chapter 15

Entry
Jon
Shanghai, China

The journey from the suffocating mines to the vibrant streets of Shanghai was surreal, as though stepping into an entirely different world. Jon chose a path along the Yangtze River, letting the brisk air fill his lungs—a sharp contrast to the dust-choked breaths of his former life. The memories of the cave-in that claimed Li Wei lingered, heavy and unshakable. Yet as the city unfolded around him, bustling and alive, it offered a fleeting sense of renewal.

Shanghai's energy pulsed like the heartbeat of a new beginning. The towering skyline, buzzing crowds, and neon lights reminded Jon of photos he'd once seen of New York and Paris in their golden ages, centers of modern civilization. His grasp of Mandarin, honed in the north, helped him navigate this eclectic world.

With the authentic identity papers tucked securely in his pocket—Li Wei's parting gift—Jon stepped into the sprawling metropolis, a man reborn. The anxiety that had once shadowed his every step in Beijing was gone, unshackled by the fear of exposure. Here in Shanghai, he had a newfound freedom, ready to pursue his calling, to seek his master and embrace his dream.

At the train station, Jon sought out a set of public lockers. He stashed a paper bag stuffed with cash into locker number 126, the day's date etched into his memory. The mustard-hued straps binding the bundles of hundred-dollar bills seemed almost out of place here, yet they were his lifeline. He dropped in the coins and pocketed the key. A flicker of reassurance swept over him—one more step in the plan he had meticulously crafted since Beijing.

As he ventured into the busy streets of Shanghai, Jon absorbed the city's dichotomies. Colorful posters advertised martial arts films from Hong Kong, their action-packed images ignited a surge of inspiration within him. Nearby, bold government posters declared the one-child policy in striking red characters, their stark messaging a contrast to the city's lively spirit. Foreign businessmen and trendsetters hastened along the sidewalks. Bicycles zigzagged through crowds, a legless man pedaling with his hands while children too young to carry such burdens moved with a haunting maturity in their eyes. The symphony of Shanghai played on, raw and unrelenting.

Jon's steps quickened as he neared his destination, Master Tong's kwoon. The traditional building stood as a testament to heritage amid urban chaos, its red lanterns glowing warmly against the twilight. The sight stirred something within him—a yearning for belonging, for purpose.

Jon rang the bell, the sound reverberating through the stillness. Moments later, a student in traditional martial arts attire opened the door and bowed respectfully. The incense-filled air hit Jon as he stepped inside, a blend of calm and focus. Weapons lined the walls alongside photos of martial arts grandmasters, each a silent tribute to the legacy Jon sought to become a part of.

"I am Li Wei," Jon introduced himself, adopting the name he had carried since fleeing the mines. The student nodded, leading him to the waiting area.

Jon's eyes wandered to the main practice hall. The last light of day had faded, and the polished wooden floors now reflected the warm, flickering glow of red lanterns hanging just outside. Inside, students moved in measured unison, their motions deliberate and composed—each stance a study in control and purpose. There was harmony in the way they shifted from posture to posture, a quiet power that resonated through the room. As Jon watched them, something within him stirred. Perhaps here, within this haven of tradition, he could begin again.

Footsteps echoed in the corridor, and Jon turned as Master Tong emerged, his presence commanding and calm. The master's steady gaze met Jon's, and both respect and apprehension stirred within him.

"Young warrior," Master Tong greeted, his voice low and resonant. "You've come seeking guidance."

Jon bowed deeply. "Yes, Master, I wish to learn under your tutelage."

A faint smile played on Master Tong's lips. "The desire is strong in you, but desire alone is not enough. Show me your forms."

Jon hesitated, his muscles tensing as he stepped into the vast practice hall. Apprehension knotted his stomach. "Master, my training has lapsed during my year in the mines. I fear my skills are not what they once were."

Master Tong gave no reply, gesturing for him to

begin. Jon took a deep breath and moved to the center of the room. His initial steps were hesitant, his motions stiff. But as he pressed on, muscle memory took over, and his movements began to flow. Each strike and stance was more natural, as if the art had been lying dormant, waiting for this moment.

When he finished, Master Tong nodded, approval glinting in his eyes. "Your skills may have dulled, but your spirit remains sharp. With dedication, you will regain your former strength—and perhaps surpass it."

Relief washed over Jon as he bowed, gratitude swelling within him. This was the beginning of something new, a chance to rebuild what had been lost. As he stood in the luminous practice hall, surrounded by echoes of a martial legacy, the certainty of his path solidified within him.

Master Tong rose, his expansive shadow stretching across the room, and gestured for Jon to follow. "Ciu will guide your initiation. He'll introduce you to the kwoon and your new comrades."

As they walked, Master Tong spoke of the kwoon's rich heritage, its legendary masters, and the trials that had shaped its legacy. Jon listened intently, each word deepening his reverence for the master at his side.

They stopped at a desk where Ciu waited. Master Tong inclined his head. "I leave you in Ciu's capable hands for your registration. Welcome to our family." With a final nod, he turned and departed.

Jon stood before Ciu, his stomach gave a slow, uneasy churn. His altered face had granted him this chance—a place among the devoted students of a revered master—but the lingering sense of fraudulence gnawed at him. He shifted his weight, steadying himself with the thought of the sacrifices that had brought him here.

"Your name?" Ciu asked, shuffling through a stack of forms.

"I am Li Wei," Jon replied, his voice steady despite the turmoil beneath.

"Will you pay monthly or annually? You save a month's fee if you pay annually."

"Annually," Jon said, placing his duffle bag on the desk with a soft thud. "In US dollars."

Ciu nodded, his expression neutral but polite. "The annual fee is five thousand five hundred. It includes tuition and lodging."

Jon pulled out a stack of crisp hundred-dollar bills and counted $3,000. "This is to hold my place. I'll bring the rest tomorrow."

Ciu recounted the money, recorded the amount, and slid the enrollment form across the desk. "Sign here."

Pen in hand, Jon paused, visualizing Li Wei's name as he had practiced so many times. With deliberate strokes, he wrote it, the characters flowing like ink on silk.

When he finished, he inclined his head toward Ciu. "Thank you. It's a privilege to begin this journey and dedicate these funds to their true purpose."

Ciu's smile softened. "Your presence honors our kwoon. Through perseverance and commitment, you will emerge as a warrior of body, mind, and spirit. Let me show you to your quarters and introduce you to our traditions."

Jon followed Ciu through the halls, a resolute determination settling over him. This was his path now, the first step in a long journey toward the mastery he had sought for so long.

Chapter 16

Strength in Pairs
Kim
Grand Rapids, Michigan

"Who's the new student?" Kim asked as she straddled the wooden bench in the newly constructed locker room, her voice light with curiosity.

Yan, pulling on her T-shirt at the far end of the room, answered without looking up, "Just visiting, like last month. His name is Ren. Handsome, don't you think? He's here to train while visiting family. Always pays in cash."

She had slipped naturally into her role as manager of the Wolf Acupuncture & Kung Fu Vitality Center—efficient, perceptive, and unshakably calm.

Kim slid into her training shoes and tightened the drawstring on her sweatpants. Something about Ren didn't sit right. She remembered his recklessness during his last visit—how his lack of control had left a training partner limping off the mat. The memory lingered, sharp and unwelcome, as she followed Yan into the training hall, determined to stay focused.

The students bowed as class began, Ethan guiding them through warm-up stretches before assigning pairs to practice the five elements techniques: earth, water, metal, wood, and fire. Kim was paired with Yan and welcomed her steady presence. Though Yan had trained since childhood under her grandfather in Beijing, she never made her feel less than. Over time, their partnership had grown into a deep and steadfast friendship—a bond Kim hadn't known she needed until Yan's calm, consistent encouragement became a cornerstone of her training.

Across the room, Ren's aggressive energy caught Kim's attention. He was paired with Bo, one of the younger but diligent students. As the drill continued, Ren's movements grew sharper—too sharp. Powerful, yes, but no restraint. No control. Ethan had spent weeks stressing the importance of intention, of listening through movement. Ren, it seemed, was deaf to that.

Kim noticed Ethan shift—only slightly, but enough. His posture straightened, his gaze narrowing as he focused in.

Then it happened.

A roundhouse kick, too fast, too hard. The snap of contact echoed through the training hall like a whip crack. Bo collapsed to the mat, clutching his ribs, his face twisted in pain. The room fell silent.

Ethan crossed the floor in a flash and dropped to one knee beside Bo with practiced calm, assessing the injury. "Control, Ren," he said, his tone steely. "Martial arts are not about brute force. They're a conversation, not a brawl."

Ren's expression didn't waver, defiance flickering in his eyes. Anger simmered as Kim's hands clenched at her sides, her gaze fixed on the scene unfolding before her. She glanced at Yan, searching for a reflection of her own concern, but Yan's face remained unreadable.

Ethan pressed a hand gently against Bo's ribs,

watching for signs of severe distress. "Take a slow breath," he instructed.

Bo winced but complied.

"Sharp pain when breathing?" Ethan asked.

Bo nodded.

Ethan scanned the injury site. "Any dizziness? Lightheadedness?"

Bo shook his head.

Ethan gave a small nod. "Looks like a cracked rib. You're not struggling to breathe, so there's no immediate danger, but you need to get checked out to rule out complications." He turned toward Yan. "Can you bring some ice?"

Yan hurried to the clinic's freezer while Ethan helped Bo sit up carefully. When she returned, Ethan handed Bo a wrapped ice pack. "Press this against your ribs—fifteen minutes on, fifteen minutes off. No training until you've seen a doctor."

Bo looked frustrated but nodded. "Yes, Master Wolf."

Ethan's gaze shifted to Ren. "In this kwoon, we protect each other. Injuries happen, but they should never come from ego or carelessness. Remember that."

The students returned to their practice, but Kim's focus remained on Ren's simmering frustration. Something about him set her on edge, and she silently vowed to keep an eye on him.

"Master, what's the most effective defensive technique?" Bo adjusted the ice pack on his ribs.

"It depends," Ethan replied with a faint smile. "Let's demonstrate. Ren, attack me using the five elements, one at a time."

The room stilled as Ren stepped forward, his

movements deliberate, his gaze hard. He launched into his attacks, each strike representing an element. Earth—his grounding kick was redirected with ease. Water—a flowing punch met Ethan's fluid counter. Metal—a slicing chop was parried and neutralized.

With each attempt, Ethan threw Ren to the mat effortlessly. Ren's strikes grew wild and sloppy. Ethan was a beacon of control in Ren's chaotic storm.

From the bench, Bo leaned forward, eyes fixed on the demonstration. His ice pack lay at his side.

Ethan turned to the class. "Martial arts teach adaptability. Each element counters another. Water absorbs fire; earth grounds water. Understanding these principles strengthens your technique and your spirit."

As the students dispersed, Yan lingered near the doorway in her gray Western Michigan sweatshirt. Kim noticed her hesitance and nudged Ethan toward her.

"Yan," Ethan said, "how are your parents?"

Yan hesitated, glancing at Ethan as though debating how much to share. "My father's health is declining. My mother has stopped working to care for him. They rely on the money I send, but it's not enough."

"Have you thought about bringing them here?" Ethan asked, his tone steady.

Yan's eyes widened. "Here? To America? I've always planned to return to them."

"What about your grandfather?" Kim interjected gently.

Yan's expression softened. "He's strong—still practices tai chi every morning. He's been my mother's strength."

"Bring them all," Ethan said. "I'll sponsor them. You're part of this community, Yan. We take care of each other."

Tears shimmered in Yan's eyes as she bowed deeply. "Thank you, Master Wolf."

When Kim emerged from her shower, the training hall was transformed. Candlelight flickered against the walls, and a low table surrounded by cushions awaited in the center of the room. Orchids floated in a bowl of water, their delicate beauty adding a touch of elegance.

"We're dining in tonight," Ethan said, his smile warm as he handed her a glass of plum wine.

"It's beautiful," she murmured, her voice tinged with surprise. "I didn't know you could do something like this."

He shrugged with a faint grin. "I had some help. I'm not exactly a pro at this sort of thing, but…I wanted tonight to be special."

As they ate, the atmosphere was intimate, their conversation easy and unhurried. At one point, Ethan reached across the table, taking her hands in his. "Thanksgiving means more to me now," he said quietly, his thumb brushing over her knuckles. "It's the day I found you again. I didn't plan to stay after that weekend, but I couldn't leave."

Her chest tightened with emotion. "I've been so happy since you came back."

He met her gaze, his eyes steady. "From the moment I saw you again, I knew I wanted to be with you. You were just…amazing. And now I can't imagine being anywhere else."

He reached into his pocket, withdrew a small box, and held it out to her. "I love you, Kim. I want us to be partners, always. Will you marry me?"

Her breath caught. Tears welled in her eyes as she

nodded. "Yes." When their lips met, a spark ran through her, an inner certainty settling over her heart. She was exactly where she was meant to be.

Chapter 17

Solicited
Jon
Shanghai, China

Jon moved purposefully through Shanghai's bustling streets, weaving around shoppers preparing for the new year. The vibrant energy of the city contrasted sharply with the somber discipline of his recent training. When he entered the teahouse, the pungent aroma of green tea and the soft trickle of water from a nearby fountain enveloped him. Jon's gaze swept the room, taking in the exits and the occupants—a pair of stocky men near the door, a high-class prostitute seated in the corner. He chose a table with his back to the wall, then sat down and ordered tea and steamed buns.

The porcelain cup warmed his hands as he took a sip, the tranquil atmosphere offering a brief escape. His thoughts drifted to the previous day's training, replaying the forms. Each movement had been a balance of discipline and pure reflex, a seamless blend of control and intent. Satisfaction settled over him, grounding him in the present.

Across the room, the prostitute caught his eye. Petite with short-cropped black hair and luminous, pearl-white skin, she exuded grace and an air of mystery. Her wide-set eyes and high cheekbones framed a pointed chin, her beauty both delicate and commanding. Without waiting for an invitation, she crossed the room and slid onto the cushion opposite him.

"I'm just here for tea," Jon said. He had no intention of prolonging the conversation.

Her smile was faintly amused. "I'm Sun," she said, her voice playful yet tinged with something hovering beneath the surface. "And you are?"

"Li Wei," he replied, using the name he'd adopted since moving to Shanghai.

Sun's laughter was soft, yet it carried an edge of melancholy. "A strong name," she said, running her fingers through her hair. "I imagine it has stories hidden behind it."

He hesitated, then deflected with a slight shrug. "Everyone in Shanghai has stories. What's yours?"

For a moment, her mask slipped. "Survival," she said simply, then quickly added, "But we all find ways to survive, don't we, Li Wei?"

Her directness threw him off balance. Rarely had anyone cut through the half-truths and veiled inquiries that defined interactions in this city. "We do," he said after a pause. "Some of us through disciplines and focus." His words nodded to his martial arts training, the anchor in his uprooted life.

"And some of us by reading people," she countered, her gaze steady. "It's not so different, is it? Both require understanding what lies beneath the surface."

He looked away, unsettled by how quickly she had pierced his defenses. He had come to Shanghai to escape his past, yet here he was, confronted by it in the most unexpected ways.

She didn't press further. "Well, if you ever wish to

share your story, Li Wei, you know where to find me." She slid a small card across the table as he was standing to leave. "No obligations. Just tea and an open ear."

As he walked away, he found himself reconsidering. Her story hinted at something deeper, something held back. Against his better judgment, he turned around and returned to find her where he'd left her. She looked up at him, her eyes brimming with tears.

"Is something wrong?" he asked, sitting down again.

Sun wiped away her tears. "I'm sorry." It's just that…I need to look like I'm with a client, or the gang on the street will demand their protection money, and I can't afford to pay it this month."

He shouldn't be shocked. Small business owners and vendors in the city commonly faced pressure to pay protection money to local gangs. Sun was an easy and vulnerable target. "Is there anything I can do?"

She shook her head. "I'll figure it out. Thank you for your kindness."

The situation was more complex than she let on, and complicating it further was the last thing he wanted. But he couldn't walk away. "Will it help if I escort you back to your place?"

She hesitated, then nodded. "Okay, it isn't far."

As they crossed the crowded street, wariness crept up Jon's spine. The sensation of being watched sharpened his focus. He placed a protective hand on Sun's elbow and stayed close, his gaze scanning the bustling crowd for anything unusual.

The streets of Shanghai were alive with the anticipation of the Chinese New Year. Red lanterns hung from every corner, casting a warm glow over the moving sea of people. Brightly colored banners bearing wishes for good fortune stretched across the roads, while performers on a grand stage captivated onlookers with music and dance, the rhythmic clash of cymbals and drums reverberating through the air.

Vendors lined the sidewalks, their calls competing with the chatter of the crowd. The aroma of roasted chestnuts mingled with the sweetness of steamed buns, creating a heady mix that tugged at Jon's memories of simpler times. But his focus remained sharp, the festive chaos doing little to soften his vigilance.

As they reached a small, unassuming apartment building, Sun paused and turned to Jon, her expression tender. She took his hand, her touch surprisingly steady. "Thank you for walking me here," she said. "I know you weren't interested in my services, but if you ever need someone to talk to, I'm a good listener."

"Are you sure you'll be okay?" he asked, glancing toward the second floor where a shadow moved behind a window. Was someone waiting for her?

She offered a small smile, tinged with sadness. "I'll be fine. Thank you for your concern."

"It's no trouble." His gaze lingered on her. "Let me walk you to your door." His mind churned with questions about what had led her to this line of work.

The door creaked open, and a young girl ran into Sun's arms.

Jon's body tensed instinctively, muscles coiled, ready to spring, until the innocence of the child registered. He exhaled, steadying himself. "What's going on here?" he asked, his voice sharper than intended as he turned back to Sun.

For a moment, she hesitated, cradling the girl protectively. "This is my sister, Xia. She's all I have. I'm responsible for her."

As understanding dawned, the tight coil of tension in his shoulders began to unwind. "Actually," he said, pausing near the exit, "I did change my mind. Let's meet outside the teahouse tomorrow at seven."

Sun blinked. "Thank you," she whispered.

"And bring Xia," he added before slipping into the night.

****

Sunlight streamed through the wide windows, casting warm light onto Jon's face as he moved through the training hall. The contrast between the sun's warmth and the cool discipline in the air sharpened his focus. A year of relentless practice had transformed him—his reflexes honed, his muscles hardened, and his mind sharpened like the edge of a finely forged blade.

At the wooden man post, Jon's strikes and blocks reverberated with power. Each impact, once jarring, now resonated through his body, strengthening his bones and solidifying his technique. The wooden dummy, a silent adversary, bore the brunt of his relentless drive. Every movement became a meditation on control and intent, the rhythm of his strikes almost reverential.

Master Tong's voice broke the intent focus of the room. "Kung fu is not merely the art of external strength and agility," he said, his tone calm but commanding. "Its true power lies within—*qi*, the vital energy that flows through all things."

Jon paused, shifting his weight, striving for the stillness the master demanded. Around him, the other students mirrored their teacher's deliberate movements, a synchronized dance of discipline. Master Tong continued, his presence almost radiating an energy Jon couldn't quite grasp.

"To master qi, you must unite mind, body, and spirit into a single current of intent," the master instructed, his movements fluid.

Jon watched, captivated by the harmony in Master Tong's demonstration. Every step and turn flowed with effortless power—grace shaped by decades of internal discipline, a mastery beyond the physical.

"Root yourself to the earth," the master instructed. "Feel the qi rise through you."

Jon closed his eyes, drawing his focus inward. A flicker of memory surfaced—a time when something powerful had moved through him, inexplicable and real. But now, all he felt was muscle strain and the weight of his breath. The flow of qi remained out of reach, leaving only the empty shell of the form.

As he continued, Jon's movements betrayed no hesitation, though inside frustration gnawed at him. He mimicked the senior students, hoping their confidence might seep into his bones. Each motion was deliberate, a projection of the mastery he longed to achieve.

Master Tong's gaze settled on him, a silent scrutiny that carried weight. Without a word, the master approached, lifting his palm just inches from Jon's chest.

"Qi is not strength alone," Master Tong murmured. "It is connection—between yourself and the ground beneath you."

In the next instant, the master shifted his stance, his feet pressing into the wooden floor, his energy coiling, gathering—then releasing. He struck with sudden force—not brute strength, but precision honed by discipline.

His fist barely moved more than two inches.

Yet the impact surged through Jon like a shockwave. His chest compressed, the breath forced from his lungs as his body lifted off the ground. He staggered back, then lost his footing entirely, tumbling across the floor in a controlled roll. The moment his back hit the mat, he sprang into a crouch, one hand braced against the ground, heart pounding.

The room was silent except for the faint creak of the wooden floor as the other students turned their attention to Jon. Their expressions were unreadable, a blend of awe and understanding, but none spoke.

"You grasp at the wind too fiercely," Master Tong said. "Qi flows around us, elusive as the morning fog yet ever present. It cannot be forced—only released."

Jon took a steadying breath, shoulders relaxing as he absorbed the master's words. He tried again, letting the tension uncoil from his body. For the briefest moment, he thought he sensed a shift—subtle, like the first whisper of a breeze.

Master Tong stepped back, his presence still heavy in the room. "Your path is not yet clear, but it is there. Through persistence and openness, you will find it."

Jon nodded, his determination reigniting. The master's lesson was more than words—it was a challenge to evolve, to move beyond the physical and into the unseen currents of the art. As he resumed his place in the line of students, a flicker of hope settled within him. The path was long, but he was ready to walk it.

Chapter 18

Lantern Festival
Ethan
Grand Rapids, Michigan

Ethan flicked the studio lights off and on, a signal for quiet. "Guo Nian Hao!" he called out, his voice bright in the dim room.

The response from the crowd was immediate. "Guo Nian Hao!" Cheers and clapping followed. Ethan had gotten the New Year's greeting just right. He locked eyes with Kim and mouthed, "Happy New Year." She returned the sentiment with a radiant smile, her red silk sheath making her stand out.

The Lantern Festival, celebrated under the night's full moon, capped off the fifteen-day Chinese New Year festivities. The studio was alive with guests—Ethan's and Kim's families, students, patients, friends—all sitting on mats and enjoying traditional dishes. The Chinese community members took turns performing lively lion and dragon dances in vibrant costumes.

In the days before, Yan had adorned every door with red and gold lanterns to usher in luck and prosperity. Auspicious symbols of wealth, fertility, and love adorned doors and windows, and kumquat trees, symbols of good fortune, dotted the space. Even the trees outside were festooned with colorful nylon lanterns, adding to the festival's joyous atmosphere.

With a grand gesture, Ethan welcomed everyone. "Tonight wouldn't be the same without all of you. I'm grateful to share in the wonder of Chinese New Year. And a special thanks to Yan for these incredible decorations and for bringing us closer to the heart of this celebration." He gave a nod toward Yan, leading the room in a round of applause.

Yan gave a shy wave, her cheeks tinted coral with a blush of bashfulness.

"Before we wrap up our festivities, I'd like to share one final tradition," Ethan announced, lifting a fully expanded sky lantern. "Tonight's perfect—clear skies, calm winds, and a full moon."

He glanced at Yan, his smile inclusive. "The Lantern Festival dates back two thousand years, starting with Buddhist monks who honored their teacher on this very night. It symbolizes light guiding us forward, casting out the dark. So everyone take a lantern and get ready to light up the sky. Once you're set, grab your coats and meet me outside."

Jen, Tu, and Bo hurried to the table where Kim handed out lanterns and lighters, Ren following. "Guo Nian Hao!" Kim greeted them warmly. Yan stepped up to help, showing everyone how to open the lanterns and attach the fuel cells.

With the group ready, Kim grabbed her own lantern and an extra one, just in case. She lit an old-fashioned metal lantern for extra light, a relic from her father's collection. Ethan then ushered the group outside into the serene night, the cordoned-off parking lot awaiting them like a stage set for their spectacle.

Ethan climbed onto a sturdy platform in the middle

of the lot, his yellow lighter in hand. "Tonight, we're part of a global celebration—the Lantern Festival. A very Happy New Year to all!" He lit the fuel cell, watching the flames carefully, ensuring they didn't lick the delicate paper. As the lantern swelled with warm air, straining for release, he let it go with a wish in his heart. His thoughts flew to Jon, hoping he, too, might be somewhere beneath the same vast sky, releasing a lantern of his own.

He stepped down and moved among friends, patients, and students, helping them send off their lanterns. Yan was right there with him, lending a hand. One lantern got snagged and started drifting toward the building. Ethan followed Kim with his gaze as she dashed after the wayward lantern. Once the sky was dotted with glowing orbs, he stood in awe at the stunning sight that unfolded above them.

Yan came up beside him, her eyes also lifted skyward. "These lanterns take me back to my hometown. To my family."

He glanced at her. "Have you spoken to your parents about coming over?"

Her smile grew. "Yes, they're looking forward to it. I'm getting all the paperwork ready to bring them here."

"That's great news. Just say the word if I can do anything more to help."

The festive mood was suddenly punctuated by a loud crack. Ethan flinched at the sound of firecrackers igniting, catching him off guard. Jen was doubled over in laughter nearby. Ethan watched, a little startled, as Bo ushered everyone back to a safer distance.

Yan laughed too. "Firecrackers are traditional, meant to scare off evil spirits and the Nian monster."

More fireworks erupted, and Bo, now on the platform, worked with Tu setting off an arsenal of rockets. The sky burst into a canvas of colors—green willows and purple spinners cascading through the air. The whistles, sizzles, and pops followed by resounding booms filled the night, but Ethan's thoughts wandered. He craved to share this with Kim but couldn't spot her anywhere.

He approached her parents. "Have you seen Kim? She shouldn't miss this."

Robert shook his head. "Let's check inside."

They combed through the building, room by room, calling her name. The booming of fireworks outside only heightened the suffocating silence within.

Panic clawed at Ethan's chest. "She would have told me if she was leaving," he said, his voice tight.

"Maybe she's out back?" Robert suggested, though doubt tinged his tone.

As they stepped outside, Ethan's heart plummeted. There, in the grass, lay one of Kim's red shoes. The fireworks finale thundered above, but its brilliance only deepened the growing dread. "Kim!" he shouted, scanning the faces in the crowd, but she was nowhere to be seen.

His pulse raced as he sprinted toward the parking lot.

"Where are you going?" Robert called after him.

"To find her," Ethan shot back without breaking stride.

Robert hurried to catch up. "I'm going with you."

By the street, Ethan froze. Kim's other red shoe lay abandoned in an empty parking space. Black tire streaks cut across the pavement like an ominous signature.

Ethan's insides roiled.

"She's been taken," he muttered, his voice raw.

Without another word, they climbed into Ethan's car. The tires screeched as they sped onto the road.

Ethan's knuckles whitened on the steering wheel. "This is the fastest way out of town," he said, his mind racing with possibilities—and dread.

Chapter 19

Escape
Kim
Grand Rapids, Michigan

Kim was in the trunk of a moving vehicle. The road roared beneath her.

Twelve minutes earlier she'd snatched the paper lantern from the hedge and stamped out the sparks. When she paused to look up at the other lanterns drifting like stars, a flicker of movement caught her eye. Before she could react, an arm clamped around her neck from behind, yanking her backward. Desperate for air, she clawed at the arm, her kicks and punches frantic.

"Stay quiet, and you won't get hurt. We're just looking for your brother and our money," a harsh voice hissed close to her ear.

Kim didn't buy it. She drove her heel down onto his foot and landed a solid punch, earning a curse from her assailant. As she struggled, another voice spoke in Mandarin, and a strong hand clasped a chloroform soaked handkerchief over her mouth and nose. Her strength ebbed away as she faded into unconsciousness.

Her pulse pounded against the restraints. Each moment took her farther from safety, from Ethan, and the chance of rescue dwindled with every mile.

Kim twisted her wrists, feeling the tape strain

against her movements. It held firm but had just enough give to exploit. Rolling onto her side, she curled her fingers inward and began working at the gag, scraping at the edges with her fingertips until she could pinch the tape between them. With slow, determined tugs, she peeled it away, finally ripping it free and gulping in deep, desperate breaths of air.

Next, she turned her attention to her wrists. Bending forward, she sank her teeth into the edge of the tape, sawing at it with sharp tugs. The adhesive stuck to her lips, the taste bitter and chemical, but she ignored it. She wrenched her arms apart, straining until the weakened tape began to split. With a final jerk, the bonds snapped. She ripped away the last sticky remnants and flexed her aching fingers.

Her mind raced. She needed to get out—but not without a plan. A sudden escape might end with her rolling onto the freeway at seventy miles an hour. She had to force them to stop first.

As Kim adjusted her position, her fingers pressed against something crinkled in her pocket—the remnants of the paper lantern. A spark of an idea flickered to life. Moving quickly, she tore the paper into smaller pieces and pressed them together with the sticky strips of duct tape, shaping a makeshift incendiary. But before she set it off, she needed a way out.

She ran her hands along the trunk's interior, searching blindly for anything useful. Her fingertips grazed the groove of a recessed handle. A surge of hope shot through her—it was the emergency release. She traced the mechanism, testing its give. It would work, but she had to time it right.

She fumbled in her coat pocket, fingers closing

around the lighter. With a sharp flick, the flame sprang to life. She touched it to the bundle. The dry paper ignited instantly, sending up acrid smoke. She hurled it forward, shoving it through the small gap between the trunk and the back seat.

The effect was immediate.

The car jerked as the driver swerved, shouts erupting from the front. Kim heard frantic coughing—thick, choking gas curling into the cabin. The vehicle lurched, slowing amid the commotion of honking horns and screeching brakes.

This was her chance.

She groped along the trunk's interior, fingers searching frantically for the emergency release. Gripping it tight, she yanked hard. The latch clicked, and the trunk lid popped open slightly. Wind rushed in, carrying the sharp, acrid stench of melting duct tape and scorched paper.

The car lurched, then skidded to a stop.

Bracing herself, Kim planted her feet against the frame and kicked with everything she had. The trunk flew open. The night sky filled her vision as she hauled herself up and out. She landed hard on the asphalt.

Cars swerved around her, tires shrieking against pavement. A horn blared inches away as she staggered to the shoulder, her breath coming in ragged gasps.

Behind her, thick smoke billowed from the car's interior, curling out through the open windows into the night. Doors flung open, and figures stumbled out, hacking and coughing. They staggered into the chaos of traffic, horns blaring and lights flashing. A semitruck skidded too late and its massive bulk collided with the vehicle and the figures in its path. The sickening crunch of metal echoed through the chaos, silencing the commotion for a split second before the world erupted into a cacophony of panic.

Kim went rigid on the shoulder, gasping for breath. Her hands trembled, soot smeared across her skin, but she was alive. She took one step forward, then another, as the adrenaline began to fade, leaving her shaken but resolute. She had survived. Now she needed to find Ethan.

The emergency response team descended upon the accident site. A state trooper approached and stopped in front of her. "Ma'am, I'm Trooper Watkins. Were you in that car?"

Her breath hitched as she nodded. "Not driving…in the trunk." Her voice cracked, the weight of the ordeal pressing down on her chest like a vice.

Watkins' expression hardened with alarm. "Were you hurt? Did they harm you?"

"They attacked me," she whispered, her body trembling as she wrapped her arms around herself. "I need a doctor."

The EMTs eased Kim onto a stretcher as the trooper reassured her. Her name and fragmented details of the abduction spilled out between gasps, but exhaustion soon overtook her, pulling her into a haze as the ambulance sped toward the hospital.

****

Ethan

The path forward was blocked by flares and police cars with flashing lights. Ethan pulled the car to the side of the service road and killed the ignition. "I'll check this out. Stay here," he said to Robert, already stepping out into the frigid night. The air reeked of burnt rubber and gasoline as Ethan jogged down the grassy slope toward the highway shoulder. A state trooper directed traffic, his radio crackling with updates. Ethan approached him, a photo of Kim clutched tightly in his hand.

"This woman—my fiancée—have you seen her?" Ethan's voice was tight, his breath frosting the cold air.

The trooper examined the photo and nodded grimly. "She was here. Ambulance took her to Butterworth—closest hospital."

Ethan's heart lurched. "Was she hurt? What happened?"

"Barefoot, bruised—she needed medical care," the trooper said, his tone softening. "Two others from the car...critical. Looks like they got hit trying to flee. You'd better get to the hospital."

Ethan found Kim in the ER, pale and bruised but conscious. Her wrists were raw from the duct tape, and a nurse was finishing drawing blood when he stepped inside. The sterile scent of antiseptic filled the room, sharp and invasive.

"We've been searching everywhere for you," he said, his voice low but steady as he kissed her forehead.

Robert leaned in, brushing a hand over her hair. "How's my girl?"

She turned her face toward them as the nurse left. "How did you find me?" she asked.

"Got lucky," Ethan murmured. "You're safe now."

Her voice was barely a whisper as she recounted the abduction. "They were looking for Jon. And their money. Then they drugged me and put me in the trunk."

Ethan's jaw tightened, and he paced to the window, staring into the night. "If Jon's mixed up in this and they think you know something, they'll come back. We need to be prepared."

"Sweetheart, I need to make a phone call. I'll be back soon." Robert patted her hand gently before exiting the room.

Ethan exhaled slowly, pressing his palms against his thighs to steady himself. "We need a story for the police. They're going to want to know who would want to hurt you." He kept his voice even despite the worry tightening his chest.

Kim sighed, her exhaustion evident. "The police said they'd be here tomorrow to question me."

The door opened, and Robert returned, his presence bringing a new energy into the room.

"Dad, we were just talking about what I should tell the police when they come to question me."

Robert paused. "Wasn't there another kung fu master who thought Ethan had moved into his territory and tried to chase you out of town?"

"Yeah, back before the office opened, during the remodeling." Ethan sat at the edge of his seat.

"After he challenged you and you beat him, he went back to China, right?"

"That's right. And his students took me as their master." Ethan nodded.

"He's the sort of character who could be seeking revenge. He certainly made threats with that intent. That's something the police can chew on for a while." Robert grinned. "Now, listen, there's someone I want you to meet this Wednesday."

Kim looked questioningly at Ethan, then back at her father. "A lawyer?" she ventured.

Robert shook his head. "No, an old friend. He once saved my life."

Chapter 20

Wishes in the Wind
Jon
Shanghai, China

Jon walked through the vibrant streets of Shanghai, the air alive with the sights and sounds of the Chinese New Year. Lanterns swayed above the crowded pathways, their red glow casting warm light over stalls brimming with wares—red envelopes, embroidered scarves, and delicate paper kites. Aromas of sizzling meat skewers and steaming baozi mingled with the sharp tang of firecrackers, wrapping the city in a festive haze.

Sun walked beside him, her sister, Xia, darting ahead to inspect each stall with uncontainable excitement. At Jon's urging, Sun had brought Xia along, and now the trio wove through the throng, their laughter mingling with the city's celebratory hum.

"She has an endless supply of energy and enthusiasm," Sun said, her tone apologetic as Xia flitted between vendors.

Jon nodded. "How long have you been taking care of her?" He wanted to know more about her story.

A wistful expression softened her face. "Since our parents passed away five years ago. She was eight then. I've done my best, but I worry I'm not strict enough. My dad—he was a general—would've thought I'm too lenient."

He watched Xia dart ahead, her excitement spilling over as she marveled at a stall displaying brightly colored kites. "She's full of life," he said. "That's a gift. Maybe she gets that from you."

Sun gave him a small smile, her eyes betraying a mix of pride and concern. "It's not easy. Sometimes, I wonder if I'm doing enough to guide her."

Xia ran to a stall where a merchant twirled scarves in the air like colorful flags. She swept a red silk scarf across her face, batting lashes with exaggerated flair. "Can I have one?"

Jon almost reached for his wallet but caught himself, remembering Sun's earlier words about being too indulgent. He glanced at her.

"Not today." Sun folded the scarf and returned it to the merchant. "But we can get something to eat. What do you think, Xia?"

Xia's face lit up. "Everything smells so good!" She took off toward a baozi stall, leaving Jon and Sun to follow, laughing.

At the stall, they ordered a generous helping of fluffy buns filled with steaming pork. For a while, the weight of responsibility lifted. The simple pleasure of shared food and the warmth of their laughter created a rare moment of peace.

As they wandered farther, they came upon a photo booth adorned with red lanterns. Jon grinned and nudged Sun and Xia toward it. "Let's make a memory."

Inside, they found traditional Chinese garments for dressing up. Xia selected a warrior princess outfit with mock armor, her eyes gleaming with mischief as she adjusted the bracers. Sun ran her fingers over the silk dresses before choosing one with intricate embroidery and a high collar, the fabric draping elegantly around her. Jon chuckled as he pulled on a scholar's robe, the flowing sleeves exaggerated with every movement. He smirked as Xia struck a fierce pose between them, clearly relishing the moment.

The printed photo encapsulated the joy of that day—a snapshot of laughter and connection amid the ancient traditions of the New Year.

As dusk fell, they joined the crowd at the riverbank for the lantern release. Hundreds of paper lanterns, each bearing wishes for the year ahead, floated into the sky—a constellation of dreams. Together, they knelt and wrote their wishes—Xia wished for endless adventures, Sun for strength, and Jon for new beginnings. With a steady breath, Jon released his lantern and watched it rise, its flickering light lifting his prayer into the night. It drifted upward beside Sun's and Xia's, joining the sea of glowing hopes above the river, yet his felt singular. Solitary. Personal.

Then the moment broke. Xia had wandered ahead to admire a nearby kite stall. Jon's vigilance heightened. A group of rough-looking youths had gathered around her, their low voices and tense stances setting off alarms in his mind.

"Sun, stay close," he murmured, quickening his pace.

The tallest boy reached for Xia's arm, his sneer brazen.

Jon stepped between them. "Leave her alone."

The boy's smirk widened. "She's Sun's, isn't she? You don't know what you're getting into."

Jon didn't flinch. "I know enough to stop you."

The gang exchanged glances before lunging. Jon's training took over. He ducked a punch. His movements had the grace of a dancer and the power of a charging bull. A swift kick sent one boy sprawling, while a hard block deflected another's strike.

The fight ended quickly, the gang retreating, battered and cursing. Jon turned to Xia, her wide eyes brimming with gratitude.

"Thank you," she whispered, clutching his arm.

Sun approached, her face pale but resolute. "We need to leave. Now."

He nodded, shepherding the sisters away from the crowd. His grip on the small, tarnished key in his pocket tightened, its weight grounding him.

****

The next morning, Jon joined the other students in the common area for breakfast. The room buzzed with laughter and the rhythmic clatter of chopsticks against bowls. The air carried the comforting aroma of steamed rice and broth, a grounding start to another demanding day of training.

"Morning, Li Wei!" Chin, a lanky student with a wide grin, called out.

"Morning, Chin," Jon replied, grabbing a bowl of rice. "You guys started without me?"

"You're late," another student teased. "Too busy perfecting that serious face of yours?"

Laughter rippled through the group, and Jon rolled his eyes. "Takes effort to look this good."

Before anyone could fire back, a hush settled over the room. Master Tong had entered, his presence shifting the air like a stone dropped into still water.

"Enough chatter," he said. "Your training awaits."

At once, the students set their bowls down, rising in practiced synchronicity. They moved swiftly from the common room, their light footsteps echoing through the corridors as they made their way into the training hall. The transition was smooth, habitual—an inherent discipline ingrained in them.

In the spacious hall, they took their places in formation, the air thick with focused energy.

Master Tong surveyed them with measured patience before lifting a hand. "Begin."

Jon fell into the rhythm of the forms, his movements fluid, his breath steady. Around him, the synchronized flow of his fellow students created a silent harmony—a unity. With each strike and purposeful step, something inside him steadied.

Belonging.

This was more than training. It was his refuge.

Chapter 21

Unexpected
Kim
Grand Rapids, Michigan

Kim met her father's war buddy, Hank
Lewandowski, three days after she was admitted to the
hospital. With a rigid posture and a gaze that seemed to
assess her every move, Hank exuded a no-nonsense
demeanor that made Kim sit up a little straighter.

"He'll be training you for two and a half hours a day,
every day, for four weeks," her father said.

She narrowed her eyes. "What kind of training?"

"Self-defense," her father replied simply.

She crossed her arms. "I'm already training with
Ethan."

"This is different," he explained. "After four weeks,
you'll be able to defend and protect yourself in ways
martial arts can't prepare you for."

Hank interjected, his voice steady. "We'll start with
basic techniques—escaping a bear hug, striking
vulnerable areas, and staying alert to potential threats.
You'll learn how to handle nonlethal weapons like
pepper spray and tasers. And," he added, his eyes
narrowing slightly, "you'll be taught how to use a knife
and a gun."

"I'm not interested in guns."

Hank studied her for a moment before responding. "They say Samuel Colt made all men equal. We'll see what he can do for a woman."

The words made her bristle, but she swallowed her discomfort, the memory of being thrown into the trunk still too fresh. "Fine. I'll do it," she said, her voice steadier than she was.

Hank nodded approvingly. "We'll start as soon as you're discharged."

After he left, she sank into the chair beside her bed, her father's reassuring hand on her shoulder.

"You're doing the right thing, Kim. This will help you take control again."

She nodded but remained silent, vowing inwardly, *I won't be a victim again.*

Her father hesitated before speaking again. "Your mother hasn't been here because…she's struggling."

Kim looked up sharply. "Struggling? What do you mean?"

"She's been shaken since your abduction," he said, his voice thick with emotion. "For her, it was like losing Jon all over again."

Her heart sank. "I didn't realize—"

"She's getting the help she needs," her father reassured. "Right now, focus on healing yourself."

She bit her lip, tears welling up in her eyes. "I just want us to be okay, Dad. I want Mom to be okay."

"We will be," he assured her, his voice firm but gentle. "It will take time, but we'll get through this together." He pulled her into a gentle hug.

Ethan arrived with lunch just as Robert left. "You're starting to look like your beautiful self again," he said, setting down a bag of takeout. "Any news from the

131

doctors?"

"Not yet, but I'm ready to leave." She turned off the TV, her focus shifting entirely to him.

"I brought Thai food. Hope you're hungry." He unpacked the containers, the aroma filling the room.

"It smells delicious," she said, digging in. "I'm actually hungry for the first time since I got here."

As they ate, he asked about her father's earlier visit. "What was that about?"

"He introduced me to his old military friend, Hank. I'll be starting self-defense training."

He nodded. "Your dad mentioned that. Special-forces-type training?"

"Something like that." She met his gaze. "Ethan, this is important. I need to feel safe."

He took her hand in his. "That's all that matters."

Before he could say more, the door opened and a nurse entered, her smile as bright as the fluorescent lights overhead. "I have wonderful news—your bloodwork shows that you're pregnant!"

For a moment, time froze. Kim's hand instinctively moved to her abdomen, her jaw slack with surprise. The nurse hesitated briefly, then offered an awkward smile and slipped out of the room, leaving them alone.

Ethan's face lit up, his hand tightening around hers. "This is great! We're going to be parents."

Kim's thoughts spiraled. The memory of her abduction still lingered, raw and jagged. And now she had more than herself to protect. "I wasn't expecting this—not yet."

He leaned closer, his eyes steady and kind. "We'll figure it out, together. You're not alone."

Her pulse slowed, his words grounding her. She

thought of Hank's training, of the skills she would gain to defend not just herself but this new life growing inside her. The fear began to ebb, replaced by a fierce resolve.

A small smile curved her lips as she squeezed Ethan's hand. "I'm scared," she admitted, her voice soft, "but I'm ready to fight for this—for us."

****

Ethan

Ethan headed to the ICU where Kim's abductors were hospitalized. Driven to uncover the mastermind behind the attack, he replayed Kim's police testimony in his mind. They'd been assured the culprits would be in a secure, surveilled room, likely handcuffed to their beds. Access to such patients was restricted to family, lawyers, and medical staff. Alone in the elevator, Ethan donned a white medical coat and draped a stethoscope around his neck, hoping this disguise would grant him entry.

But when he arrived at the unit, the rooms were not guarded by law enforcement officers. His thoughts spun in a million directions. Had the police not considered the kidnappers criminals who were a flight risk and a danger to the public or hospital staff?

As he neared the door, it opened, revealing an orderly with a cleaning cart. The room was empty, bed neatly made. Ethan's curiosity grew; the other abductor's room was also vacant. Concern flickered within him— had they been moved or taken to a more secure facility?

At the nurses' station, he sought answers and was met with shocking news—both men had died due to sudden respiratory distress during the night.

Ethan stared at the elevator buttons. The simultaneous deaths of Kim's abductors seemed too orchestrated, too convenient. The idea of both suffering fatal respiratory issues at the same time hinted at foul play, suggesting they were eliminated to keep secrets hidden. It appeared they were just pawns in a larger, more ruthless scheme, silenced by an organization desperate to protect its identity. The need to expose the ringleader and their knowledge about Jon intensified within Ethan. The importance of a deep investigation into these suspicious deaths became clear, and he recognized they were entwined in a dangerous plot.

He meandered among plush toys and bouquets in the hospital gift shop, debating whether to tell Kim the grim news. His gaze landed on a brilliantly shining faceted crystal pendant. It seemed to embody Kim's spirit—resilient, radiant, a source of strength and wonder. But the weight of his discovery pressed heavily on his mind.

"How do I tell her?" he muttered, picking up the pendant. "She's been through so much already."

He was conflicted. She deserved to know the truth, but he feared the news would shatter her already fragile sense of security. The image of her hopeful smile when he'd walked into her room made his heart ache.

She's finally starting to feel safe again. If I tell her, it might push her over the edge. But keeping it from her feels wrong.

When he returned to Kim's side, he placed the gift-wrapped pendant and a card on the table. Her calm, peaceful breathing contrasted with the storm of thoughts swirling in his mind. The unknown identity of the assailants and the looming threat to his family pressed down on him. In the stillness of the room, he clenched his jaw, his resolve hardening. He would protect her and the future they were building, no matter what it took.

For now, he would carry the burden alone, resolving

to find the right moment to tell her when she was stronger.

Chapter 22

Cinema
Jon
Shanghai, China

Jon ushered Sun and Xia out of the teahouse, glancing at his watch. "We need to hurry," he said, "or we'll miss the opening scene of the movie at the cinema." They quickened their pace, weaving through the bustling streets as they headed toward the grandeur of the theater's lobby.

Making their way to the refreshment line, Jon guided Sun and Xia through the throng of people. The opulence of the theater's lobby surrounded them. Above, intricate murals adorned the ceilings, and sculptures stood proudly beside ornate fixtures—each detail a celebration of Chinese architectural artistry. They joined the queue, enveloped by the comforting smell of popcorn undercut by the sharp tang of cigarette smoke that hung in the air.

With snacks secured, Jon, Sun, and Xia navigated through the dim aisles to their seats.

Jon grinned playfully and slipped Xia a small bag of candy. "For the full movie experience," he said in a whisper. "But let's try to make it last beyond the previews, okay?"

Xia's eyes sparkled in agreement as she clutched the

treat, a silent pact forming between them.

Sun leaned over to him, whispering a thank you, her eyes reflecting the flickering screen light. He just nodded, his attention split between the gratitude in Sun's voice and the growing anticipation for the film.

As the room hushed and the screen lit up, Jon reclined, the day's concerns melting away under the cinematic spell. He glanced at Sun and Xia, their rapt attention on the unfolding drama a gentle reminder of the connection they were building through this shared moment.

He had eagerly anticipated *Snake in the Eagle's Shadow* since he arrived in Shanghai and saw the posters plastered throughout the city. The martial arts action-comedy film emerged as a commercial success in Hong Kong cinema with a new leading actor and martial artist, Tommy Chan. Jon absorbed the story of a young orphan taken in by a beggar and trained in kung fu who found himself caught up in a conflict between a notorious gang leader and a rival kung fu school. As the movie played and the martial artists fought and leaped across the screen, Jon was mesmerized by the innovative fight choreography.

Beside him, Sun and Xia watched intently, their shifting expressions reflecting the drama on the screen. Xia's wide-eyed excitement and Sun's occasional soft smiles turned the experience into more than just a movie.

When the film ended and the lights came up, Jon turned to Sun and Xia, his smile stretching wide. "What did you think?" he asked.

"It was wonderful." Sun's eyes still reflected the excitement of the movie. "Is that what you do?"

Xia nodded enthusiastically, her face lit with

wonder. "I want to learn kung fu too."

He chuckled softly as he stood, and they followed his lead.

"I'm glad you enjoyed it," he said. "But remember, it's just a movie. Real martial arts take years of hard work and dedication."

As they stepped into the night, the aroma of sizzling street food filled the air, mingling with the chatter of the lively crowd. A vendor nearby caught Jon's attention with crispy fried wontons and skewered meat sizzling over open flames. He motioned for Sun and Xia to join him and ordered enough to share.

They ate standing under the warm glow of a streetlamp, chatting about the movie. Xia mimicked a few of the on-screen moves, her boundless energy drawing laughs from Jon and Sun. Between bites, Sun asked, "So tell me more about your kung fu school. What's it like?"

He hesitated briefly before answering, "It's rigorous but fulfilling. Every day, we train to master not just the physical techniques but the discipline behind them."

As they continued their walk back to Sun and Xia's apartment, his mood shifted. The bustling streets were alive with movement, but something about the ebb and flow of the crowd set him on edge. He glanced back and gently rested a hand on Xia's shoulder, a subtle reminder to stay close.

Sun, perceptive as ever, asked, "You look worried, Li Wei. What's wrong?"

He paused, scanning the shadows that seemed to stretch too long under the flickering streetlights. "I just want to make sure you're safe. Both of you," he said.

Sun smiled, though her gaze searched his face.

"We've been managing on our own for quite some time."

Her confidence was genuine, but it didn't loosen the knot in his stomach. The city's unpredictability gnawed at his thoughts. Every corner turned was a possible threat, and every stranger's glance lingered too long. He stayed alert, even knowing he couldn't always protect them.

As they reached Sun and Xia's apartment building, Jon hesitated at the bottom of the narrow stairwell that led to their door. The night air hung heavy, carrying the muffled hum of the city and distant laughter from revelers still celebrating the new year. He considered the possibilities—how best to prepare Sun and Xia to protect themselves, how to stay connected without exposing them further to the risks that seemed to follow him. He didn't just want to ensure their safety—he wanted to be part of their future.

****

The next morning, Jon and Ming squared off in the sun-drenched practice room of the kwoon. The wooden floor steady beneath his feet grounded him as he mirrored Ming's sharp movements. The copper gong's tone echoed through the room, signaling the start of sparring. Jon focused on Ming's quick strikes, his movements fluid yet deliberate. Each block and counterstrike came faster, testing Jon's reflexes and resolve. Sweat trickled down his temple, but he pushed forward, anticipating Ming's next move.

Master Tong's voice broke through the rhythm of their practice. "Enough," he said, gesturing for the students to gather. "Martial arts is about awareness—of your opponent, your surroundings, yourself."

His gaze seemed to linger on Jon. Did the master

sense the turmoil Jon wrestled with beyond the kwoon?

As the session ended, Master Tong called the students together. He raised his hand in a commanding gesture to silence the chatter in the room. "There is a proverb—'The wise warrior avoids the battle.' This does not mean we should be passive, but rather we should be strategic. Understand the nature of your enemy and the environment in which you fight."

With those words, Master Tong left swiftly with long, confident strides, and the class dispersed. Jon and Ming sat across from one another, peeling off their protective pads in silence. The brief look Master Tong had given him before leaving clung to Jon like a warning. Avoid the battle. The words echoed. Did Master Tong know? Had he somehow sensed that Jon was stepping into something deeper—something tied to the street?

Ming tilted his head, his tone curious as he asked, "What's bothering you, Li Wei?"

Jon sighed heavily. "I've got a friend who is being extorted and threatened by a gang here in Shanghai. They're demanding money and frightening her and her sister. It appears they're intent on collecting their 'protection' money, but they can't pay."

Ming's expression darkened. "These gangs are no joke. Some are just loose groups of thugs, but others—black societies—run entire markets and have police in their pockets."

Jon nodded, understanding Ming's point. "I know, but I can't just let them be terrorized."

Just then, Master Tong reappeared in the doorway, his presence commanding the room. "Li Wei," he called, his voice measured and thoughtful, "a word."

In the stillness of the corner, Master Tong's message

cut though him like a blade. "To protect is noble, but to act without wisdom is dangerous. Seek allies. Choose your battles. Your heart is strong, but your mind must guide your fists."

Jon nodded, the weight of the advice anchoring him. As he returned to Ming, a plan began to take shape. For the first time, he believed he could protect Sun and Xia—without losing himself.

Chapter 23

Chinese Spirit
Jon
Shanghai, China

The evening air was crisp as Jon and Sun strolled from the teahouse, their steps synchronized in a comfortable rhythm. Xia had eagerly gone to a friend's house, leaving Jon and Sun to enjoy each other's company. As they walked, the city's vibrant energy hummed around them, but within their shared space, a calm intimacy wrapped around them, making the rest of the world feel distant.

Reaching her apartment building, Sun paused, her gaze lingering on Jon. An implicit question was in her eyes, a delicate invitation. "Would you like to come up?" she asked, her voice tinged with a vulnerability he hadn't heard before.

He hesitated, his thoughts a whirlwind. "Sun, I don't want to be a customer," he said.

Her expression softened, and a gentle smile touched her lips. "I don't want you as a customer. I want you for myself," she said quietly, sincerity shining in her eyes. It was a moment of truth, a crossroads for them both.

A surge of emotion swept through him—apprehension and desire, hope and doubt. He let her take his hand, following her up the stairs, each step a silent dance toward something unknown. Inside, the apartment was an extension of Sun—warm and inviting, yet layered with untold stories.

In the soft glow of the living room, she turned to face him, her hands reaching out. He could feel the yearning in her touch, the silent hope for something more than the life she had known. They stood there, on the brink of a decision that could change everything.

He caught her hands, his heart pounding. "If we do this, you'll need to find another profession," he said. It was not just a request but a plea, a promise of something more.

She held his gaze, her expression flickering with emotions too complex to name. After a long moment, she nodded. "I understand," she whispered, her voice a blend of fear and determination. "I never wanted this life."

Her words cut deep, stirring something raw inside him. The weight of her past, of everything she had endured, settled heavily in his chest. But beneath the pain, there was relief—relief that she wanted something more, that she was ready to leave that life behind.

Sun suggested they share a bottle of *baijiu*, a traditional Chinese spirit known for its depth and warmth. They sipped the *baijiu*, its rich, fiery flavor spreading heat through Jon's chest and loosening the wordless tension between them. She spoke of dreams, pasts, and hopes, her voice growing softer as the conversation deepened. At one point, she rose and retrieved a photo album, cradling it like a fragile treasure. He watched as she turned the pages, revealing snapshots of her life. One photo caught his attention, Sun and Xia as young girls, their faces reflecting an innocence and bond that seemed unshakable. On another page, a solemn man in a military uniform stood tall—Sun's father. His proud posture and the reverent way he was framed in the photos hinted at the disciplined, structured life Sun must have grown up in.

"This was before things…changed," she murmured, her voice tinged with both nostalgia and sorrow. Her finger brushed the edge of a photograph, and for a moment, she seemed lost in it.

As Jon studied her face, he sensed the weight of subtle secrets, each one a thread woven into the fabric of who she had become. The intimacy of the moment—the sharing of pieces of her past—left him feeling honored yet acutely aware of how much he still didn't know.

When the conversation shifted to music, a spark returned to Sun's eyes. She rose again, this time pulling a beautiful instrument from a nearby stand. Its pear-shaped body gleamed in the dim light, its ornate carvings a testament to centuries of craftsmanship.

"This is my pi-pa," she said, settling it on her lap. "It's been with me through everything."

Jon leaned forward as her fingers, adorned with small plectra, brushed the strings. The first notes emerged like whispers, delicate and melodic. Then the music swelled, cascading into rapid, intricate runs before ebbing into slower, mournful strains. The room filled with sound—a haunting beauty that seemed to speak directly to his soul.

Each note painted a story, evoking images of ancient mountains, distant battles, and forgotten love. Jon closed his eyes, letting the music carry him to a world both foreign and familiar. When the final note faded into silence, he opened his eyes to find her gazing at him.

"Play another," he murmured, unable to look away

from her.

Instead, she set the pi-pa aside, stepped closer, and took his hand. Her touch was steady, but her eyes carried the same mix of apprehension and hope that stirred in him. She led him toward the bedroom, each step weighted with meaning. The night unfolded not with urgency, but with tender, deliberate connection—a fragile promise of something new.

In the soft morning light, he lay awake, his thoughts drifting to Beijing. The warmth of Sun beside him was a balm, but a yearning to reconnect with his family tugged at him like an insistent thread. He couldn't ignore the pull any longer. The memories of home and the need to bridge the distance were an urgent call he couldn't ignore. He yearned for communication from Daniel Wu.

****

Jon retrieved the mailer from his Beijing postal box with shaking hands, a deep sense of dread settling in his gut. The envelope was unusually heavy, and his heart raced as he hurried to a secluded corner of the nearby park. Sitting on a bench beneath the bare winter branches, he stared at the package, willing himself to open it. A cold wind cut through the air, but the chill wasn't what made his hands tremble.

With a deep breath, he tore it open and pulled out a folded newspaper clipping. The grainy black-and-white photograph stopped him cold.

Before him lay a scene frozen in time, a moment torn from his worst nightmares. Kim stood barefoot on a highway shoulder, her hair tangled and wild, her arms wrapped tightly around herself. Her face was streaked with soot and exhaustion, her expression distant—shock written in the slackness of her features, in the hollow set of her eyes. Behind her, smoke billowed from the mangled wreckage of a car, its frame barely recognizable. The massive grille of an oncoming semi filled the background, caught mid-motion, seconds before impact.

Jon's pulse pounded. The still image didn't capture the moment of destruction, but he saw it vividly in his mind—the blare of the horn, the shriek of metal, the final collision that had ended it all.

The chaos was frozen in the frame, but Kim stood at its center—motionless, alone, and staggered in the aftermath. The caption beneath the photo read *Freeway Escape: Woman Survives Harrowing Abduction.*

Jon's grip tightened on the paper. His sister had come that close to dying.

He unfolded the note tucked inside and scanned the lines in Daniel Wu's familiar, blocky handwriting.

Your sister is smart and strong. She used a smoke bomb to escape the trunk, forcing the car to stop. She's safe and receiving care. We have people watching over her. Stay strong, Jon. We're doing everything we can.

Relief hit first, sharp and overwhelming—but it carried a dangerous edge. A simmering fury burned beneath it. Kim had survived, but she never should have been in danger to begin with.

He exhaled slowly, forcing himself to think. He couldn't be there for her—not yet—but she wasn't alone. Daniel had people in place, keeping watch. For now, he had to trust them.

Jon carefully folded the newspaper clipping and note and slipped them into his duffel bag. His mind was a storm, his heart with Kim, an ocean away.

But he would make them pay.

Chapter 24

Honeymoon
Kim
San Francisco, California

Kim stepped out of the taxi, taking in the impressive facade of the American College of Traditional Chinese Medicine. This trip to San Francisco, their honeymoon, was her chance to bridge the gap years and grasp the experiences that had shaped Ethan into the man she loved.

Ethan led her through the hallways, his pace quick and his hand firm around hers. The hallways were adorned with traditional Chinese medicine art and artifacts, and Kim could feel his excitement in the way he moved, like he couldn't wait to show her this part of his world. They reached the open office door of his former professor, Dr. Ng, who welcomed him into a warm embrace. Kim watched as the two men exchanged greetings, their shared affection clear in the way Dr. Ng clapped Ethan's back and beamed at him.

"Congratulations on your marriage," Dr. Ng said with a wide smile that crinkled the corners of his eyes. "Ethan was a standout student."

Kim smiled, leaning in slightly. She couldn't help but be drawn in by Dr. Ng's warmth and the respect he clearly held for Ethan.

"I understand you're curious about traditional Chinese medicine?"

She nodded, eager to delve deeper. "Your passion for TCM is inspiring. What got you into it?"

He smiled, his gaze turning thoughtful. "It started when I was young back in China. I was drawn to how it's not just about healing—it's about balance, the yin and yang, how everything connects."

"How have things been since I left? What's the situation in Chinatown?" Ethan steered the conversation to current affairs.

Concern flickered across Dr. Ng's face. "The area's been troubled with increasing violence. I'd recommend being cautious, particularly after dark. Rumors suggest broader criminal activities are responsible."

Kim mulled over his words for a moment before glancing around the room, her curiosity sparking again. "Would it be all right if I had a look around? I'd love to see more of the college."

"Certainly," he said, his demeanor shifting to an educator's. "Ethan knows his way around; he'll be an excellent guide. Take care and be mindful of your surroundings."

As she stepped into the room that had once been Ethan's haven of learning, her gaze was immediately drawn to the walls where anatomical charts mapped out acupuncture points and meridians like intricate constellations. A nearby shelf displayed jars of dried herbs and roots—ginseng, licorice, and others she couldn't name—each one a small fragment of the ancient art Ethan had mastered.

She trailed her fingers over an arrangement of acupuncture needles and moxibustion sticks, and she imagined Ethan's steady hands mastering these tools. Across the room, a workstation held measuring tools and small beakers, remnants of lessons in crafting herbal formulas.

The space pulsed with purpose, a bridge between centuries-old traditions and the modern world. For a moment, Kim could almost see Ethan here—intense, hunched over a chart or a book, his sandy hair mussed from hours of study, hazel eyes flicking between notes and diagrams.

"You haven't seen the rest." Ethan was back at her side. "Come on—I want to show you where I trained when I was a student here." He led her out to the street.

YC Tsun Kung Fu School was a few blocks away within view of Golden Gate Park. The storefront windows offered a clear view inside. Ethan held the door for her.

The space inside was humble but clean, with scuffed wooden floors and a faint scent of sweat. Weapons lined one wall—staffs, swords, fans—and a row of black-and-white photos hung above the mirrors, each depicting past students in faded uniforms, their faces young and proud.

An older man stepped from the office, his posture erect, his gray hair tied back in a short queue. His eyes lit up. "Ethan—that's Dr. Wolf now," the man greeted with a smile and a slight bow. "You're taller than I remember."

"Master Tsun," Ethan said, bowing deeply. "It's good to see you."

Master Tsun's eyes shifted to Kim, curious but kind.

"This is Kim," Ethan said. "My wife."

She stepped forward and returned the older man's bow. "It's an honor to meet the teacher who helped shape him."

Master Tsun chuckled. "He was stubborn. But focused. It served him well."

Ethan grinned. "I run my own clinic and school now—in Michigan."

Master Tsun's smile widened. "Then the teachings live on."

As the master excused himself to oversee a class, Kim took in the rows of students practicing with intensity and discipline. She watched their intent focus, their coordinated forms moving as one. It reminded her of another school—Jon's school in New York.

Her thoughts drifted, unbidden, to that afternoon years ago. That kwoon had been darker, the energy more aggressive. The students, while skilled, had carried themselves with a kind of sharp-edged pride. She remembered the wary glances they'd given her, the guarded way Jon had led her through. He was proud—eager to show her the life he'd chosen—but something had been off. The sifu had been charismatic but elusive. Jon's desire to belong was evident, but Kim saw he was an outsider. She remembered a whisper of discomfort that never quite left her.

The difference between the two schools struck her with unexpected clarity. Master Tsun's kwoon was rooted, steady. There was a peace to it, a sense of tradition and balance. The other had been like a house of mirrors—reflective but distorted.

Her words of caution had fallen on Jon's deaf ears, completely engrossed as he was in his pursuit of kung fu. They had spent an afternoon together at the Pagoda Theater on Catherine Street, near East Broadway, losing themselves in the captivating realm of martial arts cinema.

Ethan's hand brushed hers, bringing her back. "You okay?"

She nodded. "This place... it's what a kung fu school should be."

They stepped back into the street as night deepened, the red lanterns swaying gently in the breeze.

"Hungry?" Ethan asked.

"Starving."

They made their way to a narrow lane where the glow of the Golden Gate Noodle House welcomed them. Ethan had spoken of it fondly, and now, stepping inside, Kim understood why. The warmth of the room enveloped her. The rich smell of broth, ginger, and scallions curled through the air. The tables were mismatched but clean, the chatter of Cantonese and laughter a soothing hum.

They slid into a booth near the back. The server greeted Ethan like an old friend, and within minutes, a stream of dishes arrived—soup dumplings, hand-pulled noodles, crispy scallion pancakes.

Ethan's face lit up as he recounted college stories—like the time he'd eaten five bowls of noodle soup on a dare and ended up asleep in the back room for three hours. Kim laughed. She watched him with something close to awe: the way he leaned in when he talked, how his hazel eyes danced between green and gray in the warm light, the freckles across his nose catching the glow.

They lingered over tea, steam rising between them, the restaurant a cocoon of comfort and connection.

As they left the restaurant, arm in arm, the cozy glow of the evening lingered—until it didn't.

The sharp crack of gunfire shattered the night. The moment splintered. Kim stopped cold. Ethan pressed her against the cold brick wall of the restaurant. Sirens wailed. A muzzle flash flared in the alley. People screamed. The sound of running footsteps, a body hitting the pavement, chaos unraveling like a torn thread.

DEA agents swarmed in seconds, shouting commands, guns drawn. Kim heard the words in pieces: *triads... heroin... surveillance.*

She stared out into the night, her breath caught. A sudden memory surged—cold vinyl against her cheek, the zip of duct tape, the suffocating dark of the trunk. Her heartbeat roared in her ears, just as it had that night. The world tilted, danger pressing in from every side.

Ethan's steady hand on hers brought her back to the present. His grip was firm, steadying her as they moved quickly out of the chaos and back toward the safety of the hotel.

Once inside, Kim collapsed onto the bed, her hand unconsciously resting on her pregnant belly. She was carrying a life. And the world outside was filled with shadows.

She leaned into Ethan. "How do we raise a child in a world like this?"

He pressed his forehead to hers. "The same way we fight every battle—with intention, with strength, and with love."

She closed her eyes, drawing calm from the certainty in his voice.

Chapter 25

Locked Away
Jon
Shanghai, China

In the evenings, as Sun enthusiastically described her day at cosmetology school, Jon witnessed her metamorphosis. She spoke vividly of the skills she was acquiring, her excitement infectious. Occasionally, she would practice her newfound massage techniques on him, and he found himself melting under her skilled hands, though he always laughed and playfully declined her offers of a pedicure or manicure. Watching her embrace her studies with such dedication and joy filled him with happiness for her. She was creating a brighter, self-crafted future.

In the solitude of Sun's apartment, away from the world's prying eyes, they had found a rare moment of peace. As they lay together, the barriers between them dissolved, replaced by a sense of trust and understanding.

An urge rose within Jon to share more of himself— the truths of his past, the life he had left behind, the struggles, the reasons for his transformation. Sun's gentle presence, her accepting gaze, softened the walls he had built around his history, making them feel less necessary, less impenetrable.

But even as he hovered on the brink of disclosure, a

deep-seated caution held him back. He could never fully let go, never completely lower the guard that had become a part of his very existence. The intimacy they shared, as genuine and deep as it was, would always have boundaries, lines he couldn't cross for her safety and his.

As Sun drifted off to sleep, her breaths soft and even, Jon lay awake, gazing at the ceiling, lost in thought. He had made the right decision, the only decision he could under the circumstances. But it didn't make it any less difficult in the darkness of the night.

****

In the dappled light of the early morning, Jon stood in the tranquil kwoon, his muscles tense, his mind focused.

Master Tong, a figure of calm authority, moved through the training space, his eyes keenly observing his pupil. "Harness the qi. Let it be your strength," he instructed, his voice steady and encouraging.

Jon nodded, breath steady as he stepped into the form. His body moved with coiled energy and effortless rhythm, striking a balance between fluidity and force.

Master Tong watched, his gaze sharp but patient. "Extend your awareness beyond the physical. Direct the energy from within through your fingertips and outward from your navel," he guided, stepping closer to correct Jon's posture subtly.

With each adjustment, Jon tried to follow the master's advice, attempting to tap into the elusive flow of qi. His movements were controlled, but the connection he sought seemed just beyond his grasp. Frustration simmered within him, a stark contrast to the calm he was supposed to embody.

Master Tong paused, placing a firm hand on Jon's

shoulder. "It is not about force. It's about letting go," he said. "Find the quiet within the storm of your thoughts."

Jon took another deep breath, trying to heed the master's words. He resumed his form, focusing on the flow of his movements, striving to find the delicate balance between doing and being.

As the session progressed, his movements gradually became more fluid, but the sensation of qi remained elusive.

Master Tong watched him in silence for a moment before stopping the exercise. "Let's take a moment for qigong. Reflect on your own being," he guided Jon to a meditative stance.

Jon closed his eyes, frustration tightening in his chest. The internal system remained elusive, just out of reach. While others seemed to channel qi with ease, the effort left him overwhelmed—burdened by the weight of his own expectations.

During reflective moments with Sun, Jon opened up about the obstacles he faced. Sun's responses, always infused with warmth and empathy, reminded him of the incremental nature of growth.

"Each step is its own journey. You are evolving, even in these challenging times," she reassured him.

Her words brought him a measure of comfort, as he found kinship in their mutual journey of change. While her path was blossoming into new beginnings, his was an arduous trial, a relentless pursuit for a profound inner awakening that continued to elude him.

Chapter 26

Good Business
Jon
Shanghai, China

The morning sun slowly crept through the cracks of the bamboo shades and into the kwoon, illuminating the space with a soft, golden glow. Master Tong guided the students through a session of qigong meditation. Seated cross-legged, eyes closed, they focused inwardly on their breathing and the subtle energy moving within them. The room resonated with the sound of deep, rhythmic breathing, occasionally punctuated by the soft rustle of clothing.

"Focus on your breath." Master Tong's voice, low and soothing, filled the space. "Inhale deeply and exhale slowly. Release your thoughts, anchoring yourself in the now."

In this tranquil setting, instead of being still, his mind was occupied with concerns for Sun's safety. Despite his efforts to dismiss these thoughts, they stubbornly resurfaced, clouding his mental clarity.

Master Tong placed a hand on Jon's shoulder. "Be present in your own life energy, Li Wei," he murmured. "Release worries and fears. They have no place here, now."

Jon inhaled deeply, endeavoring to empty his mind.

He tried to focus solely on the rhythm of his breath, rooting himself to the solid ground supporting him and the energy coursing through his body. Yet the image of Sun, possibly in danger and alone, persisted. His agitation grew, battling his efforts to remain calm and centered.

Visions of Sun confronted by the street gang tore through his thoughts, sparking a surge of anger and helplessness. He longed to protect her, but restraint held him back, every instinct urging him to move. He tried to return to his breath, to anchor himself in the present—but his mind rebelled, restless and desperate for action.

Master Tong's voice, calm and resonant, pulled Jon back from his tumultuous thoughts. "Envision an energy sphere below your navel. With each breath, see it expand, filling you with strength and peace," he instructed.

But Jon's mind spun in widening circles, slipping further from calm. His eyes opened, and with deliberate control, he pivoted to a kneeling position and bowed low to the mat before Master Tong.

Master Tong regarded him with a serene gaze. "You cannot protect others if your own emotions are unbalanced," he advised.

Jon inhaled deeply, attempting to find some semblance of calm. Bowing in respect, he addressed his sifu again. "Master, I understand the value of controlling my emotions. But what if there's a voice inside me warning of danger? Telling me someone I care about is at risk?"

Master Tong studied Jon thoughtfully. "You are released. Go."

****

Jon's heart pounded as he stood at Sun's apartment door, frantically knocking. No one answered. He then took to the crowded streets of Shanghai, driven by an unshakable sense that something was wrong. His search seemed endless until he finally saw Sun. She was limping, her body marked with bruises.

He rushed to her side. "Are you okay? What happened?"

She shook her head, her tears falling freely. "They demanded money, and I gave them everything you'd given me. But it wasn't enough. They beat me." She sobbed, her body trembling in his embrace. Her clothes were ripped and stained with blood.

"Where is Xia?" he asked, his jaw tightening as he scanned the area, his anger barely contained.

"She's safe…at a friend's place…after school." She spoke between sobs.

"We should go to the police," he asserted, his resolve to seek justice growing stronger.

But she vehemently shook her head. "No, the police won't help. They're part of the problem. We can't go to them."

He sighed, grasping the complexity of their situation. "All right, we won't involve them. We'll find another way."

Despite her pain, Sun gave a small, grateful smile. "Thank you for being here."

Gently, Jon lifted her in his arms and carried her to her apartment. He laid her down on the bed with utmost care, grimacing at the sight of her battered face. After soaking a cloth in warm water, he tenderly cleaned the dried blood from her mouth and face, his heart aching at the brutality she had endured.

She winced as he touched her swollen cheek, but she offered no resistance. He scoured her apartment for first-aid supplies and found enough to tend to her wounds. He treated her injuries with gentle hands, doing his best to ease her pain and make her comfortable.

As night fell, he prepared a simple meal for her and stayed by her side, watching over her until she drifted into a fitful sleep, her face still showing traces of her ordeal.

****

Jon spent several tense days formulating a strategy. He did not involve Master Tong or anyone from the kwoon, certain they would try to dissuade him. His plan was risky—to face the gang leader head-on, offering a significant sum in exchange for Sun's safety. It was a gamble, but he believed the lure of cash would appeal to a gang driven by profit.

With a considerable amount of money in hand, he made his way to the gang's base, a dilapidated building in the city's core. Once grand, its crumbling brickwork and graffiti-covered walls spoke of years of neglect. Shattered windows, some haphazardly boarded up, gave it the appearance of hollow, watchful eyes. Two men loomed near the entrance, their expressions cold and unyielding.

Jon approached, his heart pounding. The guards exchanged wary glances before one jerked his head toward the door, wordlessly allowing him entry.

The air inside was stale and suffocating, thick with smoke and damp. As Jon moved through grimy hallways and ascended a narrow creaky staircase, his senses remained sharp, his resolve unwavering. Finally, he entered a dimly lit room, the faint murmur of voices falling silent as all eyes turned to him. Shadows flickered across the walls, cast by the unsteady glow of a single bulb hanging overhead.

At the center of the room sat the gang leader, Fang. His broad shoulders strained against a leather jacket, and tattoos snaked down his neck and chest, each one a silent testament to a violent past. A jagged scar ran from his temple to his jaw, giving his face a permanently hostile edge. He looked Jon up and down with cold, calculating eyes. "What do you want?" His voice was rough and impatient.

"I'm Li Wei. I've come to negotiate." Jon inclined his head respectfully.

"Negotiate?" Fang's lips twisted into a sneer. "You're either brave or stupid."

Jon reached into his jacket and pulled out a thick wad of hundred-dollar bills and placed it on the table between them. "I'm here to settle things peacefully. I want Sun's safety guaranteed."

Fang's gaze flicked to the money, then back to Jon. He leaned forward slightly. "Speak."

Jon met his eyes without flinching. "Sun isn't a working girl anymore. She owes you nothing. I'm offering a settlement to ensure you leave her alone."

The leader barked out a harsh laugh, the sound echoing off the grimy walls. "They all try to quit. Once a whore, always a whore. You think you can buy us off? You are naive."

"I'm not buying you off. I'm buying protection. Isn't that your business?" He slid half the stack of cash toward Fang, the bills fanning out like a challenge.

Fang stared at the money for a long moment, his expression unreadable. "That's not enough," he finally said. "Double it, or there's no deal."

"Deal," Jon said firmly, placing the other half a strap of hundred-dollar bills on the battered wooden table.

As he walked down the dim, shadow-streaked hallway, the weight of what he'd done pressed heavily on him. No one knew he was there. If things had gone wrong, he could've vanished—just another name on a long list of the missing. The stairs groaned underfoot, each creak slicing through the silence. All he had was the word of a ruthless criminal—and even that felt like smoke, ready to dissolve with the slightest shift.

Stepping out into the sharp daylight, Jon exhaled deeply. He had done everything he could for Sun, freeing her from the grip of fear and extortion—for now. But as he walked away, apprehension lingered. How long before the gang would demand more? Or worse?

Part Three 1984

Chapter 27

The Way Forward
Jon
Shanghai, China

After nearly five years under Master Tong's discipline, Jon remained a man chasing something just beyond his grasp. In the stillness of the kwoon, a heavy hush clung to the air as he faced his teacher in Push Hands.

Their palms connected in a delicate balance of force. Subtle shifts. Controlled breath. Jon mirrored the form well—too well. He knew what it looked like. He knew how it should feel. But that feeling—the elusive current of qi flowing without resistance—never quite arrived.

Master Tong adjusted his shoulders with a light touch. "Sink into the ground, Li Wei. Let the qi move through you, not around you."

Jon nodded, as always. He wasn't resisting. He *wanted* to get it. But beneath the fluidity of his limbs, a wall remained—one even he couldn't name.

"There is grace in your technique. And yet I feel tension—not in your body, but in your center." Master Tong observed him quietly, his movements revealing no judgment.

"Some days I think I'm just better at faking it." Jon tried to laugh it off.

The master's brow lifted slightly, but he said nothing.

As Jon trained with Ming in the spiraling movements of Chan Si Gong, his form was panther-quick and leather-tough—graceful, even exquisite to the untrained eye. But beneath the fluid exterior, he knew the energy wasn't truly flowing. It was mimicry, not mastery—a dance of technique without the inner current.

"You *feel* the flow," Ming said after a set, clearly convinced. "It's in your movement now."

Jon bowed. He didn't correct him. He *wished* it were true. But there's a difference between reflecting mastery and embodying it. Inside, he was still an actor reciting lines he hadn't fully translated. Ming didn't see it—because Jon had mastered the appearance. Not the essence.

As the session wrapped up, Jon couldn't shake the question that surfaced again and again—why did Master Tong invest so much in him? He wasn't the most advanced student, still struggling to grasp the internal system as deeply as the master's top disciples. The thought settled over him, weighty and unresolved.

The zhan zhuang standing meditation practice the next morning confirmed it. Minutes dragged. Sweat rolled down Jon's back. No current rose from the ground, no effortless connection to breath or spirit—only muscle fatigue and relentless strain. Still nothing. And this time, he said so.

When Tong released the stance, Jon lowered his arms, winded and raw.

"I've tried everything," he said. "And still...I feel

nothing."

"I know," he said at last. "I have seen it for some time."

"Then why keep me here?"

"Because I've never had a student with such promise. I've tried every technique to activate the qi. In some ways, you are my greatest failure. I'm sorry, Li Wei. I have guided you as far as I can."

Jon swallowed hard.

"There is no shame in leaving a teacher," Tong continued. "There is only shame in staying when the soil no longer nourishes you. You must find the teacher who can break through this block. That is not me."

Jon bowed, his heart aching—not from rejection, but from release. "I understand."

"Seek out Master Shen in the north. He is not like me. But he may be what you need."

"I won't forget what you've taught me, Sifu," Jon said. "Not just about qi, but about resilience, patience…understanding." His throat tightened slightly. "You've given me more than I can ever repay."

Master Tong's expression remained calm, but there was warmth in his eyes. "You honor me with those words, Li Wei. A student who listens with his heart has never wasted his time."

Bowing deeply, Jon held the position longer than necessary, letting the gesture convey the gratitude he couldn't fully express in words.

That night, alone in his quarters, Jon sat in silence, the low lamplight casting a faint reflection of his face in the window. It was the face of a man who had given everything to discipline—but never dared to look too far inward.

He thought of Sun. Her presence had been gentle, steady, patient. She had never asked him to stay, but he had always known he would need to take care of her before he left. It was the least he owed her. He had loved before—Lise, Sun—but always with distance, never permanence. Each time, he remained loyal to something else entirely—the pursuit of mastery.

That pursuit had cost him more than he could admit. He was not like Ethan, who had made space for roots—for family, for love. Ethan had chosen connection. Jon had chosen motion. Always motion.

But he could not move forward until he tied off what was behind.

He would go to Beijing. Daniel Wu had promised word if there was any news of his family. He had to know they were safe. That they remembered him—or that they didn't. Either way, he needed Daniel's reports.

While in Beijing, he would provide for Sun.

And then…Gansu.

Master Shen. Reclusive. Selective. Said to accept only those with clear purpose and clean intention. Jon didn't know if Shen would take him on. He wasn't even sure he deserved the chance. But if there was anyone who could break through what Master Tong could not—who could unlock whatever still held him back—it was Shen.

He exhaled, the decision settling like a stone in his gut.

At dawn, he stood at the edge of the compound.

Master Tong placed a hand lightly on Jon's shoulder, his expression composed but warm. "You are always welcome here," he said. "And I believe you will find your way."

****

The Beijing air was dry, the city pulsing with a rhythm Jon no longer shared. He stepped into the post office and retrieved a familiar envelope from his rental box. It was thick—heavy not just with paper, but with memory. With consequence.

He crossed the street to a deserted park and settled on a bench under a row of poplars. It was nearly winter. The air had teeth.

Jon slid the contents from the envelope. The first item was a black-and-white photo. He blinked.

It was Kim's wedding.

His sister stood resplendent in a gown of silk and lace, Ethan beside her, arms wrapped protectively around her waist. Their parents flanked them, smiling— his mother radiant, his father impossibly proud. William Wolf—shorter than Jon remembered, but with a presence that defied his stature, his face lit with joy at his son's side. A family united in his absence.

Jon traced their faces with his eyes, but not with regret. He had made his choices.

They had a life. He had a path.

Underneath the photo was a second page—glossier, printed on thick stock. His own face stared back at him, the one he hadn't seen since 1978. The old face. The one with the stronger jawline, Western bone structure, and haunted eyes.

Reward $100,000. For any information on the whereabouts of Jon Fenton.

He flipped it over. Handwritten in Daniel Wu's elegant script:

You didn't just kill his son. You humiliated him.
The Flying Dragons are fractured because of you.

166

This isn't over. Sifu has not forgotten.

Jon stared at the note. Not with panic. With unshakable certainty.

They were still looking. But they were looking for the wrong man. That face? That name? Gone. Surgically erased, rebuilt from the inside out. Jon Fenton was a ghost now. A myth with a bounty on his head.

He folded the flyer in half, slid it back into the envelope, and tucked it into his jacket pocket. Slowly, he rose, scanning the park—half out of habit, half out of vigilance.

But no one watched.

He walked through the streets, blending into the blur of bodies, the clamor of life. It was easy now. He'd practiced anonymity like a craft.

But anonymity wasn't the goal. Not anymore. He wasn't running. He was searching. Not for safety. For mastery.

The flyer had reminded him that vengeance still hunted him—but it hadn't changed his direction. It had only reinforced the need to keep moving forward, not deeper into the shadows, but toward something more complete. Something earned.

Toward Gansu.

Master Tong had shown him discipline, form, internal control. But he had also seen what Jon lacked—and had named it without judgment.

"You must find the teacher who can break through the block. That is not me."

Jon was ready to find that teacher.

And if the Flying Dragons still came? Then let them. Because this time, Jon wouldn't fight from fear. He would fight from center. And the only way to reach it was through the cold hills of Gansu where a man named Master Shen lived apart from the world, offering nothing but the truth of the body and the mirror of the mind.

That's where Jon was going. Not to disappear. But to become.

Chapter 28

Failure
Kim
Zilwaukee, Michigan

Kim raked a hand through her hair. The bridge under construction was cracking, sinking into the ground—just as she'd warned. As a geotechnical engineer for the Department of Transportation, she knew the language of soil and structure, the way earth and steel resisted and yielded. Her meticulous studies, her urgent recommendations—they'd been dismissed like whispers in a storm.

Now cost-cutting had led to collapse. The fix would cost a fortune. She might as well have been shouting into the wind—unheard, her expertise squandered.

She kicked at the dirt with the toe of her steel-capped construction boot and squatted down, the fabric of her denim jeans stretching taut over her knees as she set to work with her boring equipment. These samples were historical records of the earth, a silent narrative of ages encapsulated in layers of dirt.

As she drilled into the earth, each rotation echoed her mounting exasperation. She seemed caught in a relentless loop, with her crucial warnings and recommendations consistently dismissed. The truth was right there, in the soil, as tangible as the dirt now smudging her gloves.

She rose, having completed her borings, dusting her knees with a rough swipe of her hands. A sudden breeze caught her hair, sending loose strands dancing across her face, but a prickling sensation on the back of her neck gave her pause. The hairs stood up, a silent alarm, and an eerie feeling crept over her. She was being watched.

She straightened, every muscle in her body tensing. The unsettling sensation of being watched was too familiar, too tangible to ignore. Her pulse quickened, each heartbeat echoing the terrifying memory of her abduction five years ago. She was abruptly yanked back to the claustrophobic confines of the car trunk, a memory she'd rather leave buried. Yet here she was, enmeshed in a drama far greater than soil analysis and structural failures.

Beneath her gloved hand, she felt the imprint of the ankle holster carrying her parting gift from Hank Lewandowski, a small, elegant pistol with a sleek, compact frame—the kind James Bond famously carried. Her father's military comrade, who had sworn to help her reclaim her confidence, had been true to his word. The awareness of the weapon's presence, hidden beneath her pant leg and her ability to use it, bolstered her courage.

Kim tightened her grip on the hilt of the eight-inch tanto knife secured to her belt. Determination burned within her—she would live long enough to be there for her son, no matter what it took. Her thoughts often drifted to her four-year-old son, Logan, especially during the long hours her work as a soil analyst and structural engineer kept her away. She missed the simple joys of motherhood—bedtime stories, bicycle rides, and the small, everyday triumphs of watching him grow.

Logan's peaceful image filled her mind, his small body curled up under a blanket, surrounded by glow-in-the-dark stars stuck to his ceiling. The thought always hit her with the same ache—the fragility of time. She wanted to be there for every scraped knee, every curious question, every little victory.

Balancing her career and motherhood had never seemed like a choice before. But now, standing on the edge of the unknown, Kim found herself yearning for the smaller, simpler moments that mattered most. The cuddles before bed. The laughter shared over silly jokes. The chance to be part of his journey, not as a visitor, but as a constant presence.

She swept her gaze over the horizon, her jaw set with determination. Where her truck had once stood solitary, an array of vehicles now lined the shoulder of the bridge approach. Cars and trucks of all kinds, some bearing news outlet emblems and others conspicuously plain, impervious to the dust and grime. They had all been drawn to the collapsed structure like moths to a flame.

Kim was unsettled as she noted the growing crowd of reporters. What had started as her discreet investigation was now an unexpected spectacle.

A cluster of reporters broke away, striding toward her with determined focus. Her heart skipped as their microphones, marked with local station logos, extended toward her like unwanted offerings.

"Ms. Wolf! Can you comment on the collapse?"

"Is the bridge safe to continue construction?"

Her name floated through the air, tangled in a chorus of urgent questions. Kim stiffened. She wasn't just an anonymous engineer anymore—she'd become the center of an unplanned media storm.

She steeled herself against the onslaught, her mind hastily piecing together the best way to address the persistent reporters. They wanted answers, explanations, perhaps even someone to blame. Even as she prepared to speak, her gaze flickered uneasily to the horizon, a silent acknowledgment of the shadows that seemed to grow longer and more sinister with each passing moment.

Kim took a steadying breath, raising a hand to silence the clamor. The crowd hushed, a wave of anticipation settling over the reporters.

"The Zilwaukee Bridge," she began, her voice calm and steady, "was a project born out of necessity. By the 1960s, it was clear that the existing bridges across the Saginaw River couldn't handle the growing traffic or the increasing sizes of ships navigating the waterway."

She gestured toward the damaged structure. "Construction began in 1979, with an expected completion date three years later. But challenges— including budget constraints and construction—pushed the timeline back."

She paused, her gaze dropping to the soil samples at her feet. "We're investigating to understand why this happened. The goal remains the same, to ensure the bridge's long-term safety."

A heavy silence followed her explanation. Reporters jotted notes, their questions momentarily stilled.

But even as Kim spoke, unease lingered at the edge of her thoughts. There was a bigger story here, one that extended far beyond the failure of the Zilwaukee Bridge, and it seemed to be circling closer with each passing moment.

Her gaze swept over the crowd, and her pulse

quickened when she noticed them—four figures dressed in black jeans, turtlenecks, and mirrored sunglasses. Their stillness stood in stark contrast to the eager movements of the reporters. The opaque lenses hid their eyes. Something cold settled low in Kim's gut, still but insistent.

Who were they? Government agents? Corporate watchdogs? Or perhaps something far more dangerous—shadows from Jon's past, hunting for a man they still believed was alive?

A reporter from the *Grand Rapids Journal* stepped forward, curiosity sparking in his eyes as he looked at the soil samples in her hands. "Can you explain the significance of these borings, Ms…?" he asked, holding out a sleek, digital recorder.

"Wolf, Kim Wolf," she replied, forcing a polite smile. "The borings provide a snapshot of the ground beneath us. They reveal soil properties and how they interact with the structures we build. In this case, they may help us pinpoint what went wrong and how to prevent similar failures."

As she finished, an idea struck. "Listen, I hate to impose, but my truck's acting up. Would you mind giving me a ride back to Grand Rapids?"

The reporter hesitated, exchanging glances with his cameraman. After a moment he said, "Sure, Ms. Wolf. Happy to help."

Relief flooded Kim as she climbed into their vehicle.

"That's quite the knife you have there, ma'am." A playful smirk played across his lips while his eyes held a hint of curiosity.

"Field work can be unpredictable," she responded with a soft laugh. She cast one last glance toward the bridge. The crowd of reporters was shrinking in the distance, but her eyes lingered on the glint of sunlight reflecting off the sunglasses of the men in black.

As the vehicle pulled away, her stomach tightened, as if her body sensed something her mind hadn't yet named. Her impromptu press conference would no doubt stir a hornet's nest back at the Department of Transportation. She could almost hear her boss's voice now, sharp with irritation, reprimanding her for speaking to the press.

Her employment contract flashed in her mind— confidentiality clauses prominently underlined. She might have just crossed a line.

Yet, strangely, she didn't care. The bridge was a failure because warnings had been ignored. If her employer wanted to fume, so be it. A rebellious spark ignited within her, a fiery determination she refused to suppress. Let them stew. She had spoken the truth, and she'd do it again.

Chapter 29

Square Envelope
Jon
Shanghai, China

Jon arrived at Sun's apartment, taking a deep breath before knocking on the door. He couldn't ignore the knot in his stomach—moving on was hard.

Her face lit up with a warm smile as the door opened. "Li, you're here." She hugged him tightly.

He hugged her back, trying to maintain his composure. "Sun, we need to talk." His voice was low and serious.

She gazed at him, concern etched on her face. "What is it? Is everything okay?"

"I'm leaving Shanghai." He tried to keep his voice steady. "And it's time for you and Xia to leave too."

Her face fell, confusion and disbelief evident in her expression. "What? Leave Shanghai? Why?"

He had kept his ongoing payments of protection money a secret, not wanting to worry her unnecessarily. However, he could no longer hide this from her. She needed to know what was going on and the dangers they faced. Less than a year after he had reached a deal with the gang's leader, the extortion resumed.

The fear crept back into Sun's eyes, like the prey seeing the predator after a long hunt.

"I was thinking you'd like to be close to your friends in Beijing. You can enroll Xia in university there, and the demand for spa services is high and expected to grow." He made a conscious effort to avoid alarming her.

Motivated by his encouragement, Sun had pursued and completed her education at a vocational school, earning her cosmetologist and massage therapist licenses. She'd spent several years working at an elegant spa in the heart of Shanghai, building a dedicated clientele who insisted on her services exclusively. He surveyed the well-appointed apartment and its tranquil ambiance. She had journeyed a long way from the shadowy and perilous life she once endured to the stability and success she enjoyed now.

He sat across from her, his fingers anxiously twirling a square envelope. "There's something important I need to tell you."

A faint smile touched her lips as she leaned in, her sadness still evident. "Tell me," she said softly, her voice tinged with curiosity despite the weight of the news.

"I've bought a small spa in Beijing," he revealed, handing her the envelope. "It's situated in a neighborhood near the university that's becoming popular among young professionals."

She pulled out the deed to the spa, and her eyes widened as she examined the document. "Li, this is too much," she said, her voice trembling slightly.

He shook his head firmly. "No, we're going to be partners." He gestured to the papers in her hands. "Inside, you'll find a business registration certificate issued by the Administration for Industry and Commerce. It's proof of our legal ownership. There's also a sales contract. We just need your signature on the ownership register at the AIC to make us official co-owners."

She stared at him, her expression unreadable for a moment before her lips parted. "Thank you, Li, I...I'm speechless." Her voice was soft, but he could hear the emotion in it. After a brief pause, she asked, "So when will you come to Beijing?"

He looked away briefly. "I won't be joining you in Beijing for a while," he murmured. "I need to go...elsewhere."

Confusion crossed her face. "What do you mean?" Her voice rose an octave.

"It's time for me to move to another kwoon," he explained, his gaze shifting to avoid hers.

Her expression remained steady, though he could see the questions in her eyes, urging him to continue.

"I'm heading northwest to seek guidance from a master," Jon disclosed, squeezing her hand in reassurance. "But it's crucial for you and Xia to start in Beijing right away."

She blinked, her lips pressing into a faint tremble before she spoke. "I understand," she whispered, her tone steady. "Thank you for everything—for helping us find a new life. This spa is more than I ever dreamed. I promise I'll make it a success."

He offered her a soft smile. "I have no doubt you will. Just promise me you'll leave Shanghai as soon as possible—for both your sakes."

She nodded, and a single tear slipped down her cheek. Jon reached out and gently wiped it away with his thumb.

For a moment, they stood in silence, a weighty understanding passing between them. Then with a tender embrace that spoke volumes, they parted ways, the timing of their next meeting uncertain.

Jon arrived at the bustling train station, the chaotic energy mirroring his own state of mind. Announcements echoed overhead as travelers rushed past with suitcases and bags in tow. He moved through it all with purpose, navigating toward a familiar set of public lockers.

He reached locker number 126, inserted the key, and pulled the door open. The hinges creaked, slicing through the station's din. Inside sat a plain paper bag, its edges worn with time. He retrieved it and counted a few bundles of hundred-dollar bills secured with mustard-colored straps. As he slid the bag into his duffle, the weight pressed down—not just the heft of cash, but of memory.

Five years ago, he'd left this behind, a contingency plan for a life of uncertainty. Now it felt like a relic from another self. His fingers brushed a second key in his pocket—the one for a locker in Beijing. He paused, tracing its edges, his thoughts drifting to what awaited him there.

It wasn't just a key. It was a beginning. A reminder of the choices that had brought him here—and the road still ahead.

He slung the duffle bag over his shoulder and stepped onto the train platform. Moments later, he boarded the train and settled into a seat by the window. The station faded into the background as the train rumbled to life.

Jon stared out at the passing scenery, his thoughts fixed on Gansu. He was headed to a master who, he hoped, could offer the guidance he'd been seeking for so long. What that guidance might be, he didn't know—but for the first time in years, the path before him was clear. Northward. Forward.

Chapter 30

Sifu
Jon
Dunhuang, Gansu, China

Jon sipped strong, bitter coffee in the corner of the Silk Road Dunhuang Hotel dining room, watching the desert light rise through the windows. The decision to splurge on this hotel was strategic—it offered proximity to Master Shen's compound, nestled at the base of the Mingsha Mountain, just ten minutes away along the Silk Road.

Earlier that morning, he had rented a locker at the Dunhuang train station and stashed his cash inside—an offering he intended to present if Master Shen accepted him as a student, payment for instruction and lodging. He kept only what he needed for daily expenses. Everything else—his future, his body, his path—he was prepared to entrust to Master Shen.

At the compound gates, the desert silence deepened. Crescent Spring shimmered in the distance, a mirage carved in sand. Beyond the training plaza, figures moved with the serene, exacting rhythm of forms. Jon crossed the wide courtyard and entered the reception hall.

Inside, an immaculately dressed young man sat behind a carved mahogany desk. "Welcome," he said. "How may I help you?"

"I am Li Wei. I've come to train. May I meet Master Shen?"

The receptionist looked him over without judgment. "Please, take a seat."

Jon turned to find three others already seated on the long black leather sofa. They looked like travelers—students, perhaps—each of them watching the door, waiting. He took the last available seat and settled in.

Minutes passed. Hours. No one came.

Eventually, the receptionist returned. "Master Shen is unavailable. Come back tomorrow."

And so Jon did.

The second morning, he arrived earlier, the sky still blue-gray, the courtyard empty. The others joined him one by one. They sat, silent and respectful, until the receptionist appeared. The routine repeated.

Day three, he brought water and a small lunch. By afternoon, only one of the others remained.

By day five, Jon arrived at six a.m. and sat alone. The others had stopped coming.

He waited twelve hours, unmoving, only breaking for the bathroom or a brief stretch outside. His body ached by evening, but he didn't complain.

On the seventh morning, the receptionist greeted him with the faintest nod of acknowledgment. "You may join the courtyard practice."

Jon stood and bowed with gratitude. "I'd like to meet Master Shen," he added.

"Don't think he won't be watching you," the receptionist said, his voice even.

Outside, Jon joined the students training in the sand-paved courtyard. No one greeted him. No one corrected him. Days passed. He blended in yet stood apart.

On the fourth day of courtyard practice, without announcement, it happened. A gong sounded. A pause in the drills. Master Shen stepped into the yard. He was smaller than Jon expected—lean, compact—but his presence filled the space like thunder. His gaze swept over the students and landed on Jon. "Come forward, Li Wei."

Jon bowed and obeyed.

"Show me your favorite form."

Jon centered himself—breath steady, arms loose. The courtyard fell silent. He launched into the five animals—dragon's fluid power, snake's precision, tiger's raw strength, leopard's speed, crane's grace. Then, without pause, he shifted into the five elements. Each movement carried the imprint of every master who had shaped him—years of discipline woven into motion.

When he completed the final stance, chest heaving, the silence stretched.

Then a wooden staff hurtled through the air. He caught it cleanly, barely thinking. Two senior students charged.

He pivoted, staff rotating in smooth arcs—deflecting, redirecting. His rhythm was exact, reactive but calm. The encounter lasted under a minute. Shen raised a hand. The attack ceased.

"Do you wish to know who my masters were?" Jon stood tall, staff at his side.

"I already know." Shen's eyes narrowed.

Jon held his gaze without flinching.

"There is no hiding in kung fu," Shen said. "Your lineage is in your spine, your breath, your fists."

"Then I hope I have honored them." Jon bowed low.

A tense beat passed. "Come back tomorrow," Shen

said at last.

Jon nodded, his pulse settling. He turned to leave, but Shen added, "At this level, Li Wei, the world is smaller than it seems."

Jon paused mid-step, Shen's words settling in. Not a warning—just the way of things. Among martial artists, reputations moved faster than footsteps.

Outside, the cold desert wind hit his face. He stood a moment beneath the darkening sky, watching the courtyard behind the gates, still alive with movement.

He would return tomorrow.

Chapter 31

No, Not Yet
Jon
Dunhuang, Gansu, China

Jon lingered over a second cup of coffee in the Jiexing Pavilion, his duffel packed and ready at his side. For once, he allowed himself a slow morning. No rushing. No pressure. Just warmth and the comforting certainty of a plan set in motion.

He left a generous tip, bundled up against the biting cold, and made his way down the Silk Road toward Master Shen's kwoon.

A dusting of fresh snow clung to the rooftops. As Jon passed the dunes, he spotted silhouettes of camel riders against the rising sun. The scene was almost unreal—a foreigner walking alone through ancient lands, chasing an uncertain future.

Pinch me; I'm living the dream.

The thought settled deep, fortifying him. If he could get this far, he could go the rest of the way.

By the time he reached the compound, students were already warming up for the six a.m. tai chi class, their movements fluid and deliberate in the crisp morning air. Jon crossed the courtyard, eager to begin his training, and stepped into the reception hall.

"Good morning," he said, nodding to the young

receptionist.

"Good morning. How may I help you?"

"I met Master Shen yesterday," Jon replied, placing a neat stack of bills on the desk. "He told me to return today. I've brought my belongings and would like to arrange payment for accommodations and training."

Before the receptionist could respond, Master Shen entered the hall, his presence shifting the energy in the room. The receptionist immediately stood and bowed deeply, and Jon straightened reflexively.

Shen's piercing gaze landed on Jon. A long silence stretched between them.

"I accept payment only from students," Shen said at last. "I have not yet decided if you are one."

Jon hesitated. "How long until you decide?"

"One year."

"One year?"

"Maybe, six months."

"Six months?"

"Perhaps, thirty days."

Jon exhaled, relieved. "I can live with thirty days."

"It's not about whether you can live with it." Shen motioned toward the desk. "Take your money."

Heat rose to Jon's neck as he scooped the bills back into his pocket. The receptionist avoided his eyes.

Shen turned and walked away, leaving Jon standing there, uncertain whether he'd passed a test—or just made a fool of himself.

Jon's thoughts churned as he wandered back down Silk Road.

What had gone wrong? Was it the money? The arrogance of assuming he could pay his way in?

His aimless steps carried him to the Silk Yododo

Inn, a modest, sand-colored concrete-block building on the outskirts of Crescent Moon Lake. The area was sparse, the distant dunes rising like frozen waves in the morning light.

Inside, the air was stale, the dim lobby uninviting. The clerk barely looked up when he asked for an extra blanket. His room was worse—cramped, cold, the type of place that magnified isolation. He thought of his family. But reaching out wasn't an option. He had made sure of that.

With no bicycles to rent and no breakfast offered, he set out for the Shazhou Night Market, hoping for a hot meal and a distraction.

The market plaza was alive with fluttering flags and lanterns, though the winter chill kept most visitors indoors. He sat down at a food stall and ordered a steaming bowl of spicy beef noodle soup.

As he ate, the server, a round-faced man with bright pewter eyes, wiped his hands on a rag and leaned in. "You're not local, are you?"

Jon swallowed a bite of broth-soaked noodles. "I've come to train with Master Shen. Name's Li Wei."

The man introduced himself as Tai, the proprietor, a lifelong resident of Dunhuang. He launched into an animated description of the upcoming Lunar New Year Celebrations—fireworks, dragon dances, and a grand festival at Master Shen's kwoon.

"You'd be lucky to be part of it," Tai added, his eyes twinkling.

Jon wiped his mouth with the back of his hand. "Do you know Master Shen?"

"In a way."

Jon leaned forward. "Any advice on how to win his

favor?"

"With Master Shen, it's impossible to pretend to be something you're not," Tai said, polishing a glass. "Many seek to be his student."

Jon raised an eyebrow. "He seems unable to make up his mind."

Tai chuckled. "Don't take this the wrong way, but Master Shen is never the confused one." He wiped the counter clean. "I suggest you embrace the Lunar New Year traditions and let go of your ego."

Jon hesitated. "Have you known him a long time?"

Tai's smile grew. "All my life. He's my uncle."

Jon blinked. The man he had been casually pumping for information was Shen's nephew. Heat rose in his cheeks. "Then can you tell me how to sway his opinion of me?"

Tai met his gaze. "Be trustworthy and humble. That's all I can say." Without asking, he flipped a glass upright and poured Jon a bottle of beer.

Jon took a sip and exhaled slowly. "I'm not seeking enlightenment, just kung fu instruction."

"Then you may have come to the wrong place," Tai said, amusement in his voice.

Jon gave a half-smile, still unsettled. "I thought mastery came through control—discipline, precision. That's what every master I trained with believed."

Tai leaned on the counter. "Sure. That works—everywhere else." He grinned. "But here? It starts with surrender. Welcome to Gansu."

Jon let the words settle as Tai flipped the neon sign to closed.

Later that night, under the moonlight, Jon moved through hung gar's five animals—tiger, crane, snake, leopard, dragon—each strike sharp, each transition seamless. But the cold gnawed at his fingers, and something in his chest remained locked tight.

He flowed through the forms again, chasing exhaustion, trying to outrun the silence in his mind.

Hours later, back in his room, spent and aching, he stood under the shower—the water ran hot, then cold. The towels reeked of cigarette smoke.

Lying on the stiff mattress, he stared through the sky window above his narrow bed.

Shen had not said no.

And that meant he still had a chance.

Chapter 32

Worthy Replacement
Ethan
Grand Rapids, Michigan

Ethan glanced up as a news van rolled to a stop outside the center. The *Grand Rapids Journal* logo spanned the side in bright red, a satellite dish perched like a crown. He put down a patient file and stepped to the window just as Kim climbed out, arms full of gear.

She was supposed to be driving the pickup.

He stepped outside. "What happened to your truck?"

Kim's shoulders lifted in a shrug, the kind that said she'd rather not get into it. "Long story. Short version? It's staying behind. I caught a ride with the news crew."

He tilted his head. "Is everything okay?"

Before she could answer, the low rumble of an approaching engine drew their attention. A black limousine pulled up to the curb.

A tanned man stepped out, sharp as a blade in a slate-gray blazer. Polished and self-assured, he strode toward Ethan with his hand extended. "Ethan Wolf, I presume? Frank Castle. Sunset Pictures."

Ethan accepted the handshake, his brow rising. Castle's name rang a bell—Sunset Pictures had produced half the action films in theaters over the last decade.

"Mind if we talk?" Castle gestured toward the

189

center.

Inside, the space was warm and quiet, wood floors lit with late-afternoon sun.

Frank paced slowly, absorbing the room with a practiced producer's eye. "I'm putting together a martial arts film," he said, tone casual but practiced. "And I want it done right. No wire-fu fakery, no stuntmen slapping the air. We want truth. Real training. Real movement. Real philosophy."

Ethan crossed his arms. "Hollywood doesn't exactly have a track record for that."

Frank smiled. "This is going to be different."

Kim emerged from the back of the room, sliding off her jacket. "Ethan, you've spent your life teaching people what martial arts is. This could show the world."

Ethan looked at her, surprised by the certainty in her voice.

"And to be honest, coming here wasn't my idea. Master Hin turned down the job. But he told me 'Call Ethan Wolf. He's the one you want.' "

The name stopped Ethan cold. Master Hin wasn't one to hand out compliments—or recommendations. He rubbed the back of his neck. "I've got responsibilities. A full clinic. Students. My son."

"I know," Kim said. "But I've made a decision."

Ethan turned to her fully.

She held his gaze. "I'm resigning. I'm done with engineering. I'm committing to this—us, the center, my training. This is where I want to be."

For a moment, he couldn't speak. Kim had never done anything halfway—but this? This was more than dedication. It was belief. In him. In the future they were building.

Frank tilted his head. "Sounds like you've got your operations manager."

Ethan cracked a smile. "Sounds like I do." He turned back to Frank and nodded once. "All right. I'm interested. Let's talk details."

Chapter 33

Thirty Days
Jon
Dunhuang, Gansu, China

Jon's heart raced as he arrived at the kwoon, the dawn still fresh in the air. It was minutes before six a.m., the time for tai chi to commence under the watchful eye of Master Shen. The plaza, already bustling with students warming up, emanated a vibrant energy that Jon yearned to be a part of.

As he entered, his path intersected with Master Shen's. The master's presence was imposing, a formidable figure with deep-set, piercing eyes that seemed to look right through him. "You are adept with a knife?" His voice was calm yet carried undeniable authority.

"Yes, Master," Jon replied, a flicker of hope igniting within him.

"Good. You will assist Loki in the kitchen."

Shen's words echoed in Jon's ears as the master walked toward the plaza. For a moment, Jon couldn't move. His hands tightened into fists at his sides, the disappointment hitting him like a physical blow. *Kitchen duty.* He hadn't traveled all this way, poured every ounce of his determination into this journey, just to wash dishes and chop vegetables.

Heat surged through him, frustration threatening to bubble over. *I came here to train—to push myself, to prove myself—not to scrub pots.*

He exhaled sharply, the breath leaving him like steam off an iron. His gaze followed Master Shen as the students assembled around him, a stark reminder of the goal he was chasing. He rolled his shoulders back and let his hands fall open at his sides, the tension easing by degrees.

If this is the price, then I'll pay it. Every second, every task. I'll show him what I'm made of.

With a deliberate step forward, he turned toward the kitchen, his resolve hardening. The disappointment still lingered, but it no longer defined him. He would prove his worth, even if it started behind a sink.

He navigated the kwoon's maze-like corridors, finally pushing through the swinging doors into the kitchen. The compact space was a flurry of efficiency, dominated by a gleaming wok station and steel counters. At the pantry, a stocky man in a white apron and black skull cap was hefting a bushel of Chinese cabbage.

"Morning. Are you Loki?" Jon asked, hesitating in the doorway.

The man turned, his round face breaking into a crooked smile. "That's me. You're the new guy, huh?" He handed Jon an apron. "You'll be chopping today—cabbage, ginger, garlic, spring onions, chilis. We serve at noon, so no time to waste."

Jon stepped up to the counter, eyeing the daunting array of ingredients. He picked up the cleaver, gripping it with uncertain confidence, and started on the cabbage. The sharp blade thudded against the cutting board, uneven slices piling up.

Loki glanced over, his smile widening. "Not bad—if we had all day." He grabbed a piece of ginger and demonstrated how to peel and slice it with quick, practiced ease. "Watch this. You want speed and control."

Jon tried to mimic him, the ginger slipping slightly under his knife. "How many are we cooking for?" His clumsy attempts at chopping needed a distraction.

"Fifty." Loki's hands moved in a blur as he demonstrated a better method. "Main meal. And you're a bit slow, my friend."

Jon winced but nodded. "First day." He offered a sheepish smile.

Loki laughed, a warm, hearty sound. "Fair enough. But Chinese New Year's coming, and things only get busier from here."

The kitchen came alive as the clock ticked toward noon. Loki's hands flew as he kneaded dough and pulled it into thin noodles, while Jon worked his way through the garlic, the pungent aroma stinging his nose. When Loki showed him a quick trick for peeling, Jon muttered a grateful, "Thanks," and tried to pick up the pace.

"How long have you been here?" Jon's knife clinked against the cutting board.

Loki paused as he rolled out the dough. "Me? Been here years. Started in the kitchen, just like you. Took me a while to prove I was serious about training." His voice carried a note of pride. "Master Shen doesn't make it easy—he's not supposed to. But if you stick it out, it's worth it."

Jon nodded, silently filing away the advice. He finished chopping the chilis, then rubbed his nose absentmindedly. The burn hit immediately, a searing pain that spread like wildfire.

"My nose—it's on fire!" Jon dropped the cleaver and fanned his face. He stumbled around the kitchen, his eyes watering.

Loki doubled over with laughter. "Amateur mistake!" He handed Jon a napkin and a small dish of vegetable oil. "Dab this on your nose. It'll dissolve the capsaicin. And remember, never touch your face after chopping chilis."

Jon followed his instructions, and the burn subsided.

Loki clapped him on the shoulder. "You'll survive. But you'd better pick up the pace tomorrow, or the chilis will be the least of your worries."

By noon, the kitchen work was done. Loki arranged platters of steaming food with practiced ease, while Jon leaned against the counter, his arms heavy from hours of chopping.

"You staying for lunch?" Loki asked, his tone light but encouraging.

"I'd like that."

As he watched the dishes disappear through the kitchen doors, Jon wiped his hands on a towel, the scent of ginger and garlic still clinging to his skin. This wasn't how he'd imagined his training beginning, but something about the rhythm of the work was grounding—and Loki's easy way was unexpectedly steadying.

Exhausted, Jon returned to the Silk Yododo Inn at three p.m. He collapsed onto the hard wooden bed and quickly drifted into a deep, dream-filled sleep.

In the dream, he found himself standing in a vast, ethereal training hall, its high ceilings stretching into an endless golden haze. The walls shimmered with intricate carvings of mythical creatures—dragons coiling around phoenixes, tigers locked in eternal battle with cranes. A figure emerged from the shadows, radiating wisdom and quiet authority—the grand master.

Jon moved through a mantis form, each strike and sweep deliberate, yet something was off. His balance wavered, his timing a breath behind. Without a word, the grand master stepped in, offering the slightest touch, adjusting his stance, refining his flow. Jon followed, his body responding with a surprising ease. The longer he moved, the more natural it became—like a rhythm he had always known, just momentarily forgotten.

He woke with a start, the dream lingering like a whisper in his chest. The sensation of the master's guidance still pulsed through his muscles, as vivid as if it had truly happened. He sat up slowly, rubbing his face. Had it been just a dream or something more? A message? A memory yet to be created?

With that thought still turning over in his mind, he rose and splashed cold water on his face, shaking off the last remnants of sleep. Refreshed, he set out for the Shazhou Night Market.

The Silk Road was alive with festive energy, the approaching Chinese New Year infusing the streets with anticipation. Lanterns swayed overhead, their warm glow casting flickering light onto the bustling crowds. The scent of roasted meats and spices filled the air, mingling with bursts of laughter and the rhythmic clang of street performers' gongs. Families moved together in tight clusters, children tugging at their parents' sleeves, eager for festival treats.

Jon let himself be carried by the pulse of the market, but his thoughts remained tethered to the dream. Perhaps, in ways he hadn't yet realized, his path had already been set before him.

At the bar, Tai greeted him with a grin and slid a cold beer across the counter. "Good day at the kwoon?"

Jon took a sip and let the cool drink settle him. "Master Shen put me in the kitchen."

"With Loki?"

"You know him?"

Tai chuckled. "Cooked with him for years before I opened this place. Loki's a good man. Fast with a cleaver and faster with his jokes. Here—take a look." He passed Jon a menu card.

Jon waved it off. "Surprise me with your best noodle dish."

Tai's grin widened. "You got it." As he turned toward the kitchen, he added over his shoulder, "Used to be a chemist. Cooking's not so different—get the balance wrong, and it all blows up."

Jon shook his head, amusement tugging at his lips as Tai vanished through the swinging doors. Around him, the market swelled with noise and motion— clinking dishes, laughter, the sizzle of woks. He took a slow pull of his beer, his gaze drifting to a nearby chessboard where two men hunched in silent focus. In an instant, he was back across the table from Kim. She was always five moves ahead—the one who saw the whole board while he chased pieces.

The melody of live traditional music pulled Jon from his thoughts.

Tai reappeared, placing a steaming bowl of noodles in front of him. "Best in Dunhuang," he said, leaning on the bar.

Jon took a bite, the spices hitting his palate with a

satisfying kick. "Perfect." He raised his glass in thanks.

Their conversation shifted to martial arts. Tai with his easygoing manner shared snippets of his journey. "I trained at the kwoon for years." He refilled Jon's glass. "But eventually, I had to find my own way. Kung fu's still a part of my life, just not the same way it is for my uncle. Master Shen's incredible, though. A true master. And how's your training going?"

Jon chuckled. "Let's just say my chopping technique needs work. I'm frustrated. I feel alive when I'm training. But I'm still waiting to see if Master Shen will accept me as a student."

Tai studied him for a moment, then nodded. "If Sifu Shen is testing you, it's because he sees something worth testing. He doesn't waste time." He paused, then grinned. "We're closing up soon. How about we get in some training? I may not be at the kwoon these days, but I still work out—and my uncle's lessons stuck."

Jon sat up straighter, setting his glass down. "Absolutely." The word left his mouth before he even thought about it. This was why he had come to Gansu— to train, to sharpen his edge.

"Finish your drink. I'll lock up, and then we'll get started."

As the market emptied and the lanterns cast softer, flickering light over the square, Tai led Jon into the open plaza. With the crowds gone, the space was vast beneath the night sky, hushed, still, and ready.

Tai moved first—fluid, controlled, his years of training evident in every step. Jon followed, not tentative, but sharp, his body responding without thinking.

"You don't need to force it," Tai said as they circled

one another. "It's already in you."

Jon adjusted, letting his breath guide the rhythm. Strike, pivot, breathe—each motion carving away the rest of the world. The frustration, the waiting, the questions—they all dissolved. In this moment, he wasn't trying. He was simply doing.

When they finished, sweat clung to his skin, breath coming steady and deep.

Tai clapped him on the shoulder. "You're ready. Whether he sees it yet or not."

Jon let out a dry chuckle. "Let's hope he sees it soon."

As they gathered their things, Tai gestured toward the sky. "Look at that," he said.

A handful of lanterns had risen above the rooftops, golden and slow against the night. Jon watched them drift, their light fading into the dark.

For the first time in weeks, he wasn't waiting. He was moving forward.

Chapter 34

Spring
Jon
Dunhuang, Gansu, China

Every morning before sunrise, Jon moved through the kitchen in methodical rhythm—measured, focused, waiting—only tolerable because of the nightly training with Tai. The clatter of knives and the scent of ginger had become a meditation, the routine anchoring him in the long silence of not knowing. He hadn't questioned it; the waiting had become its own kind of discipline. But on this morning, as the pale blush of spring light crept across the tiled wall, something shifted.

The kitchen door flew open. Master Shen strode in, a bright-red sash tied across his brow. "Time to join class, Li Wei!" he called out, eyes bright with bait. "Chop, chop, quickly!"

For a moment, Jon froze, cleaver in hand. "You mean…"

"Yes! No more kitchen!" Master Shen's laughter echoed through the small space as Loki looked on, smirking.

Jon fumbled to untie his apron and tossed it to Loki, who caught it midair.

"Try not to miss me too much," Loki called after him, the grin in his voice impossible to miss.

As Jon followed Master Shen through the courtyard, a rush of excitement surged through him. The white dunes shimmered under the clear blue sky, and the air carried the scent of spring blossoms and freshly swept stone. Students were stretching in the plaza, their movements slow and deliberate against the backdrop of desert and awakening trees.

Master Shen led the morning tai chi, his motions fluid as drifting mist—weightless yet grounded. Jon moved with the group, allowing himself to fall into rhythm. He focused on the breath, visualized an imaginary opponent, and moved like he had no arms.

As the session ended, students bowed in unison, their sleeves whispering through the air. Jon rose, steadier than he'd been in days.

Instead of dismissing the group, Shen picked up a staff and called Jon forward with a subtle tilt of his chin. "Li Wei," he said. "Come."

The students stepped back, creating a wide circle.

Jon approached, pulse quickening. He bowed, then stood at attention, ready for instruction.

Shen didn't speak. He simply moved—slow at first, then sharp, a lightning-quick series of strikes that blurred the lines between form and function. His feet barely seemed to touch the ground, yet each step shifted the air with force. His final move ended in perfect stillness, staff tucked neatly against his forearm.

Then he handed the staff to Jon. "Now you."

Jon accepted the weapon with both hands. Shen's form was still fresh in his mind, but he moved not with mimicry—but with purpose. Each strike was deliberate, every motion clean. His body understood what his mind no longer needed to overthink—staff slicing, pivot landing, breath following breath. He finished in Shen's final stance, heart pounding.

A long silence followed.

Then Shen moved again—this time straight toward him. Without warning, his hand darted out, striking toward Jon's centerline.

Jon blocked, barely.

Another strike. A sweep. A grab.

Instinct surged. Jon countered, turned, spun with the staff. Around him, the students watched in taut silence. Shen advanced—fluid, unrelenting. Jon stayed with him—not overpowering, not yielding—moving with muscle memory and the urgency of reflex.

Shen withdrew with the suddenness of a gust. He nodded once. "Not bad."

Murmurs ran through the group. Shen rarely offered praise.

Jon exhaled, the rush in his blood still cooling. No meditation could have taught him what this exchange had—how power didn't always announce itself. Sometimes it came quiet, sharp, unyielding.

Shen turned to address the group. "Skill is forged in silence. In repetition. In the willingness to be tested."

Then, as quickly as it had begun, class was dismissed.

Jon moved to breakfast with the others, energy thrumming beneath his skin. The disquiet that had haunted him the past few weeks had dissolved in that courtyard. Not because he had proven anything.

Because he'd finally found a place where he belonged.

That evening, Jon returned to the Shazhou Night Market, the lanterns swaying above a hum of laughter and clinking bowls. He found Tai at the bar, sleeves rolled, drying glasses beneath a string of red lights.

"How's training going?" Tai asked, sliding him a beer.

Jon smirked. "Better than chopping vegetables all day."

They chatted about the kwoon, about spring festivals and courtyard drills.

"I trained with Master Shen for years," Tai said, his gaze fixed on a point past Jon's shoulder. His tone had shifted. "But not anymore. We...had a falling out."

Jon paused mid-sip. "I didn't know that. What happened?"

Tai shrugged, not quite casually. "It's a long story. We didn't see eye to eye. He cut ties. I haven't been back since."

Jon paused. "Do you think he'd ever...change his mind?"

Tai shook his head and barked a short humorless laugh. "Doubt it. I regret how things ended. But I've found other teachers—other people still willing to fight for something that matters."

Jon didn't know what unsettled him more—the bitterness in Tai's voice, or the calm conviction beneath it. He let the silence settle.

Eventually, the market thinned. Lanterns bobbed lower. The night air cooled.

"The night's still young. Want to train?" Tai's offer came with a glint of mischief and something steadier beneath it—respect.

Jon's mood lifted. "Absolutely."

Under the moonlight, the market square transformed into their training ground. Tai guided him through layered forms, correcting stances with quick hands and a calm authority Jon hadn't noticed before. Jon moved harder, sharper—pushing through the burn in his thighs and the ache in his back.

By the time they finished, sweat soaked his shirt and his breath came hard. But as he stood beneath the starlit sky, chest heaving, there it was again—progress.

For all the questions that remained, this moment was solid. This bond, real.

****

A month after Master Shen invited Jon to join class, he offered him a place to stay at the kwoon. "It will be better for your training if you live here and sleep in the bunkhouse."

Jon bowed deeply. "Thank you, Master Shen."

That afternoon, he returned to the Silk Yododo Inn to pack his few belongings. As he left the room, duffel slung over one shoulder, a strange weight settled over him—not weariness, but the gravity of a new beginning.

Back at the kwoon, Zhang greeted him at the gate and led him up the long, winding ramp to the communal sleeping quarters.

"Master Shen's strict about the rules," Zhang said. "Break them, and you could be asked to leave."

"What kind of rules?"

"Respect instructors. Show loyalty to the kwoon. No unsupervised fighting. No stealing. No smoking. No prostitution. And always bring honor to the art."

Jon nodded, listening closely.

"Only the most committed students stay," Zhang added. "This place runs on discipline. We're a family here. We protect that."

Something in Jon's chest tightened—pride, maybe.

Or hope.

The bunkhouse was pristine. Neatly arranged bedrolls lined the bamboo floor like driftwood washed ashore. Cabinets, polished to a soft sheen, hugged the walls.

Zhang handed him a rolled-up mat. "Pick any open spot. And a cupboard for your things." He pointed to a carved doorway at the far end of the room, its dragon relief shimmering in the light. "Bathhouse is through there."

Jon followed him inside—and paused. The air was warm, herb-scented. Steam drifted lazily over four large stone tubs, their surfaces mirroring the carved ceiling above. Along one wall, neat rows of basins and squat toilets. Against another, glass jars labeled with salts, roots, and powders for pain, circulation, and recovery.

Jon ran a hand along a basin's smooth edge. The bathhouse wasn't just a place to cleanup—it was a sanctuary, a place to mend.

Later, back in the bunkhouse, he chose a secluded spot near the rear. He laid out his bedroll with care, tucked his duffel into the cupboard, and took a long breath.

Through the window, the last light of day spilled into the room. Outside, the courtyard glowed gold beneath the fading sky. For the first time since arriving in Dunhuang, a calm assurance settled over him—he was exactly where he needed to be.

Chapter 35

Timing
Jon
Dunhuang, Gansu, China

The sharp crack of fists meeting padded gloves echoed through the kwoon courtyard. Nearly two years under Master Shen's tutelage had forged Jon into a far more capable fighter—but today, against Zhang, he was struggling. Sweat trickled down his back as he braced for the next flurry of strikes.

Zhang attacked hard—relentless, fast. Jon blocked a high punch, the impact jolting his arm. He countered with a straight punch, but Zhang sidestepped and swept his leg. Jon hit the ground hard, the air whooshing from his lungs.

"Enough." Master Shen's voice rang out, firm and final.

Zhang immediately stepped back and bowed. Jon rose more slowly, frustration simmering beneath his ribs. Another loss. Again.

Master Shen approached, his gaze assessing but not unkind. He rested a hand lightly on Jon's shoulder. "Li Wei, you rely too much on force. Zhang is stronger than you. You cannot win that way."

Jon looked down, wiping sweat from his brow. "What should I do, Master?"

"The one who wins in combat is not the strongest, nor the fastest, but the one who can change the quickest." Master Shen gestured for Jon to step aside and took his place opposite Zhang. "Watch closely."

Zhang lunged forward, throwing a rapid combination of punches and kicks. But Master Shen moved like smoke—untouchable yet solid. Shen didn't meet strength with strength. Instead, he shifted, redirected, flowed around Zhang's attacks like water slipping past stones. No brute resistance. No hesitation. Only seamless adjustment, moment to moment.

Jon's gaze sharpened as he searched for the secret. It wasn't about strength. It wasn't even about speed. It was about *timing*—feeling the shift before it landed, moving before the opponent could commit.

After a few exchanges, Shen stepped back, raising a hand to end the demonstration. Zhang bowed, flushed and breathing hard. Master Shen barely looked winded.

Jon, however, stood rooted to the spot, his mind racing. How had Master Shen averted every attack? It seemed almost supernatural.

After class, Jon approached the master. "Master Shen," he began, hesitant, "how did you know where Zhang would strike? How can I learn that?"

Master Shen smiled. "Combat is not a contest of strength. It is a dance. When you are attuned to your partner, you will know where the next step must fall. You will move before you think to move."

Jon nodded, the weight of the lesson pressing down on him. For a split second, he caught a glimmer of what Master Shen might mean. He remembered scattered moments in past fights when time had seemed to stretch—when he had sensed an opening or a strike before it happened, moving without thought. Those flashes had come and gone without control, like sparks in the dark. Could he learn to summon that awareness at will? The thought both stirred hope and left him daunted.

Later that evening, he returned to the dormitory, his body sore from the day's training. As he entered, his gaze scanned the familiar rows of bamboo mats and cupboards. Something wasn't right. He paused, counting the bedrolls—only seven remained.

His brow furrowed as he scanned the room—his bedroll wasn't where he'd left it. It had been moved. Footsteps echoed behind him. Jon turned to find Hanying leaning against the doorframe, a smirk playing at his lips.

"What's so amusing?" Jon asked, his tone sharper than intended.

Hanying stifled a laugh. "Nothing."

"Did you move my bedroll?"

Hanying shrugged, still half smiling. "It was just a joke."

"How is that a joke?" Jon's tone flattened.

Hanying shifted. "I'll move it back, all right?"

Jon nodded and watched as Hanying quickly returned his bedroll to its original place. "Thank you," he said, though his annoyance lingered.

In the bathhouse, Jon eased into a steaming stone tub, the scent of eucalyptus rising in the humid air. He sank deeper into the heat, letting it unknot the day's tension.

Hanying entered a moment later and settled into the stone tub beside him. At first, Jon considered ignoring him, but the warmth of the water softened his irritation.

"About earlier," Hanying said, "it was just a joke. No hard feelings?"

Jon exhaled, nodding. "No hard feelings."

They soaked in companionable silence for a while.

"I heard something today. About Min," Hanying whispered.

Jon straightened slightly. "What about Min?"

"He's gone." Hanying glanced at Jon. "Stripped of his rank and expelled. They say he broke one of the rules."

Min. Gone. No ceremony, no explanation. Just erased. Jon sank lower into the tub, the warmth suddenly less comforting. The rules weren't just words on a wall. They were a blade—swift, final.

Part Four 1989

Chapter 36

Crossroads
Jon
Dunhuang, Gansu, China

The Shazhou Night Market buzzed with life when Jon arrived—later than he'd planned. Since he'd moved into the kwoon, weekends were the only time he could catch up with Tai, and he'd been looking forward to the familiar rhythm of their training sessions. When he finally spotted Tai behind the bar, Jon's shoulders eased at his friend's easy grin and the casual wave beckoning him over.

Tai slid a cold beer toward Jon, the glass sweating in the warm market air. "Good to see you, my friend," he said, clinking the bar lightly with his knuckles.

Jon nearly drained the cold brew. "I thought we were training tonight."

"We will," Tai said, lowering his voice with a conspiratorial smile. "But first, come to a private gathering. Just a small group—like-minded people. I think you'll find it interesting."

Jon hesitated, surprised. Their training had always been straightforward—no distractions, no games. But something in Tai's tone, something purposeful, caught him. He set his glass down and nodded. "All right. Lead the way."

Tai guided him through the bustling market into a private back room, where a loose circle of people were deep in conversation. They welcomed him with nods and handshakes, a current of silent familiarity running between them. He settled in, curious about what he had just agreed to.

The conversation quickly turned to politics. The group spoke passionately about the changes sweeping through China—the rise of private companies, foreign investment, and the government's attempt to modernize the economy. But they also discussed the darker side: rampant corruption, rising inequality, and the growing discontent among the people.

Jon sat in silence, listening as their voices grew more fervent. He hadn't expected a political gathering. The frustration in the room was palpable, and though their words were compelling, politics had never been Jon's concern.

The sharp clink of a glass silenced the room. Jon looked up to see Tai standing on a small platform, a spoon in hand and a thoughtful expression on his face.

"Imagine a world without censorship," Tai said, his voice calm but commanding. "What would that mean for us?" He swept his gaze across the room, his dark eyes locking briefly with each person. "Imagine being able to express ourselves freely—no fear, no suppression. To have open and honest discussions. That is what makes a society truly free."

The room murmured in agreement.

"It won't be easy to achieve," Tai continued, his voice growing stronger. "But it's a goal worth fighting for. We need to raise our voices together. We're not alone in this—we have each other. And together, we can make change happen."

Applause rippled through the group, the room alive with energy. Jon clapped along, but the fervor was distant. He'd grown up with the freedoms Tai spoke of—freedoms he'd never had to defend. Only now did he realize how much he'd taken them for granted. The idea of fighting for something as basic as free speech struck him as both foreign—and deeply unsettling.

As the applause died down, Tai's expression turned somber. "Friends," he said, "today we mourn the loss of Hu Yaobang. He believed in democracy, in a better future for our country. But for those beliefs, he was purged from the communist party. I invite you all to join me in Tiananmen Square tomorrow to honor his memory. Let us stand together and show the world that his fight wasn't in vain."

The room buzzed with energy, whispers of agreement spreading like wildfire. Jon's gaze shifted to Tai, who stood tall and resolute, his words igniting something in everyone around him.

But Jon wasn't sure what to think. He admired Tai's passion, his determination, but a warning bell echoed in the back of his mind. This wasn't his fight. He didn't belong in their struggle, and he couldn't afford distractions that might derail his own path.

Still, as the crowd began to disperse, Tai approached him. "You should come," Tai said. "It would mean a lot."

Jon hesitated, his gaze dropping to the floor. He thought about the march Tai was planning, about the risks and the symbolism. He didn't feel the same fire these people did, but Tai was his friend. If he went, it wouldn't be for politics—it would be for him.

"I'll think about it," Jon said finally.

Tai nodded, his expression softening. "That's all I ask."

Jon stayed a while longer, listening to the group's stories, their frustrations and hopes for the future. But even as he nodded along, a part of him remained on the outside, cautious and detached.

When he finally stepped back into the cool night air, a restless pressure built behind his ribs, thoughts circling without shape or answer. Tai's words had been earnest, but their direction felt precarious. Jon wasn't one to chase causes or movements. Trusting someone, letting himself be drawn into something larger, carried risks he couldn't ignore. Yet beneath the caution, another truth stirred. Tai had offered more than friendship—he had offered belief. And now Jon had to decide whether to return that trust, knowing that once he crossed that line, there might be no way back.

Chapter 37

Protest and Reunion
Jon
Beijing, China

As Jon stepped off the train and onto the streets of Beijing, the city buzzed with an energy that was equal parts hope and unrest. Thousands of voices rose in chants, weaving through the wide avenues, their words echoing off government buildings. Banners fluttered in the breeze, bearing messages of defiance and longing for change. The smell of food, motorbike exhaust, and summer sweat mixed with the metallic tang in the air.

Jon glanced at Tai, who strode with purpose, his face alight with determination. The man radiated conviction, his steps quick and confident as they wove through a throng of students.

"Down with the dictatorship! Long live freedom, long live democracy!"

The chants grew louder as they approached Tiananmen Square. Jon kept pace beside Tai, his hands flexing and releasing at his sides, as if searching for something solid to hold on to. He hadn't wanted to come—this wasn't his fight. But Tai had asked for his support, and Jon, reluctant as he was, had agreed.

The square opened before them like a vast stage, alive with a sea of people. Students stood on makeshift platforms, shouting into megaphones, their voices cracking with passion. Others held signs high above their heads, their messages painted in bold strokes. *Democracy Now! No More Corruption! Hu Yaobang's Legacy Lives On!*

Jon moved carefully through the crowd, his eyes scanning the masses. The protesters were young, full of fire, their faces flushed with excitement and resolve. But there was an undercurrent of something darker—a tension that prickled at the edge of his awareness.

Police stood at the periphery of the square, their uniforms crisp and their expressions unreadable. Their presence was a silent reminder that the protests were being watched, judged, and perhaps counted.

Tai slowed as they reached the center of the square, his gaze fixed on a group of students clustered near the towering Monument to the People's Heroes. Without a word, he turned to Jon and gripped his arm. "Stay here for now," Tai said, his voice low but firm. "I'm going to speak."

Before Jon could respond, Tai stepped onto one of the makeshift stages. He took the microphone from a wide-eyed student, and within moments, the crowd's noise dimmed.

Jon watched as Tai's voice carried over the square, his words impassioned, his gestures sweeping. He spoke of Hu Yaobang, the former communist party leader whose death had ignited the protests. He called for reform, for freedom, for the end of corruption. Each phrase drew cheers from the crowd, their voices rising like a wave crashing against the silent government buildings.

Jon admired Tai's courage, but a dull tightness crept

across his chest, each breath catching just slightly as if something half whispered at the edges of his thoughts. The energy in the square was electric but unstable, as though one wrong move could spark a fire that no one could contain.

As Tai stepped down from the platform, another student eagerly took his place, rallying the crowd with fresh fervor. Tai pushed through the gathering, finding Jon near the edge of the square.

"I need your help," Tai said quickly, his eyes scanning their surroundings. "There's a package that needs to be brought back here. It's important."

Jon gave him a wary look. "What package? Where is it?"

Tai pressed a scrap of paper into Jon's hand. "Memorize the address. Then destroy this. It's close by, in a neighborhood near the university. Tell anyone who asks that you're visiting a friend."

Jon unfolded the paper, his stomach tightening as he read the address. His breath caught. It was Sun's spa.

He looked up sharply, searching Tai's face for any hint of recognition. Did he know about Jon's connection to Sun? Had he known all along? If so, why send him? The questions coiled in Jon's mind, but Tai's expression remained unreadable, his urgency unwavering.

The door chime jingled softly as Jon stepped inside, the spa's familiar scent of lavender and sandalwood wrapping around him like an old memory. He paused in the entryway, the still serenity of the space at odds with the chaos he'd left behind in Tiananmen Square.

For a moment, he hesitated, unsure of what he would find—or how Sun would react to seeing him after so much time.

The rhythmic clicking of machinery drew his attention. He followed the sound down the hall, his pulse quickening with each step. At the end of the corridor, he found a door slightly ajar, the mechanical whirring loudest here.

"Sun?" he called softly. The noise stopped. The door swung open.

Sun stood in the doorway, her hands full of freshly printed papers. Her eyes widened as they met his, and for a moment, she froze. A wave of surprise and joy washed over her luminous face. The papers slipped from her fingers and scattered across the floor as she stepped forward and threw her arms around him.

"Li," she whispered, her voice trembling. "It's really you."

Jon held her tightly, her warmth and the faint lavender scent of her hair pulling him back into a time when things had been simpler, easier.

When she finally stepped back, her eyes shimmered with unshed tears. "I can't believe you're here."

"It's been too long," he said. "You look...you look amazing, Sun."

She smiled softly, a laugh escaping her lips. "You always had a way of showing up unannounced."

He chuckled, the tension in his chest easing slightly. "Some things never change."

But his gaze drifted to the counter behind her where bundles of brown paper-wrapped flyers were neatly stacked. His smile faltered. "What's all this?"

Sun's expression sobered. She glanced at the stacks of flyers, then back at Jon. "You're here for those, aren't you?"

"Tai sent me," he admitted. "Said they were

important."

"They are," Sun said. She stepped back, closing the door behind her.

"The government has been cracking down hard. They've shut down the university press, arrested students for distributing protest materials. These flyers are one of the few ways we can get the message out."

He blinked, absorbing the weight of her words. "And you're risking yourself for this?"

"It's not just me," Sun said. "Xia's been working with the student newspaper since the protests began. She's in Tiananmen Square every day."

The mention of Xia hit Jon like a blow. He struggled to reconcile the image of the wide-eyed little girl he remembered with that of a young woman standing in the middle of a volatile protest.

"This is dangerous, Sun," he said, his voice low. "If something happens to you or Xia—"

Her gaze didn't waver. "We all have our roles to play, Li. This is bigger than us."

Jon stared at her, searching for the right words. But before he could speak, she handed him the bundled flyers, her hands brushing his as she passed them over.

"Take these back to the square," she said. "They're waiting for them."

Jon nodded, his throat tight. He hesitated for a moment, wanting to say more—to convince her to stay out of harm's way, to ask more about Xia—but the weight of the task Tai had entrusted to him pressed him forward.

The humid dusk air wrapped around him as he stepped out of the spa and back into the streets of Beijing. The noise of the square grew louder as he approached, the chants blending with the occasional crackle of a megaphone.

He moved through the crowd, his heart pounding as he scanned the faces around him. His voice grew hoarse as he called Xia's name, weaving between students holding banners and others sitting cross-legged in quiet defiance.

Where was she? Was she safe?

Jon's mind raced with questions he couldn't answer. As the crowd swelled and the sky darkened, a terrible sense of helplessness settled over him. For the first time, he understood the precariousness of the movement— how quickly hope could shift to chaos, and how easily a life could disappear in the crush of history.

Chapter 38

The Letter
Jon
Beijing, China

The walk to the post office stretched endlessly.

Jon's mind churned with the events of the past eight hours—the sea of protesters in Tiananmen Square, Sun's unflinching defiance, and the gnawing worry for Xia. Each step was weighed down by the heaviness in his chest, a tight knot of anticipation pulling him forward.

As he rounded the final corner, the familiar red-and-white sign of the post office came into view. He slipped inside, the cool air a brief reprieve from Beijing's heavy summer heat. Rows of steel postal boxes lined the walls like sentinels. He approached his, key in hand, and turned the lock with a soft click.

Inside was a single thick mailer, Daniel Wu's handwriting sharp across the front. Jon tucked it under his jacket and left without lingering.

Moving quickly, he crossed to a small tree-shaded park to open the mailer, and passed a group of soldiers from the People's Liberation Army. Their stern faces and rigid postures were a stark contrast to the chaotic energy of the protestors. He kept his head down, moving swiftly past them. The noise of the city faded slightly under the shelter of gnarled branches. He slid onto an empty bench and tore the envelope open.

Two photographs slid into his hand.

The first stopped him cold. Ethan stood in a familiar training hall—the Wolf Acupuncture & Kung Fu Vitality Center—beside a boy in a crisp training uniform, small but proud. His nephew. Jon didn't need anyone to tell him; he could see Kim's features woven into the boy's face. Ethan's hand rested protectively on the boy's shoulder, pride and warmth shining through the photo.

Jon's throat tightened. His family was alive. Thriving. It was a balm to the deep loneliness he rarely allowed himself to feel.

He reached for the second photo—and his relief turned to ice.

The same training hall. But this time, empty. A bloody message was smeared across the mirror. *We will find you, no matter where you hide.*

Jon stared, every muscle in his body locking tight. They were going after Ethan. After Kim. After the boy.

For a long moment, he sat frozen, the photographs trembling slightly in his hands. But then training, survival, some unspoken need kicked in. He gathered the photos and mailer, scanned the park quickly—no one close enough to notice—and moved toward a deserted corner near a crumbling stone wall.

There, he knelt, struck a match, and fed the photos to the flames. The paper curled and blackened, the images vanishing into ash. Only when the last ember died did Jon stand, wiping his hands clean against his jeans.

He had hidden himself well. His enemies hunted a face that no longer existed. But Ethan, Kim, the boy— they were vulnerable.

Jon stared down at the small pile of ashes. He couldn't reach out directly—not without bringing more danger to their doorstep. Ethan would protect them. Jon trusted that. Not just because of the bond they shared since childhood, but because Ethan had the strength, the skill, and the will to defend those he loved—with his life if he had to.

He turned away from the ashes and headed toward Tiananmen Square. Tai was still out there, swept up in the protests. Jon needed to find him, get him out of the city before the inevitable storm broke.

Chapter 39

The Reed and the Storm
Jon
Dunhuang, Gansu, China

The train sped westward through the dark mountains, the steady clatter of its wheels battling the harsh blare of news updates over the loudspeakers.

Jon sat beside Tai, his arms crossed and his head resting against the cold glass of the window. His mind raced, replaying the events of the day: the overwhelming chants of the protesters, the defiance in Sun's eyes, and Xia's commitment to the cause. He couldn't shake the image of Xia as a child, darting from stall to stall during the Chinese New Year celebration. Now she was a young woman, standing in the middle of a firestorm, fighting for ideals that could cost her everything.

The knowledge of his nephew—the child he had seen in the photograph—added a deeper layer to his thoughts. Each protester in Tiananmen Square became more than just a face in the crowd; they were someone's son or daughter, someone's sibling, someone's hope for the future.

Beside him, Tai stared out the window, his usual chatter replaced by a contemplative silence. The earlier fervor that had burned so brightly in Tai during the protests seemed to have dimmed, replaced by a burning intensity.

"You still believe this will change everything?" Jon asked, breaking the silence.

Tai turned to him, his eyes bright with determination. "I know it will. What we did today, what the students are doing, it matters. It's bigger than you or me, Li Wei. This is history being written. We're part of it."

Jon studied his friend, seeing the unwavering passion that had drawn him into the protests in the first place. Tai's belief was almost intoxicating, but Jon couldn't ignore the danger that came with it.

"History isn't written without a cost," Jon replied, his voice low. "And sometimes, that cost is too high."

Tai shook his head, his expression resolute. "Some things are worth any cost."

Jon didn't respond. He stared out at the shadowy mountains, the train winding through their rugged terrain like a thread pulled taut.

At some point, Jon dozed off, the exhaustion of the day overtaking him. He was jolted awake by a commotion echoing through the train car. Reports of the protests—and the government's tightening grip— echoed through the crowded cars, a grim soundtrack to the anxious whispers of the passengers.

"They're clearing the square," someone murmured. "Police…violence…arrests."

Jon sat up, his pulse quickening as he listened. The details were fragmented, but the message was clear. The protests had turned violent. Tiananmen Square, once a place of unity and defiance, was now a scene of chaos and desperation.

The gravity of the situation sank in as the train

pressed on through the night. The passengers fell silent. Jon's worry for Xia intensified, the uncertainty of her fate gnawing at him.

By the time they reached Lanzhou West Railway Station, a heavy weariness had settled over him.

Tai, still brimming with passion despite the grim news, clasped Jon's shoulder as they parted ways. "Don't forget what we stood for, Li Wei. This is just the beginning."

Jon nodded, though his mind was elsewhere. The memory of the bloodied message on Ethan's training hall mirror loomed in his thoughts, a chilling reminder that his fight wasn't just with the present but also with the ghosts of his past.

The familiar sight of Master Shen's kwoon brought a sense of solace Jon hadn't expected. As he stepped into the courtyard, the desert air dry against his skin, the weight of the day began to lift. The rhythmic sounds of students training in the distance reminded him of why he had come here in the first place.

Back in the bunkroom, Jon noticed his bedroll had been moved again—this time to the center of the room. Irritation flared, sharper than ever. He snatched up the bedroll and returned it to its usual spot in the corner, his movements stiff with frustration. Sitting down, he clenched his jaw, his mind churning with thoughts of who might be behind this. The repeated disturbance gnawed at him, leaving no room for peace.

The next day, Jon approached Master Shen, his frustration simmering just beneath the surface. He bowed respectfully, but his voice carried a sharp edge. "Master Shen, may I have a word?"

Master Shen turned to face him, his expression calm

and attentive. "Yes, Li Wei. What is on your mind?"

Jon hesitated for a moment, then pressed on. "For the past few weeks, someone has been moving my bedroll every day. At first, I thought it was a joke, but it hasn't stopped. I've confronted Hanying about it, and he denied it. I don't understand why this keeps happening—but I can't ignore it any longer. Do you know who's behind it?"

Master Shen met his gaze, calm and unwavering. "I do."

Jon paused. "You know who's doing it?"

Master Shen nodded. "It was I."

Jon blinked. "You? But…why?"

Shen clasped his hands behind his back. "You are attached—to routine, to control. Each time your bedroll was moved, frustration ruled you. Instead of bending, you resisted."

Jon opened his mouth to argue, then closed it again, the truth settling uncomfortably in his chest.

Shen turned to face him fully. "The reed that yields to the wind survives the storm."

Jon let out a slow breath, the lesson cutting deeper than any rebuke. He bowed his head. "I let my anger control me. I see that now."

Master Shen placed a hand on Jon's shoulder. "True strength lies not in resisting the storm, but in shaping oneself within it."

Jon bowed deeply, gratitude threading through his shame. "Thank you for your teaching, Master."

Shen nodded once, the faintest trace of approval in his eyes. "Now go. Your true training has just begun."

Chapter 40

Unity in Motion
Kim
San Francisco, California

The chants echoed through Union Square, rolling over the crowd like waves. Kim tightened her grip on Logan's hand as they pressed closer to the rally's main stage. Around them, banners for free speech and political reform fluttered in the breeze, blending with the hum of drums and the sharp crackle of megaphones. Logan's eyes darted from one colorful sign to the next, his excitement barely contained. Kim glanced ahead and spotted Ethan weaving through the crowd with Yan and her family in tow. She leaned down to Logan. "Look, there's your dad."

Logan perked up instantly, gripping her hand tighter. "He's with Yan!"

Ethan reached them first, crouching to meet Logan's gaze. "Hey, buddy," he said. "We're here because sometimes the people we care about need to know we're standing with them. When we show up, we're telling them and their families that they're not alone—that we've got their back."

Logan nodded, his wide eyes locked on Ethan's. "Like we're part of their team?"

"Exactly," Ethan said, smiling as he ruffled Logan's

hair. "One big team."

Before Kim could say more, Yan emerged from the throng with her parents and grandfather. She introduced them quickly, pride brightening her voice. Kim's gaze landed on Yan's grandfather, Dali—a wiry man with silver hair gathered in a traditional topknot. Even amid the bustling crowd, he moved with effortless grace, gliding through the chaos as if untouched by it.

"Your grandfather's a kung fu master, isn't he?" Kim asked, her voice low with respect.

Yan smiled. "He's been teaching longer than I've been alive."

Kim glanced at Dali again, feeling a deep admiration stir within her. Amid the swirl of energy around them, his steady presence was like an anchor.

"I'm so glad your family made it here from China," Kim said. "It must mean the world to have them with you."

Yan's smile deepened, her eyes shining. "It does."

The rally surged forward, as a Stanford student climbed onto the stage and tapped the microphone. The crowd hushed.

"Fellow students, friends," the speaker began, his voice ringing out over the square—clear and passionate. "Today we stand not just for Stanford but the global community. Our hearts are united with our Chinese brothers and sisters demanding democracy and freedom. Their courage has sparked a revolution, and we must not let their efforts be in vain."

Logan's grip on Kim's hand tightened. She looked down. His brow was furrowed.

"Just two weeks ago, there was a glimmer of hope with promises from Zhao Ziyang that 'reasonable demands' would be met. But now we hear troops are surrounding Beijing, and a crackdown seems imminent. We have no weapons, only our conscience. We stand for free speech, for reform, for justice."

The crowd erupted into applause. Beside her, Ethan and Yan raised their fists in solidarity. Kim glanced down at Logan, watching as his small chest puffed up with pride while he clapped along with the crowd.

Logan leaned closer and whispered, "Dad, you were right. Yan knows we're on her team."

"As we stand here, others are gathering at Chinese Embassies and Consulates across the nation." The student's voice swelled with passion. "We may be far from Beijing, but our hearts and voices are united with the demonstrators. Let us cry out for the students and activists in China. Let us show the world we will not be silent in the face of oppression. Together, we demand freedom and justice. Thank you."

Applause and cheers erupted across Union Square, a powerful wave of unity sweeping through the crowd. As the rally moved into a march, Kim fell into step beside Ethan and Logan. Yan's family carried signs, their expressions resolute. The chants for freedom rang in Kim's ears, a reminder of the courage it took to fight for change—whether in Beijing or San Francisco.

Over lunch, conversations drifted between martial arts, politics, and the uncertainty surrounding China's future. The rally's energy lingered in the air, a reminder that battles were fought in many arenas. But as they made their way to Kezar Pavilion, another kind of battle awaited—one of skill, discipline, and honor.

Logan darted ahead in Golden Gate Park, chasing pigeons and laughing as they scattered. Kim and Ethan walked side by side, their conversation easy, still reflecting on the powerful connections during the sympathy demonstration.

"Look at this," Kim said, nodding to the growing crowd outside the pavilion. "So many people, from so many places, all brought together by martial arts."

"It was fortuitous that the tournament brought everyone together at this time," Ethan said.

As they neared the pavilion, Yan glanced over her shoulder at Kim. "I knew today would be special. But seeing it—the speeches, the spirit—it reminds me why my grandfather teaches. Strength is in the spirit, not just the body," Yan said.

Dali, walking steadily beside them, gave a small nod. "Martial arts connects us. Across countries, across languages. A community without borders."

Kim smiled, watching Logan sprint ahead. His wide-eyed excitement earlier at the rally still lingered. She hoped he would carry the day's lesson with him— not just about martial skill, but about belonging to something bigger. Inside the pavilion, the tournament unfolded in a blur of skill and energy. Kim watched as Logan's gaze darted from one competitor to the next, his excitement bubbling over. When Ethan's turn came, Logan's cheers rang out above the crowd, his small voice carrying across the arena.

A familiar ache stirred in Kim as she watched Ethan move—fluid, powerful—a reminder of the days when he and Jon trained side by side. But she shook off the pull of the past. Today was about the future, Logan: his pride, his joy, and the subtle lessons he was learning from his father.

As the crowd began to thin, one of Ethan's earlier

opponents stepped forward, his movements tense, his face clouded with anger. "I seek to restore Master Gong's honor," the man said, his voice cutting through the murmur of conversation.

Ethan turned to face him fully, his composure steady. "I have no quarrel with Master Gong. My clinic was never a threat to his livelihood."

Kim turned to Dali, a knot forming in her stomach as the challenger circled Ethan. "When Ethan won Master Gong's challenge ten years ago, his students were ready to switch masters the next day. Half of Ethan's students are Master Gong's former students."

Dali nodded slowly, his expression serious. "In martial arts, losing students to another master is not just a practical loss—it's seen as a loss of face. For Master Gong, the defeat would have been deeply humiliating, not just in his community but to his students as well. For some students, loyalty to their master goes beyond logic or fairness. This man likely sees it as his responsibility to restore what he perceives as a stain on Master Gong's legacy—even if the cause of that loss was Master Gong's own actions."

Before Kim could respond, the challenger launched into a fierce attack. Logan pressed himself tightly against her side. The crowd around them froze.

Ethan sidestepped the man's strikes, his movements swift and controlled. Then, with a sharp snap kick to the knee, Ethan brought the challenger down. The man crumpled to the ground, a dragon tattoo on the back of his neck visible as he fell.

Dali stepped forward. "Honor is not restored through anger or bitterness. It is upheld through respect and discipline."

"Your loyalty is clear. Now show your strength by moving forward with honor." Ethan stepped closer and extended a hand.

The man hesitated, his expression still guarded.

Ethan held his gaze. "What's your name?"

"Zheng Mu," he answered as he took Ethan's hand. For a moment, he hesitated. Something in his eyes shifted.

As the crowd dispersed, Ethan ruffled Logan's hair and laughed. "What'd you think, buddy?"

Logan's face lit up. "You were awesome, Dad."

Kim's heart lifted, but her eyes were trained on the retreating figure. Her gut told her this wasn't over. Not yet.

Chapter 41

Hunger Strike
Jon
Beijing, China

Three weeks after first standing with Tai in Tiananmen Square during Hu Yaobang's funeral protests, Jon moved through the swelling crowds once again. Heat shimmered off the stone plaza. His gaze swept over a sea of colorful headbands and banners, scanning for Tai. The square, usually pristine and orderly, had transformed into a chaotic city of voices. The air was stifling, thick with sweat, tension, and the acrid tang of garbage collecting in corners.

Finally, he spotted him—sitting on the ground near the Monument to the People's Heroes, his back slouched, a red band tied around his forehead.

"Tai!" Jon called, picking his way through the crowd.

Tai looked up slowly, his face pale and drenched with sweat. He offered a weak smile as Jon crouched beside him.

"You look like hell," Jon muttered, handing him a bottle of water.

Tai chuckled hoarsely. "Hunger strikes aren't meant to be pretty." He took a small sip before setting the bottle aside. His voice was barely audible. "What's happening outside the square?"

"The barricades are holding, and tens of thousands of people have gathered to block the army's advance." Jon's voice dropped as he leaned closer. "Some soldiers are refusing orders—saying they were sent to stop a riot that doesn't exist. And…there are rumors that Zhao Ziyang has been stripped of power," Jon said after a pause, his voice dropping to barely a whisper. "Some are saying he's under house arrest."

Tai's expression tightened, a flicker of anger breaking through his exhaustion. "Zhao was the only one willing to talk to us. If he's gone, who's left to listen?"

Jon didn't respond, his gaze drifting to the filthy ground beneath their feet. The square was a patchwork of discarded flyers, food containers, and debris. The stench of waste and overflowing latrines filled the air, carried by the occasional breeze.

"But this movement is bigger than Zhao, bigger than any single leader," Tai said, his voice hoarse but filled with conviction. "It's about all of us, Li. Change is coming—I can feel it. Are there enough volunteers at the communication center to keep everything running?"

Jon nodded. "Calls are pouring in from all over— Shanghai, Los Angeles, Boston, DC, Beijing. Students at American universities are sending funds for food and supplies. Princeton raised over two thousand dollars. And when Chinese students at Columbia learned the government shut down the printing press that produced student newspapers, they arranged for a high-speed copier to be delivered to a storefront here in Beijing."

Tai's lips curved into a tired smile. "It's incredible, isn't it? The whole world standing with us." His voice softened, heavy with sincerity. "No matter what happens, we'll stand side by side. We're in this together."

Jon didn't share Tai's optimism. He had seen the soldiers—rows upon rows of them—and he couldn't shake the ominous sense that the government's patience was nearing its end.

The oppressive heat bore down as Jon sat with Tai, listening to the surrounding whispers of protesters. The rumors were rampant: troops were advancing underground through the subway system; the army would use tear gas to clear the square; and the most outrageous—200,000 people would be killed to restore order.

"Do you believe any of it?" Tai asked, his voice barely above a whisper.

Jon leaned in, his voice low but urgent. "I believe we're running out of time. I saw soldiers on the move—not just a few, but hundreds. And not with riot gear. With rifles."

Tai didn't hide his skepticism. "They wouldn't dare. Not with the whole world watching."

Jon shook his head. "They will. And when they move, it won't be to scare anyone. It'll be to crush this." He scanned the packed square, the students singing and waving flags. "You need to get out while you still can."

Tai's smile faltered, but he lifted his chin stubbornly. "I can't leave."

"You can," Jon pressed. "And you must. Find a way to disappear into the city. Lay low. If you stay here, you're gambling with your life—and theirs." He gestured toward the clusters of students around them. "This isn't a protest anymore. It's about to become a battlefield."

Tai shook his head. "American news anchors are

still here, broadcasting everything. As long as Gorbachev is in the country, they'll think twice about doing something drastic."

"Gorbachev's leaving soon, Tai. And when he's gone, the international spotlight goes with him. The foreign press? They're already being restricted—kept in their hotels, their broadcasts cut off. No more live footage, no one left to stop what's coming."

He swept his gaze across the crowded square, tension coiling in his chest.

"The soldiers aren't just standing by. They're closing in, surrounding us. You think they're here to negotiate? They're preparing to clear this place—with force if they have to. You need to leave now. Before it's too late."

Tai met Jon's urgency with a steady gaze. "We need to hold the line," he said. "No matter what happens, we stand together. If we back down now, everything we've fought for, everything we believe in—it'll mean nothing." He glanced around the square, at the faces young and old filled with stubborn hope. "They can surround us. They can threaten us. But if we stand together, they can't erase us."

By evening, Jon made his way to Sun's spa, the knot of worry in his chest tightening with every step. The streets leading away from the square were filled with a brittle tension—soldiers posted at corners, armored vehicles rumbling in the distance, pedestrians only speaking in hushed tones.

When he arrived, he found Sun stuffing a bag with bottled water and food, her movements brisk and determined.

"Sun, stop." He stepped into the room, urgency in

his voice. "You can't go to the square. It's too dangerous. Troops are closing in. They won't hold back."

She didn't even look up. "I have to find Xia."

Jon moved closer. "Listen to me," he said, his voice low. "Most of the students have already pulled back to rest. Xia's probably returned to her dorm. Let me find her—I'll bring her to you. But you—you have to stay clear."

She zipped the bag and finally faced him, her eyes bright with emotion. "You don't understand. Xia won't leave. She's stubborn. She's fighting for something bigger than herself. I can't just stay behind while she risks everything."

"And if you walk into that square now, you'll be risking everything too. You can't help her if you're caught in the crossfire. Let me go instead."

For a long moment, she wavered. Then she reached out and rested a trembling hand on his arm. "Li, I know you care about us. I know you want to protect us. But this is my choice. I need to stand with her—even if it's dangerous."

Jon searched her face, willing her to reconsider. But he saw the determination there—the same fire he admired. Slowly, he nodded, though the weight of it nearly crushed him. "Then at least be smart," he said, his voice low. "Stay near the edges. Watch for signs. If anything feels wrong, you get out—promise me."

A faint smile touched her lips, though tears shimmered in her eyes. "I promise." She slung the bag over her shoulder and slipped out into the night.

Jon stood there a long time after she was gone, listening to the echoes of the city readying itself for something it could never undo.

His journey to the train station was a gauntlet of silent warnings. Soldiers lined the streets—stoic and unblinking—while the distant clatter of tanks echoed like approaching thunder. He kept his head down, avoiding eye contact as he moved through the oppressive atmosphere.

At the platform, the approaching train rumbled closer—but Jon barely heard it over the hammering of his own pulse. Rows of soldiers from the 27th and 28th armies marched past, their faces blank, their tanks and guns angled toward Tiananmen Square.

Jon's fists tightened at his sides as he boarded the train. He sank into his seat, staring out the window at the vanishing city. Tai, Sun, Xia. They were still out there, standing in the eye of the storm. And all he could do now was pray the storm would pass without destroying everything in its path.

Chapter 42

Overseas Link
Ethan
Grand Rapids, Michigan

Ethan leaned against the desk in the communications room, surrounded by the constant hum of ringing phones and chattering fax machines. Exhaustion gnawed at him, but he refused to leave until the next shift arrived. Yan stood nearby, scanning a list of international numbers, her calm focus never wavering despite the long hours they'd been working.

"Dali and a few students should be here soon," Yan said, checking the time. "He wants to make calls, especially to a former student who's active in Beijing."

Ethan nodded, stretching his arms to ease the ache in his shoulders. "Makes sense. It's been chaos over there. Did you see *48 Hours* on CBS last night? Dan Rather was live from Tiananmen Square, but honestly, it's impossible to tell what's really going on inside the government."

She gave a weary smile. "It's like a family feud spilling out into the front yard for the whole world to see." Her voice softened. "But the stakes aren't political—they're life and death."

He let out a dry chuckle. "Too many factions. Too many hidden agendas."

"We can't untangle it from here," Yan said. "All we can do is help where we can." She gestured to the phones and fax machines around them. "This wouldn't have happened without you. International calls aren't something this community can afford, and allowing them a link to their loved ones has been a gift."

Heat rose to his cheeks at her words. Before he could respond, the door opened and Dali entered the room, his silver hair tied neatly into a topknot. Despite the gravity of the moment, he moved with composed, almost regal grace.

"Good evening, Dr. Wolf, Yan," Dali greeted them, pressing his palms together in a gesture of respect.

Ethan returned the greeting. "Good to see you, Dali. Let me know if you need anything."

"I appreciate it," Dali said, his tone polite but steady. "I have two calls to make. First to an old friend—a professor. Then to one of my former students who's been involved in the protests."

Ethan stepped aside as Dali settled by the speakerphone and dialed carefully from a worn scrap of paper. The line connected with a few static pops.

"Master Dali," said a serious voice from the speaker. "It is good to hear from you."

"Professor Bai," Dali said warmly. "What is the situation on the ground?"

"Barricades have gone up. Some soldiers refuse to act against the people, but the party leadership is divided. The hardliners are gaining ground. We are expecting a crackdown—soon." The professor's tone was grim.

Dali's jaw tightened. "Then the people must endure. Tyranny must be resisted."

The conversation ended with subdued words of

solidarity. Dali immediately placed the next call, his fingers steady. "This is a former student," he explained to Ethan and Yan.

The phone rang several times before a young man answered. "Hello, this is Pan Qigang." His voice was weary but composed.

Dali leaned in. "Pan! It is Dali calling from the United States. I am trying to find out about Tai. Has there been any news?"

There was a brief pause. Then Pan answered carefully, "I spoke with Li Wei today—a friend of Tai's. He saw him this afternoon at Tiananmen Square. Tai's still there, helping the students. But…it's dangerous. The government is preparing something. We can feel it."

Ethan exchanged a glance with Yan, the grim confirmation tightening the room's already heavy air.

"Thank you, Pan," Dali said. "Tell Tai—tell all of them—to stay safe. We are proud of them."

"I will," Pan said. "And…thank you, Master Dali. Your words mean more than you know."

The line went dead, leaving a charged silence behind.

Dali sat for a long moment before slowly rising to his feet. "Tai is strong. And he is not alone."

Ethan cleared his throat. "He's lucky to have had a teacher like you behind him."

Dali inclined his head. "We plant seeds, Dr. Wolf. It is for the young to carry them into the storm."

As the moment settled around them, Ethan's thoughts shifted to the urgent work still ahead—the calls to make, the support to organize. There would be time for questions later.

Chapter 43

Bloody Sunday
Jon
Beijing, China, Tiananmen Square

Jon moved through the darkened alleys like a shadow, slipping past soldiers, tanks, and barricades that had turned Beijing into a fortress. The air was thick with smoke and tension, and each step closer to Tiananmen Square tightened the knot in his gut. He had sworn he would never return here—not after that night three weeks ago, standing shoulder to shoulder with Tai during the hunger strike, pleading with him to leave before it was too late.

Back then, during the desperate days of mid-May, there had still been hope. Students had believed they could force change without bloodshed. Jon had seen the cracks forming even then—the government's patience thinning, the soldiers moving into place, the whisper of violence growing louder. He had tried to pull Tai out. He had warned him that the clock was running out.

Now the clock had struck midnight.

It was June 4th. The army wasn't just maneuvering anymore. It was moving in. And this time, Jon knew, no camera crew or peaceful song would stop them.

Somewhere inside the square, Tai was still out there. Stubborn. Brave. Blind to how quickly hope could turn into slaughter. Jon pushed forward. He had come back for one reason. To find Tai. To get him out—if there was still time.

The piercing sound of the government announcement shattered the still of the night. At four in the morning, Jon was jolted awake from a restless slumber in the students' tent city encampment on the square's northern side. Beside him, Tai sprang to his feet with a start.

The broadcast blared across loudspeakers, declaring a "counterrevolutionary rebellion" and accusing the protesters of attacking the army and setting fires. It warned that the troops would use any means necessary to clear Tiananmen Square—and that anyone who remained would bear the consequences.

Jon locked eyes with Tai, his mind already racing. Time had run out.

Around them, groggy students stumbled from their tents. Panic rippled through the crowd. Jon scanned the confusion, his heart hammering, until he spotted familiar faces—Sun and Xia, banners gripped tightly in their hands as they joined a tightening circle around the new Statue of Liberty replica, hastily erected just the day before. The slogans on their banners shouted into the dawn's sickly light. *Long live Freedom, Down with Dictatorship! Give me democracy or give me death.*

Tanks appeared from both the east and the west, engines snarling as they converged on the square. Before Jon could react, Tai broke away, running forward to stand between the advancing tanks and the students clustered around the statue. He raised both arms high—defiant, unyielding.

For a breathless second, it seemed as if even the

tanks would hesitate. Then a sharp burst of gunfire split the morning. Soldiers atop the tanks opened fire.

Tai staggered backward, blood blooming from his chest. Jon bolted toward him, adrenaline surging, and dragged Tai's limp form out of the tank's crushing path. All around him, the world dissolved into chaos. Gunfire cracked the air. Screams rose, raw and terrified. Students scattered or dropped where they stood. A mother and daughter, hands entwined, collapsed under a volley of bullets.

In the madness, Jon's gaze locked onto Sun. She stepped forward, away from the group, and lay down before the lead tank—soon joined by an old woman and a scattering of others. He shouted her name, desperation tearing from his throat, but the tank lumbered forward, indifferent. Jon watched, helpless, as the machines crushed the bodies beneath them, blood and dust rising into the already choked sky.

The People's Liberation Army—meant to defend the people—was massacring its brightest sons and daughters. Bullets struck down anyone who tried to flee. There was no mercy.

Breathless, battered, Jon dropped beside Tai in the square's blood-soaked heart. Tai's chest rose and fell in ragged gasps. Blood trickled from his mouth, his ears, his nose.

Despite everything, Tai looked up at Jon with a peaceful expression. "We never expected that soldiers would kill students like that. Tell my uncle he was right."

With those final words, he took his last breath.

Tears blurred Jon's vision as he cradled Tai's still body. Above the chaos, the image seared into him: Tai standing before the massive tank, arms spread wide; Sun lying down in defiance, shielding her sister—Xia's fate swallowed in the smoke and screams.

The ground shook with the relentless advance of tanks, their treads crushing stone, banners, and bodies alike. Riot police followed, a dark wave wielding sticks and cattle prods. They struck at anyone still breathing.

Jon threw himself onto the blood-slicked pavement, face down. A crack of pain lanced through his arm as a baton smashed across his forearm. He bit back a groan, forcing his body to go limp, willing himself into stillness.

Blow after blow rained around him, but none struck his head. He kept his face pressed into the cold stone, his breathing shallow, pretending to be just another corpse.

Finally, the shouts and boots grew distant.

Jon shifted his weight experimentally. His left arm hung useless at his side, a dead weight of throbbing pain. Gritting his teeth, he pushed up awkwardly with his good hand and began crawling forward, dragging the injured limb against the rough stone.

The square was a graveyard. Torn banners fluttered weakly from broken poles. Blood pooled beneath crumpled bodies. The acrid stench of smoke, gunpowder, and death coated the air.

Keeping low, Jon moved west along the southern edge of Tiananmen Square. His every movement was agony. Each meter he gained was a victory ripped from the jaws of hell itself.

He passed the twisted wreckage of bicycles, crushed under tank treads. Shoes abandoned mid-flight. A young man sprawled across a protest sign, his hand still curled around its battered pole.

Jon didn't dare look too closely. He couldn't afford to.

At the towering columns of the Great Hall of the People, he turned north, slipping through the shadows cast by the grand facade. His breath came in ragged gasps. His vision blurred from blood loss and exhaustion.

By the time he reached the Xidan intersection west of the square, the soldiers had pushed farther east. The streets were eerily silent now—punctuated only by the distant crackle of gunfire.

Jon staggered upright, cradling his injured arm against his chest, and forced himself toward the Beijing train station.

Inside, the terminal was chaos—frantic travelers and stunned students pressed against ticket counters. Somehow, Jon thrust a few grimy bills at a clerk and secured a ticket north.

When the train finally lurched forward, Jon sank into a seat by the window, cradling his broken arm.

The city slipped away behind him—its smudged lights a ghostly reflection against the glass.

He did not look back.

He carried the faces of the fallen with him, and the weight of their sacrifice pressed against his chest, heavier than the pain of his shattered bones.

Jon closed his eyes. He had survived. Now he had to make it mean something.

Ahead lay Gansu, the silent deserts and the kwoon where he'd found refuge. He vowed he would reach Master Shen and deliver Tai's final message.

Chapter 44

Beaten
Jon
Dunhuang, Gansu, China

Jon dragged his feet along the dusty Silk Road, his body and soul battered. As he made his way across the kwoon's courtyard, his injured arm, immobilized and plastered to his side, throbbed with every heartbeat. The recent memory of soldiers' batons striking him, a punishment for his refusal to leave Tai's side, haunted his thoughts.

As he stumbled through the entrance, his appearance drew immediate attention. Zhang hurried over, his face a mask of concern. "What happened?" he asked, eyes scanning Jon's injuries.

"I need Master Shen," Jon managed, his voice strained with effort.

"You need the infirmary," Zhang insisted, assessing his condition.

But Jon was adamant. "Master Shen, please," he said, his body trembling from pain and fatigue.

With a supporting arm around Jon, Zhang guided him through the corridors of the private residence wing to Master Shen's chamber. At the door, Zhang knocked firmly while Jon called out, "Master Shen, it's Li Wei. I need you."

The door soon opened to reveal a surprised Master Shen. "Li Wei, what happened?" he asked, ushering them into the chamber rich with the scent of burning incense. The walls were adorned with calligraphy and ancient scrolls, and the air was heavy with sandalwood, creating a calming, almost otherworldly atmosphere.

Jon collapsed onto an ornate chaise lounge, its silk fabric worn from years of use. Tears streamed down his face as he choked out the words, "I have a message from your nephew Tai."

Master Shen's face darkened. He gestured for Zhang to leave, then sat beside Jon, placing a comforting hand on his shoulder amid the soft glow of the chamber's dim lighting.

"Tai is dead. With his final breath he said, 'Tell my uncle he was right.' "

"Tell me everything," Shen said.

Jon recounted the events, his voice breaking with emotion. As he spoke, Master Shen's face reflected a growing sorrow, illuminated by the flickering of a small oil lamp on a nearby table.

When the story ended, Master Shen stood, his eyes ablaze. "You broke rules and dishonored the kwoon," he said, pacing on the woven bamboo mat flooring. But soon, his anger gave way to sorrow, tears welling in his eyes. "Tai was stubborn…his dreams led to this tragedy. I warned him many times. His actions put the entire kwoon in danger. But Tai was naive and headstrong, convinced that his ideas were worth fighting for. He lured you into his false hope."

Jon, tears flowing, spoke of Tai's bravery. "He died a hero."

Master Shen gazed at him, sadness and pride on his

face, the lines of age and wisdom more pronounced under the soft light. "I knew my nephew from the day he was born," he said. "You are correct, he had courage. He spoke truth when all were silent, and he had the talent to have been my successor one day. His life was precious…and lost to those who value only power and wealth. Now he feeds worms and maggots."

They were connected in grief.

"Is there no honor in Tai's sacrifice?" Jon asked tentatively.

"He is a martyr, but we don't study martial arts to become martyrs. Tai had the potential to make a greater impact in life than in this death."

Master Shen turned his attention to Jon's injury, carefully examining the arm. Jon winced but remained still.

"Can you move your fingers?" Master Shen asked, gently flexing them.

Jon gritted his teeth. "Yes."

With practiced ease, Master Shen prepared a poultice of herbs and minerals, crushing them in a stone bowl. The sharp earthy scent filled the air as he spread the cool paste over Jon's arm. Relief seeped in, easing the throbbing enough for Jon to unclench his jaw.

"This will help reduce the swelling," Shen said, wrapping the arm with a clean strip of cloth to secure the poultice, which hardened like a cast. "But you'll need rest. Overuse will make it worse."

"I know I broke the rules," he spoke hesitantly. "I'll do anything to make it right."

"I had great hopes for you," Master Shen said, his voice heavy with disappointment. "But you must leave."

Jon's chest tightened. "Would you cast me out for

one mistake? Please, Master Shen, give me another chance to prove I can bring honor to you and the art."

Master Shen held his gaze for a long moment, his expression unreadable. Then he exhaled deeply. "I wish it were that simple. But the CCP has declared the protests a counterrevolutionary riot. They are arresting and punishing participants and anyone connected to them. Keeping you here puts everyone at risk."

Jon's heart sank like a stone. "Isn't there another master, another kwoon?" he asked, his voice barely above a whisper.

"Go home, Li Wei. The consequences if you're caught are severe." Master Shen's voice softened, but his tone remained resolute.

Jon hesitated, his fingers curling into fists. "I…I can't go home," he finally admitted, conflicted and ashamed. "People are looking for me because of something I did. At the time, I thought it was justified, but now…I'm not sure anymore."

Master Shen studied him in silence before turning away. At his small desk, he pulled out a sheet of paper and began writing. The scratch of his pen filled the room, each stroke deliberate and steady. Finally, he folded the letter and held it out to Jon.

"This is a letter of introduction to Grand Master Peng in Hong Kong. It is your next step," he said.

Jon took the letter, the paper warm in his hands. "Thank you, Master."

"In three days, you'll leave for Hong Kong," Master Shen said, breaking the silence. His tone was final, leaving no room for argument. "Use this time to heal and prepare."

Part Five 1993

Chapter 45

The Turning Point
Ethan
Grand Rapids, Michigan

Ethan glanced at the wall clock just as the door swung open. Logan stepped inside, his backpack slung over one shoulder. His black eye and split lip told a story before he said a word.

Robert Fenton, Logan's grandfather, reached him first. "Logan, what happened? Are you all right?" His voice was tight with concern as he inspected his grandson's face.

Logan shrugged, avoiding eye contact. "I'm fine, Grandpa," he mumbled.

But Ethan wasn't convinced. He had been leading a class and immediately passed the reins to one of his senior students and crossed the room. Standing nearly eye level with his thirteen-year-old son, Ethan placed a firm but comforting hand on Logan's shoulder. "Talk to me," he said, his voice calm but resolute.

"It's nothing," Logan muttered, then hesitated. "Just Billy Dusen and his friends. They cornered me after school. Billy hit me a couple of times, but it's no big deal."

D.G. Schulman

"It *is* a big deal. No one has the right to put their hands on you. Did you try to defend yourself?" Ethan kept his tone steady, though heat rose in his chest and his jaw tightened.

"I *did*, but there were three of them," Logan said, his hands balling into fists. "Billy's friends held me down so I couldn't even try to fight back."

Ethan exhaled. "All right, we'll figure this out together." He rested a hand on Logan's shoulder. "You know how to defend yourself—but it's not just about fighting back. It's about knowing when to stand your ground. We'll talk more."

Logan's shoulders squared slightly, a flicker of determination returning to his eyes.

As Ethan guided Logan through the reception area toward the door, his attention caught on Yan at the desk, smiling as she accepted a small gift from Zheng Mu. Something about Mu's demeanor—his polished grin that stopped short of his eyes—stirred a flicker of concern in Ethan. But with Logan at his side, he pushed the thought away. Tonight, his focus was entirely on his son.

Later that evening, after a simple dinner at home, Ethan and Logan agreed to confront Billy and his father directly. The Dusen residence was a modest ranch-style house in the neighborhood. As Ethan and Logan approached the door, the air was crisp, and the streetlights cast long shadows across the yard.

When Bert Dusen answered the door, he was chewing a mouthful of food, his jaw working slowly. He looked from Ethan to Logan, his broad frame filling the doorway. "You're ruining my steak dinner," he grumbled before adding, "What's this about?"

Ethan extended a hand, but Bert ignored it. "We

need to talk about your son, Billy," Ethan said, keeping his voice steady.

Bert leaned lazily against the doorframe. "What about him?"

Ethan gestured to Logan, his bruised face evident in the porch light. "Your son attacked mine after school. This kind of behavior needs to stop."

Bert glanced at Logan's injuries and gave a chuckle that set Ethan's teeth on edge. "Boys will be boys," he said with a dismissive wave. "They'll figure it out on their own."

Ethan's patience wore thin, but he kept his composure. "Bert, this isn't about boys being boys. It's about teaching our kids right from wrong."

Bert shrugged. "Why don't we let them have it out in the yard? Old-school style. No need for all this talking."

Ethan's jaw tightened, and he glanced at Logan, whose eyes reflected a mix of apprehension and resolve. Without breaking eye contact with his son, Ethan gave a slight nod, their silent communication speaking volumes.

"If that's how you want to handle it," Ethan said, stepping back. "Logan's ready."

The Dusens' front yard became an impromptu arena, the fading light of the day casting long shadows over the two boys. Neighbors began to gather, drawn by the commotion. Billy stood across from Logan, his chest puffed out and a smug grin plastered across his face.

"Let's see what your kung fu's worth, loser," Billy sneered, cracking his knuckles for effect.

Ethan's gaze scanned the gathering crowd, their murmurs of anticipation rippling through the air. The fight unfolding in a sleepy suburban yard unsettled him—it was something primal, raw, and uncomfortably familiar. But he pushed the thought aside, focusing on the significance of the moment. This wasn't just a scuffle; it was a lesson in standing tall, a test of restraint and courage in balance.

Logan, standing opposite Billy, took a deep breath. He raised his hands in a guarded stance, his feet planted firmly on the grass. Ethan could see the focus in his son's eyes, the restraint in his movements.

Billy lunged first, throwing a wide, sloppy punch. Logan sidestepped easily, his movements fluid. He didn't counter, simply watching and waiting as Billy charged again, his strikes wild and uncontrolled.

"Come on, fight back!" Billy growled.

Ethan watched closely, his heart swelling with pride at Logan's discipline. He wasn't letting anger control him; he was thinking, strategizing.

Then Billy landed a lucky punch—a wild swing that grazed Logan's jaw. Logan staggered slightly but recovered quickly. Ethan saw the change in his son's posture, the subtle shift as Logan decided it was time to act.

Billy charged again, and this time, Logan didn't dodge. He stepped into the attack and delivered a controlled sidekick to Billy's midsection. Billy doubled over, winded, and before he could recover, Logan followed with a strike to his shoulder, which sent him sprawling to the ground.

The crowd fell silent as Billy lay there, clutching his side. Logan stepped back, his breathing steady, his fists still raised. No one restrained him now—Billy was completely at his mercy.

"This ends here. I don't think you'll try this again—but if you do, you'll regret it. I won't hold back next time. And you won't have your friends to back you up." Logan crouched down beside Billy, his voice calm but firm.

The fight drained from Billy's eyes. After a beat, he gave a stiff nod. Logan stood and extended a hand. After a moment's hesitation, Billy took it, and Logan helped him to his feet.

As they walked away, Ethan glanced back at the yard now emptying of neighbors. He wasn't sure if allowing the fight had been the right call. But when he looked at Logan—his stride steady, his head held high—a deep reassurance settled in. Some lessons weren't taught in classrooms or training halls. Some unfolded in the unlikeliest places.

Chapter 46

The Gift
Ethan
Grand Rapids, Michigan

The next morning, Ethan arrived at the center early, his thoughts still lingering on the previous night's confrontation at the Dusen residence. He hoped to focus on his classes, grounding himself in the familiar rhythm of teaching.

As he passed through the reception area, a familiar voice drew his attention. Zheng Mu was again standing at the counter, a neatly wrapped gift in his hands. Yan, always poised and gracious, stood on the other side, her expression bright with curiosity.

"Yan, I've brought you something special. A token of my affection." Mu's electric smile spread across his face as he handed her the gift.

Ethan slowed his pace, watching their interaction unfold.

Yan opened the small package carefully and lifted out a stuffed dog with a heart-shaped name tag. Her laugh was warm, lighting up the room. "It's adorable," she said, cradling the toy in her hands. "Thank you, Mu. What's the story behind it?"

"There's more to this little dog than meets the eye." he replied, his tone tinged with intrigue.

Ethan lingered by the edge of the room, straining to catch their words. His curiosity mingled with a flicker of disquiet. There was something calculated about the way Mu spoke, as though every word was chosen for effect.

Her brow furrowed slightly as she tilted her head. "What do you mean?"

Mu's voice dropped, forcing Ethan to move closer under the guise of checking a clipboard on the wall. He caught fragments of the explanation—something about loyalty and devotion, but the rest was lost in the hum of morning activity in the center.

Ethan's gaze shifted between the two. Yan's expression softened as Mu spoke, her smile genuine and unguarded. Ethan couldn't help but feel unsettled. How had he missed the deepening connection between Yan and Mu?

Yan placed the stuffed dog on a nearby shelf, nestling it beside a pig and a platypus that seemed to match as part of an unlikely trio. The whimsical set fit right in with her growing collection of small gifts and trinkets from students and staff, a subtle testament to how deeply adored she was by everyone around her.

Mu's smile lingered as he stepped back from the counter. "I thought it would brighten your day."

Yan glanced at the stuffed dog on the shelf, a small smile playing at her lips. As Mu turned to leave, his jet-black hair shifted, revealing the dragon tattoo etched into his neck. The ink caught the light for a moment before disappearing beneath his collar.

Ethan's shoulders stiffened, a heaviness settling in his chest he couldn't quite shake. The sight of the tattoo brought back memories of their first encounter at Kezar Pavilion where Mu had sought to restore his former master's honor. Back then, his movements had been fueled by anger and pride, his strikes wild and undisciplined. But after the tournament, Mu had come to Michigan—not just for treatment, but to learn under Ethan, to train as one of his students.

Ethan's mind wandered briefly to the weeks following that tournament. He had treated Mu with acupuncture, focusing on the "Spirit Gate" point at Heart 7 to calm his anger and balance his emotions. The work had been painstaking, addressing not just the physical pain but the emotional turmoil that drove Mu.

Yet, as Ethan watched Mu now, he couldn't shake the feeling that the transformation was incomplete. Discipline and focus had replaced the wildness in Mu's demeanor, but beneath the surface, there was a craftiness that put Ethan on edge.

At that moment, Dali entered the reception area. His sharp eyes immediately zeroed in on Mu, narrowing slightly. Mu offered a polite nod in greeting before stepping out of the building.

"Yan, my dear, be careful with Zheng Mu. There is an air of deception about him." Dali leaned in close to the counter, his voice low but firm, his movements steady and deliberate.

She chuckled lightly, brushing off her grandfather's warning. "Grandpa, Mu has changed. He's committed to the center, to improving himself. You always taught me that people can grow—that redemption is possible."

His expression softened, but his eyes remained watchful. "Redemption is proven through actions, not words. Trust, but never blindly. Not everyone who seeks a new path has truly left the old one behind."

From where he stood, Ethan observed the exchange,

sensing the veiled friction between Yan's optimism and Dali's cautious wisdom. Yan's belief in the center's mission—to heal and transform—was unwavering, but Dali's intuition hinted at something more complicated.

Ethan's thoughts returned to his own experiences with Mu. He had seen progress, yes, but change was never a straight path. Years of ingrained habits couldn't be unraveled overnight—not by discipline, nor by the careful application of meridian work. True transformation required more than skill or time; it demanded intent.

As Yan returned to her work, Ethan stepped closer to Dali. "Do you really think Mu is a threat?" he asked, keeping his voice low.

Dali turned to him, his expression unreadable. "I don't trust what I can't see. Zheng Mu may have learned discipline, but his heart—his true intentions—are still hidden."

Ethan nodded, wariness settling deeper in his gut. "I'll keep an eye on things."

Dali gave a small nod of approval before heading to the training hall.

Ethan lingered in the reception area for a moment, his gaze drifting to the stuffed dog now sitting proudly on Yan's shelf. The gift unsettled him—not for what it was, but for what it might mean. It didn't feel like a simple gesture of gratitude. There was an intention behind it, one he couldn't quite name. As the morning classes began and the hum of activity filled the center, Ethan pushed the thought aside—but not away. The center was a place of healing and growth, but even within its walls, trust had to be earned.

For now, he would focus on his work. But

something told him that Zheng Mu's story was far from over.

Chapter 47

Dual Existence
Jon
Hong Kong, British Crown Colony

The blistering heat of Hong Kong's summer wrapped around Jon like a suffocating blanket as he squared off with Brother Wang inside Master Peng's kwoon.

Across the polished floor, Wang's grin flashed—cocky and teasing. "Li Wei," he said, circling. "Think you can keep up today?"

"You know my name?"

"Sure. You're the guy making me look good."

Jon didn't get the chance to answer. Wang lunged, delivering a series of lightning-fast strikes that Jon countered with equal intensity. The exchange sent a wave of energy rippling through the room, drawing subtle nods of approval from Master Peng. Despite over a year of sparring together, Jon never forgot that his opponent wasn't just a martial artist; he was a star. A figure larger than life, a symbol of perfection that Jon was constantly measuring himself against.

But just as Jon found his rhythm, the sliding doors opened. A man in a tailored suit entered, breaking Jon's concentration. Wang's next punch nearly clipped him before Jon refocused and swept him clean to the floor.

Wang landed with a grunt but pushed up, grinning. "Not bad."

The suited man didn't smile. "Wang, we have a problem."

Jon's eyes darted toward the suit. He recognized the man immediately from the way Wang straightened. This was Tsui Ho, producer of Wang's latest film.

"One of the actors broke his leg. We're stalled. We need a replacement."

"Use Li Wei," Wang said without hesitation.

Jon blinked. *Did he just—*

Tsui Ho turned. "You one of Peng's students?"

Jon nodded slowly.

"Good enough." Tsui didn't wait for agreement. "It's a small role, just a few fights. You in?"

Jon glanced at Master Peng, who gave a single nod.

"All right," Jon said, unsure what he'd just agreed to.

What started as a favor turned into something bigger. The role led to another, then another. Days were spent at the kwoon under Master Peng's relentless eye. Evenings were spent under hot lights, retaking fight scenes, trying to match Wang's effortless charisma.

He'd come to Hong Kong to train, not act. Four years ago, he'd fled Gansu with a backpack and a locker key to a bundle of cash hidden in Beijing. He'd had no plan beyond finding a new master and burying his past. The kwoon had given him structure, purpose. But now?

Now he was tired.

The film work wasn't bad. It paid well—something he had to think about more lately. His funds from that locker in Beijing were almost gone, and for the first time in years, money had crept back into his decisions. Rent, food, training—none of it was free.

Wang had noticed. He saw the way Jon never turned down a gig, no matter how small. He saw the extra hours, the side conversations with production managers, the careful counting of cash after shoots. But Wang also saw something else—*talent*. "You've got the skill," he said one night after filming. "But you're tight. This isn't the kwoon. Loosen up. Let the emotion through."

Jon took the note. He always did. Still, he couldn't shake the question. *Have I taken on too much?*

Jon's days blurred—caught between two lives. He was the disciplined student, bowing respectfully before Master Peng in the sanctity of the kwoon, and the performer hitting his mark under the glare of studio lights.

By 1995, Jon stood on the rooftop set, wind tearing at his costume, the neon skyline blazing behind him. In *Rise of the Shadow Warrior*, he played a supporting role. In tonight's scene his character confronted the film's villain, a figure who cloaked himself in lies and silence.

The director shouted, "Action!"

He launched into the choreographed fight sequence, movements sharp and deliberate. For the first time, flow took hold—not just in his body, but in his presence. In the way he stepped into character. In the way the mask no longer felt like a mask at all.

On screen, he was decisive. Expressive. Unafraid.

In life, he'd spent years holding back—his past, his face, even his voice.

"Cut."

He stepped away from the lights, tugging at the collar of his costume as the crew reset behind him. The city shimmered in the glass wall ahead—his reflection caught between motion and stillness, half-lit by neon and shadow. For a long moment, he stared at it. He touched his chest lightly, feeling the steady rhythm of his breath. He was still doing kung fu—only now, it came with a voice.

The stunt coordinator clapped Jon on the back. "Perfect. We'll get that last kick in slow-mo."

Jon nodded absently. The sweat on his skin had already begun to cool, but something else still burned underneath.

He had trained for years to disappear—to master silence, to mimic, to suppress. That was kung fu, the version he had known: restraint, repetition, control. But this…this *required* him to be seen.

Emotion, presence, vulnerability—it was what the camera demanded. And it was exposing things his martial discipline had long buried.

He wasn't sure yet if he was becoming someone new or finally becoming who he had always been. But as the crew called reset and lights flared back to life, Jon turned from the glass.

He didn't look back.

****

The humid air outside the small post office was thick with the scent of brine and diesel from the nearby harbor. Jon moved through it without hurry, the small key in his hand warm from his pocket. The box had once been a safeguard—a buffer between him and the world he'd left behind. Now it was a checkpoint. A comforting ritual. A reminder of the lines he still walked.

Inside the box, a single envelope. The handwriting was unmistakable—Daniel Wu.

He stepped aside and opened it beneath the low

awning, careful with the folds.

Jon,

This will be my last communication. I am retiring—heading to Florida, where I plan to spend my days on a deep-sea fishing boat. A life of peace and simplicity. Enclosed is the name and address of a retired cop in Michigan, now a private investigator. He's been watching over your family. I've paid him in advance. If you need anything, he'll be your point of contact now.

I also used the last of your retainer to pay off your mother's hospital bills. Consider it a gift from an old friend.

One more thing—Sifu is gone. With no son to succeed him, his daughter, Mei, will lead now.

Enclosed is a recent photograph of your parents. Take care, my friend.

Wu

Jon read it twice, then pulled out the photograph. His parents stood together at Meijer Gardens—hand in hand, mid-stride, unaware of the camera. His mother, thinner, but smiling. His father, a little stooped, hair streaked with silver. Time had softened them but not dimmed them.

He let the image settle in his hands for a while, then folded the photo carefully and slipped it back inside. As he reached in again, his fingers brushed against something else—a newspaper clipping, Swedish, *Svenska Dagbladet.* He recognized the masthead instantly and read the article.

Break-In at Stockholm Clinic: Confidential Medical Records Stolen.

Authorities in Stockholm are investigating a break-in at a private medical clinic known for its discretion and high-profile clientele. Among the items stolen were

*confidential medical records, leading to concerns over
the privacy of former patients. The clinic has refused to
comment on the extent of the breach, but sources indicate
that the stolen records include sensitive information
related to reconstructive surgeries. The incident has left
many former patients on edge, fearing the exposure of
their private lives.*

Jon exhaled slowly.

No fear this time. No panic. Just clarity.

The past had a long reach. He knew that. And
whoever had taken those files—whether they were
Flying Dragons or someone else—would come looking
eventually.

But he'd spent years preparing for that.

His gaze drifted toward the harbor, where boats
bobbed in the swell and the scent of the ocean hung thick
in the air. This city, this life—it wasn't borrowed
anymore. He'd earned it. Brick by brick. Blow by blow.

If someone wanted to drag him back into the dark,
they'd have to reckon with the man he'd become.

He tucked the envelope into his shirt and stepped out
into the heat, the sun sharp off the pavement.
Somewhere, someone had his name on a piece of paper
and thought that would be enough.

Chapter 48

Safe With Me
Kim
Grand Rapids, Michigan

Yan's eyes sparkled as she laced up her kung fu shoes.

"What is it?" Kim asked, unable to hide her curiosity.

"You have to promise not to tell anyone." Yan lowered her voice.

Kim paused, surprised by the shift in tone, then nodded. "Of course. Your secret's safe with me."

Yan grabbed her hands. "I'm engaged to Zheng Mu."

Kim blinked. "Wow. That's...big."

"Grandfather would never approve," Yan added quickly. "Mu's working on a way to win him over, to show how much we respect tradition. But we need time. You can't tell anyone."

Kim met her gaze. "Dali's a wise man. If Mu's intentions are sincere, maybe there's a way."

"We'll find it. We have to." Yan's eyes betrayed the worry still beneath the joy.

The weight of the secret settled between them. Kim said nothing more—she'd given her word.

They stepped into the training hall, and the world

narrowed to the sound of breath, movement, rhythm.

In the stillness of the training hall, Kim and Yan moved in harmony. Their motions were sharp, fluid, and disciplined—strikes and counters practiced into muscle memory.

Kim's style was forceful, deliberate. Yan flowed like water, each movement a seamless continuation of the last. Together, they formed a rhythm that needed no words.

Kim caught their reflection in the mirrored wall—two bodies moving in sync, until they seemed like one.

She let the repetition ground her. The secret she now carried pressed heavily on her mind, but in motion, there was clarity.

As they landed the final sequence, Kim exhaled. She and Yan bowed in unison, a gesture of respect, but also of tacit understanding.

After changing, Kim lingered at the edge of the training hall, drawn by the sight of Ethan and Dali moving through an intricate form. Their footwork, timing, even the pauses—they weren't just performing. They were communicating.

Dali's corrections were few but exact. Ethan absorbed them with the ease of a longtime student. Watching them, Kim was struck by how much could be passed through quiet repetition—how mentorship, trust, and strength could be contained in a simple exchange of movement.

Watching them stirred something in Kim. Trust. Legacy. The sense that martial arts was more than form—it was lineage. Family. The weight of her promise to Yan pulled at her again.

As she was about to leave, the front door opened.

Zheng Mu stepped in, carrying a tray with a porcelain tea service. He stopped short when he saw her. "Kim. I didn't expect anyone else here tonight."

"I was just leaving," she said. "That's quite the elaborate setup."

He smiled, though it didn't quite reach his eyes. "A small gesture of respect—for Master Dali and Sifu Wolf. I thought they might appreciate some tea after training."

She studied him. "I'm sure they will."

The silence stretched.

Then she gave a small nod and stepped past him, her pulse steady.

Outside, the cool night wrapped around her. She didn't look back—but the image lingered. Mu, ceremonial, laying the groundwork for something deeper.

Was it tradition? Love? Strategy?

Whatever it was, she had made a promise. And she would keep it.

But she'd be watching.

Chapter 49

New Wave
Jon
Hong Kong, British Crown Colony

On June 4th, four years after Tiananmen, a somber crowd gathered in Victoria Park to pay homage to the lives lost on this day. Candlelight stretched across the lawn in trembling halos, and Jon stood among them—still, silent, his callused hands cradling a single flame.

The night was thick with heat and memory. Around him, faces blurred in the soft glow, each one marked by grief or defiance, or both. The flicker of his candle pulled him inward—to Tai.

Boisterous, brilliant Tai. Jon could still hear his laughter at the Shazhou Night Market and see his arms outstretched before the tank, fearless. That memory burned brighter than the flame in his hand.

Then Sun. The last glimpse of her—a figure walking calmly forward to meet the impossible. She hadn't just followed the cause; she'd walked into its fire.

And Xia. He didn't know what had become of her. That silence gnawed at him more than the answers he already carried.

His grip on the candle tightened.

Back in Gansu, after telling Master Shen everything, he had never spoken of the massacre again. But tonight, under Hong Kong's dark sky, memory broke through. Not just of Tai and Sun—but of those still living.

Kim. Ethan. His parents. Their voices were close, even here. The distance he had built—out of necessity—was suddenly thin.

The vigil began to dissolve. One by one, candles dimmed. The crowd drifted toward bars and teahouses, their footsteps muted on the concrete.

"Aren't you Li Wei, the film star?" A soft voice startled him.

Jon turned to find a young woman standing nearby, a tentative smile on her face. He nodded, unsure how to respond.

"Won't you join us at The Tap Room? They've got a great selection of craft beers. It's just a casual gathering—some of us from the vigil."

He managed a polite smile, shaking his head. "Thanks, maybe another time," he said before turning away.

The crowd scattered as Jon made his way out of the park. The humid Hong Kong night pressed against his skin like a warm and sticky veil. Wang's heated words on the set of Golden Cinema that afternoon replayed in his mind, each one laced with bitterness and accusation.

Golden Cinema had become a second battlefield for Jon—a space where the competition for stardom was as fierce as any martial arts duel. He hadn't sought out the world of film; it had found him, capitalizing on his martial arts background and what directors called his "screen presence." To Jon, it was strange to think of himself as a leading man, but the opportunities kept coming. Wang the longstanding lead in the studio's action blockbusters, had not taken kindly to Jon's rise.

271

His frustration had boiled over when Jon was cast as the romantic lead in a new motion picture, a role that marked a departure from the studio's traditional formula. Wang had taken it as a betrayal—a blow to the camaraderie they'd shared as martial artists.

Jon's senses sharpened as he exited the park. A prickling sensation crept up the back of his neck, a telltale sign that someone was watching. He glanced over his shoulder and caught sight of a figure lingering in the shadows, mirroring his steps. Wang. Even in the dim light, his distinctive stride and the tension in his posture gave him away. The way he moved, deliberate and steady, carried a latent menace that sent a chill down Jon's spine.

Jon's heart quickened as Wang trailed him through the city streets. The vibrant energy of Hong Kong had dimmed into hush, leaving only the occasional hum of passing cars and the distant clang of harbor cranes. The path led them to the isolated shipping docks where rows of stacked containers loomed like silent sentinels. Under the harsh glare of neon lights, the two men finally stopped, facing each other.

"Why, Li?" Wang demanded, his voice raw with emotion. "How could you betray our years together like this?"

Jon's mind raced, but he held his composure. "Wang, I'm sorry. I never meant for this to happen. Golden Cinema is changing direction, yes, but not at the cost of our friendship."

"Friendship?" Wang spat the word as if it burned his tongue. "You call this friendship? Stealing the spotlight while I'm cast aside like an old relic?"

"It wasn't my intention," Jon said. "You know how

this industry works. It's not about loyalty but who fits the role. I didn't ask for this."

"Loyalty," Wang repeated bitterly. He stepped closer, his movements sharp, his voice rising. "You could have shown loyalty! You could have held back, made me look better. Instead, you left me in the shadows. To me, that's betrayal."

Jon didn't flinch, meeting Wang's heated gaze. "I held back, Wang. I've tried to honor our bond."

"Honor?" Wang's fury ignited further. "You think leaving me in the dust is honor? You've taken everything from me—my spotlight, my legacy. Your journey ends here, Li Wei!"

Wang lunged, his movements wild but dangerously fast. Jon shifted into a defensive stance, years of training snapping into place. Wang's strikes came hard and relentless, forcing Jon to block and counter. Each blow sent a jolt up Jon's arms, the brutal force of the fight grounding him in its stark reality. This wasn't the practiced choreography of a movie set—it was raw, chaotic, and far too real.

Wang's rage blurred his technique. His strikes turned wild, leaving openings. Jon saw his moment—snapped a kick to the chest that sent Wang stumbling back.

In an instant, Wang's foot caught on the edge of a metal dock cleat, and he fell. His head struck the sharp horns of the cleat with a sickening thud. The sound echoed across the empty docks, followed by a heavy silence.

Jon froze, his breath caught in his throat. He stepped closer, his gaze falling on Wang's motionless form. The man's eyes stared blankly into the night, the spark of life extinguished.

A cold weight settled over Jon's chest as the reality sank in. Wang was dead.

His pulse thundered in his ears. Every instinct screamed at him to leave. He scanned the area. Shadows stretched long across the docks, the harbor lights flickering against the water. No witnesses. Jon turned and walked away, forcing his movements to stay measured despite the tension coiled in his chest. The weight of what had just happened pressed down with every step.

By the time he reached the vigil crowd at the edge of the park, their soft murmurs and candlelit faces were a world apart. Someone recognized him, called his name. Another group invited him to The Tap Room. This time, he didn't refuse.

The blast of air-conditioning hit him like a slap as he stepped inside, cooling the sweat still clinging to his skin. He shivered, but it wasn't from the cold. The images from the docks stayed with him, vivid and unrelenting. No matter how loud the bar grew around him, the silence he left behind was louder.

****

The city awoke to the shock of the dockside tragedy the next morning. News of Wang's death rippled through Hong Kong, reaching the kwoon and the Golden Cinema set where cast and crew faced intense questioning.

Jon watched it all unfold like an outsider in his own life. His world, once defined by martial arts and acting, had shifted into something unrecognizable—a space dominated by police interviews and a truth he couldn't share. The memory of Wang's final moments clung to him like a second skin.

By noon, Jon's alibi was ironclad. He was no longer a person of interest. Dozens of witnesses from the vigil, along with the patrons of The Tap Room, confirmed his presence miles from the docks. Napkins and forearms scrawled with his autograph added further proof. The city speculated on the cause of Wang's death. Headlines shifted, the investigation continued.

Wang's absence was a ghost that moved through the kwoon and the Golden Cinema set—unseen, but always present. The camaraderie among the martial artists had shifted, muted by grief and uncertainty. Training continued, but something essential had fractured.

On set, Master Peng stood motionless in the shadows, arms folded, his presence a steady anchor amid the noise of lights, cranes, and shouted directions. He said little, but his eyes missed nothing.

Then Frank Castle arrived.

The American filmmaker, from Sunset Pictures, stepped on the set with authority. Where others moved with urgency, Castle moved with intent, taking in the actors, the choreography, the pacing. His gaze landed on Jon and stayed there.

He approached. "Li Wei," he said, extending a hand. "Frank Castle, Sunset Pictures. I've heard good things. You're exactly what we need."

Jon accepted the handshake, surprised by its firmness. Castle's tone carried confidence without arrogance—an offer wrapped in inevitability.

Jon's thoughts raced. Wang's death, the coming handover to China, the unease that had settled over the city—all of it made the offer feel like a door cracking open. Not just escape. Renewal.

Castle didn't pitch it like a salesman. "We're putting

together something real. A US co-production. We need authenticity. You've got it."

Jon glanced at Master Peng, who stood watching them. Without hesitation, Jon crossed to him and bowed. "Sifu, I've been offered a role. It may take me away from the kwoon for a while. But I won't accept without your blessing."

Peng studied him. "You came here to train, not to chase fame," he said. Then his expression softened. "But life is movement. If this is the right next step for you, take it. You'll know if it's not."

Jon bowed again, the weight of the decision lightened by the master's trust.

He returned to Castle. "I'm in."

Castle nodded. "We'll get the paperwork started. We'll be in touch soon."

As Castle walked away, Jon looked once more at Master Peng, who gave the faintest of nods.

Chapter 50

Synchronicity
Ethan
Hollywood, California

Frank Castle swept an arm around Ethan's shoulders as he guided him across the bustling film set. Equipment and crew members buzzed around them like bees in a hive. Spotlights cast long shadows that danced on the backdrop of makeshift skyscrapers. Castle's smile was as polished and brilliant as a Hollywood marquee sign.

"Ethan"—he gestured toward a man standing some distance away—"I'd like you to meet someone vital to this production."

They moved closer, and Ethan sized up a figure built like a fortress, broad shoulders set atop a formidable frame. The man stood like a monolith amid the chaos, his gaze intense and discerning, his stance one of disciplined power.

"Li Wei is a martial artist from Hong Kong," Castle continued, gesturing toward him. "His screen presence and martial arts expertise is exactly what we need."

Ethan extended a hand, and Li's grip conveyed a silent message of strength. His stance was economical, grounded—like someone who knew how to move without wasting energy. Something in his posture and the feel of his handshake tugged at Ethan's memory, though he couldn't quite place it.

"Li, meet Ethan. He's not just any fight choreographer. He's a protege of Master Hin from San Luis Obispo. The guy's a legend. Ethan's got a gift for turning rough fighters into graceful combatants. His moves are pure poetry." Castle clapped Ethan on the back, his confidence in the pair unmistakable.

Castle's gaze ping-ponged between the two men. "You will collaborate over the next three weeks, orchestrating the fight sequences for *Shadow Fist Chronicles*. This movie, gentlemen, is set to redefine martial arts cinema."

Weeks unfolded in a blur of sweat, camera lights, and combat choreography. Paired with Li Wei, the martial arts star from Hong Kong, Ethan threw himself into the work—mapping out sequences that blended brutal efficiency with cinematic grace.

From their first rehearsal, something about Li's movement tugged at Ethan's memory.

As they practiced, their rhythm synced naturally—it wasn't just skill. It was something deeper. Familiar.

During a break, Ethan wiped sweat from his brow and said, "Your technique feels…known. Like déjà vu."

Li's hands stilled. "I've trained under many masters," he said evenly.

Ethan tilted his head. "It's not just the form—it's the way you move. Like I've seen it before."

"Perhaps our paths crossed without us knowing. The martial world is smaller than people think."

Ethan narrowed his eyes slightly, studying him. "Ever been to San Francisco? Unity in Motion? Tiananmen solidarity rally?"

For a beat, Li's expression faltered—something

flashed across his face. Then it vanished. "I was in China. During the real thing."

The answer was clipped but true—honest with something unsaid beneath it, heavy with implication.

"Maybe I remind you of someone," Li added and looked away.

Ethan opened his mouth but stopped. The conversation had shifted—walls rising as quickly as they'd almost come down.

At the end of the day, Li bowed low. "Our work is complete."

Ethan returned the gesture, a knot of questions tightening in his chest. "I have a feeling our work's just beginning."

As Li disappeared into the bustling set, Ethan stood motionless, the sense of mystery surrounding the man gnawing at him like an itch he couldn't scratch. There was something there—something unspoken, just out of reach.

Ethan drove the winding coastal road toward San Luis Obispo, seeking the man who had taught him how to stand still inside a storm. The ocean shimmered beyond the cliffs, steady and immense, its rhythm familiar after all these years. He wasn't the young man who used to train barefoot on these beaches at dawn, hungry for praise or progress. Now he was a father, a husband, a teacher. But something inside him still turned like a compass needle toward his old master when the center of things began to shift. He needed to see Master Hin—not for answers, exactly, but for the inner clarity that had always followed their time together.

Ethan pulled off his shoes and stepped onto the sand, the grains warm underfoot. Master Hin stood facing the sea, arms crossed behind his back, watching the surf with a stillness that seemed carved from the landscape itself. He radiated the focus of a man who had long since made peace with what he couldn't control.

Ethan crossed the sand without calling out. As he approached from behind, the wiry man addressed him, never looking away from the sea.

"Ethan, you carry something heavy," the old man said.

"Something's been nagging at me since LA," Ethan said.

Hin didn't turn. "Li Wei."

Ethan stopped short. "You know?"

Hin turned to fully face him. "Show me the last kata I taught you."

Ethan hesitated, then took his stance. With a deep breath, he moved into the form—fluid, focused, the sequence a part of him. His arms cut clean lines through the air. His feet sank and pivoted in the sand with practiced power. Each strike and sweep landed sharp and grounded.

When he reached the end, Hin gave a quiet nod. "Good. But not finished. Try again—with intention."

Ethan bowed and began again, this time leaning into the transitions, letting his breath guide the shifts. By the final step, his skin glistened with sweat and his pulse thudded in his ears.

"Now," Hin said, gesturing him to follow, "something new."

Master Hin stepped into a stance Ethan didn't recognize—a tight coil of tension that exploded into a series of low sweeping kicks and deflective strikes. The movements were compact, circular. No wasted energy.

No show. Just economy and control.

"Internal style," Hin said as he slowed. "Silk-reeling, spiral power. Useful when strength and speed fail—when the body ages but the mind sharpens."

Ethan mirrored the form. It was deceptively difficult, demanding coordination that resisted brute force. Hin corrected his alignment with light touches, barely brushing his shoulder or foot but changing everything.

As the session stretched on, the kata began to unfold in Ethan's body like a puzzle snapping into place. He moved with growing confidence, drawing deeper into the spiral patterns, anchoring his mind in breath and intention.

They stopped only when the tide crept toward them.

Hin studied him. "Still thinking about Li Wei?"

Ethan nodded. "There's something about him I can't place."

Master Hin said nothing for a while, watching the slow curl of waves along the shore. Finally, he asked, "Did he say where he trained?"

"Hong Kong," Ethan replied. "But he was vague. Careful. And there were moments—little gestures, certain phrases—that triggered something. It was like sparring with someone I'd fought a hundred times before."

"Then maybe you have," Hin said. "Not in body, perhaps. But in spirit."

Ethan gave a half-smile. "Sounds like one of your riddles, Sifu."

Master Hin tilted his head, the faint smile lingering. "The world of kung fu is like a river. It has many branches, many tributaries, but they all flow toward the same sea. When two streams meet, it is not by accident. It is by nature."

"Thank you, Sifu." Ethan bowed and absorbed this in silence.

As they packed up, the sun dipped low on the water, casting a golden sheen across the waves. And still, Ethan's thoughts churned.

****

The phone was ringing before Ethan even stepped foot into his hotel room. The insistent sound cut through the stillness. He tossed his bag onto the bed and snatched up the receiver.

"Ethan, where have you been? I've been calling all night. You need to come back, now," Kim said, her voice strained.

A knot formed in his chest. "What's going on? Are you and Logan all right?"

"It's Dali."

Everything inside Ethan stilled.

"He collapsed." Kim's voice broke. "The doctors aren't sure what's wrong. Neurological, maybe something toxic—they're running tests, but it's bad."

The clarity Ethan had found moments ago scattered like sand in the wind. He clenched the phone, his chest constricting. "Why didn't you call me sooner?"

"It started small," she said, her voice cracking. "Just nausea and vomiting. Then a student noticed his speech slurring. By this afternoon, he was so confused and weak he could barely stand. And then—" She faltered. "He collapsed, Ethan. He had a seizure. We called an ambulance."

His pulse raced, his thoughts a jumbled mess of images—Dali teaching at the center, animated, telling a

282

story, his hand firm on Logan's shoulder. "He's in the hospital now?"

"They've run every test they can think of—heart problems, kidney failure—they don't know what's causing it. The doctors say...he could fall into a coma."

He gripped the edge of the desk, his knuckles whitening. "I'll get the first flight out."

Chapter 51

The Poisoning
Ethan
Grand Rapids, Michigan

Ethan pushed through the hospital's cold white corridors, Kim's midnight call still echoing in his ears. "He's in ICU. It's bad."

At the reception desk, the nurse barely glanced up as she rattled off the room number. Ethan moved quickly, his footsteps echoing, but he faltered just outside the doorway.

The beeping monitors broke the hush as Ethan stepped to Dali's bedside. His skin was pale under the fluorescent lights, stretched thin over sharp cheekbones. The calm strength that had once filled every room, now lay silent. Ethan reached for his hand—cold, too still.

"Dali?" His voice barely rose above a whisper.

Nothing.

"Are you family?" the nurse asked gently as she approached.

"I might as well be." He swallowed hard, his throat dry. "I need to speak to a doctor. Now."

Minutes later, Dr. Matthews, a serious-looking man with kind eyes, pulled him aside. "I understand you're close to Mr. Guo," he began. "I won't sugarcoat it. Dali ingested a significant amount of ethylene glycol. The damage is severe."

Ethan's stomach lurched. "Antifreeze?" The word didn't belong here, not in this sterile hospital, not in the same sentence with Dali. "How?"

"We're not sure yet. We haven't been able to reach his daughter. What we do know is that it's highly toxic. We administered fomepizole and started dialysis," Dr. Matthews said. "But he's in a coma. You should be prepared."

Ethan's legs buckled, and he dropped into the chair. His breath came fast, shallow. His mind clawed for answers, but all he could hear was the relentless beep of Dali's heart monitor.

"What are his chances?"

Dr. Matthews shook his head. "It's too soon to tell. He could stabilize, but...you should prepare for the possibility that he won't."

Dali had always been the unshakable one—the steady presence, the guiding hand. And now? Reduced to machines keeping him alive.

Dr. Matthews placed a reassuring hand on his shoulder. "Stay as long as you need. If he wakes up, familiar voices might help."

Ethan barely nodded. *If.* That single word carried too much weight.

Ethan absently moved back to Dali's bedside and clasped his friend's hand again, rubbing his thumb over the rough, calloused skin. It didn't make sense. Dali was meticulous about what he put in his body. This *wasn't* an accident.

He blinked, and a long-buried memory surfaced— the still figure of Scotty, his childhood dog. Ethan and Robert had found him stiff in the garage, a faint, frostlike residue clinging to the fur around his nose and mouth. Sweet. Odorless. A silent killer.

Now here he was again, staring at someone he loved, watching poison steal their life.

He clenched his jaw, forcing down the raw ache in his throat.

Who would want to hurt Dali?

Back at home, Ethan paced while Kim sat motionless on the couch, her silence louder than any apology.

"He's in a coma." His voice was hoarse, the weight of the words pressing down on him. "No one can find Yan, and I need to talk to her. Where is she?"

She flinched, guilt flickering across her face. "Ethan… I should have told you."

He turned sharply, the hair on his neck rising. "Told me what?"

She hesitated, her fingers tightening in her lap. "Yan's on a business trip with Mu."

Ethan froze. "A what?"

"She left before Dali fell ill," she rushed on. "Mu convinced her it would be an adventure," Kim said.

Ethan stared. "While her grandfather's dying?"

"They're picking up knockoff Beanie Buddies in California, selling them to distributors in New York and Canada."

The words barely registered.

He stared at her. "You're joking."

She shook her head.

Ethan ran a hand over his face, his pulse thrumming. *Mu convinced her.*

The words lodged in his chest like a blade. Too convenient. Too perfectly timed.

He looked at Kim, searching her face. "Have you spoken to her?"

"I'm trying. Her cell goes straight to voicemail." Her eyes shone with worry. "I don't understand any of this, Ethan."

Neither did he. But a storm was building in his chest, and for the first time since stepping off the plane, he knew one thing for certain.

This wasn't just bad timing. It was too clean. Too orchestrated. Ethan looked at Kim and saw it in her face, too. They were already in the middle of something—and the worst was still ahead.

Part Six 1997

Chapter 52

Fame
Jon
Los Angeles, California

"Cut!" Frank Castle hollered from the aerial platform, his voice slicing through the noise of the set. "That's a keeper." He was already leaning toward the cameraman, animated as they reviewed the flawless take.

Jon stayed in position, breath steady, muscles still buzzing from the exertion. As he straightened, Frank clattered down the metal staircase, his face lit with approval.

"That fight scene was extraordinary!" Frank slapped Jon on the back. "One take—you've still got it!"

Jon allowed himself a brief grin. "It felt right."

Frank motioned toward the open lot beyond the soundstage. They stepped outside, and the late afternoon sun hit like a hammer. Jon lifted a hand to shield his eyes. After weeks inside under artificial lights, daylight was almost foreign.

"I've been thinking about the ending," Frank said. "Ethan's choreography is next level—the final sequence will blow people away. But I want to tweak something. You're the only one who can nail it."

Jon's thoughts were drifting. The staged fights, the relentless hours, the perfect hits—they were starting to feel hollow. Like fighting shadows.

"I'll give you something unforgettable," Jon said suddenly. "But I need the rest of the day. Recharge a bit. Tomorrow—you'll get something better than extraordinary."

Frank raised an eyebrow, then chuckled. "I trust you, Li. Go on. You've earned it."

Jon stepped barefoot across the parking lot, the rough pavement grounding him in a way the studio never could. His body, trained for violence and discipline, was restless. The sun bore down, and for the first time in a long while, it was real.

At Alta Vista, his mansion on the hill, he showered quickly and changed into fresh clothes. As he stepped toward the front door, Thomas, his house steward, met him with a travel mug.

"Your favorite tea, for the road. Be safe, Li Wei."

Jon accepted it with a nod, then paused. "One more thing—send a check to Master Peng in Hong Kong. Enough to keep the kwoon running for a year. Don't put my name on it."

Thomas hesitated, but only for a second before nodding. "Of course, sir."

Jon lingered in the doorway. "He gave me more than I paid for. It's time I gave something back."

"Very good," Thomas said.

Jon slipped into the red convertible, and the leather seats were hot from the afternoon sun. He turned the key, and the engine growled to life. He pointed the car north toward San Luis Obispo, the Pacific glinting beside him as the cliffs peeled away like the edge of a film reel.

For four years, fame had scripted his life—press tours, premieres, fight scenes, applause. He had everything. Yet the silence of Alta Vista rang louder than any ovation. He couldn't remember the last real conversation he'd had with anyone but Thomas, who brought tea, not questions.

The coastline blurred past, wild and open. Jon's thoughts drifted to Ethan—and the past he'd buried under new names and bright lights. He wasn't sure what he was chasing. Only that he couldn't keep pretending it wasn't missing.

Jon pulled into the driveway of Master Hin's beach house, his heart hammering. The property was simple, almost spartan—weathered wood, sun-bleached stone, and a garden of carefully placed pebbles and shells. Clusters of Mexican firecracker burst between the rocks, red blossoms vivid against the sand.

He hesitated, then made his way toward the beach. There, beneath a swaying palm, sat Master Hin.

Cross-legged, motionless, the old man seemed as vast and still as the ocean behind him. His face bore the softness of age, but his eyes were ancient—deep and unflinching.

"I am Li Wei," Jon said, bowing.

Master Hin barely looked up. "The famous martial artist. And why does Li Wei seek me?"

"To deepen my mastery, as I did in China and Hong Kong."

The master finally met his gaze, his eyes piercing—searching. "Show me."

Jon took a breath and moved. One kata. Then another. His body flowed through each with practiced control, honed by years of training and performance.

Every stance, every strike—measured, exact, complete.

When he finished, Hin gestured for him to sit.

Then, without a word, the master reached forward and cupped Jon's face in his hands.

Jon tensed, startled by the intimacy of the gesture. Hin's thumbs traced his cheekbones slowly as he studied him—deeper than Jon expected or wanted.

Finally, he said, almost whispering, "Your hands are strong, but your heart is hollow."

Jon flinched. "I don't understand. What's missing?"

Hin let go. "Who is Li Wei, truly?"

Jon straightened. "I am Li Wei. The martial artist."

Hin's gaze didn't waver. "And when the name fades? What remains?"

The words cut deep. Jon clenched his fists. "I don't know."

Hin exhaled, the breath slow and deliberate. "Then you are not ready."

Jon's pulse roared in his ears. "What?"

"Go," Hin said. "Return when you have your answer."

Jon stood abruptly, anger rising to fill the sudden emptiness. "This is ridiculous."

But as he stalked away, the master's question echoed inside him.

Who is Li Wei, truly?

The red convertible surged up the highway, engine snarling beneath him. The wind tore at his hair, but Jon barely noticed.

His name, his fame, the life he'd built—smoke slipping through his fingers.

He had choreographed every move, controlled every word. And now one man's question had shattered that illusion. His chest tightened. His breath hitched.

For years, he'd run from his past. Reinvented himself. But what if Li Wei was just another disguise? The name had been his fortress. But now, the walls were crumbling. And for the first time, he didn't know who he was.

Chapter 53

Coast to Coast
Kim
Grand Rapids, Michigan

Kim followed Yan to the locker room after a hard sparring session. After nearly two decades of training together, she knew the signs—tight shoulders, slow exhale, a guarded silence. Yan was worn down, and not just from the fight.

"These trips are draining you," Kim said, lowering herself onto the bench. "We haven't trained in months."

Yan gave a faint laugh. "You wouldn't believe the Beanie Buddy craze in Canada and New York. Mu's knockoffs are flying."

Kim blinked. "Seriously? You're hauling toys cross-country?"

Yan nodded. "In person. Mu insists on face-to-face connections, especially for the Canadian buyers. Says it builds trust."

Kim frowned. "Seems like something a shipping company could handle."

Yan hesitated, then brushed it off. "He just likes doing it this way. And…he wants me there."

Kim studied her. "Just be careful. You know how to read people. Does any of this feel right to you?"

Yan's smile came too fast. "It's just toys, Kim."

Kim didn't push. Not yet.

That afternoon, the training hall pulsed with motion. The air buzzed with the slap of feet on mats, the pop of punches on pads. Across the room, Ethan guided Logan through a balance drill—spin, stop, strike. The boy wobbled, caught himself, and laughed.

"Again!" Ethan called. Logan turned too fast and toppled.

"Remember to breathe," Kim said, hands on her hips.

"I *am* breathing," Logan shot back, smirking through the sweat.

Ethan tossed him a towel. "Your mom's right. She usually is. You know she took gold in three divisions at her last tournament, right?"

Kim rolled her eyes. "Don't start."

"I want to hear that story," Logan said, eyes wide.

Ethan grinned. "She outpaced a field of black belts half her age. Lightning-fast hands, perfect control—every match was textbook."

Kim shrugged, trying not to smile. "It's not about strength. It's about timing—and knowing when to strike."

Logan nodded, reset, and tried again—stronger, steadier.

As he trained, Kim exchanged a glance with Ethan—the kind of look they shared after years of trust. But behind her smile, Kim's thoughts were elsewhere.

That night, after the house had settled, Kim curled into Ethan, their bedroom dim but for the soft glow from the hallway.

"Something's wrong with Yan," she murmured.

He turned to face her. "You've noticed it too."

"She says it's Beanie Buddies, but Mu's dragging her cross-country, even into Canada, all by car? No shipping, no tracking? It doesn't add up."

He held the pause. "I've had my own suspicions."

She sat up slightly, her voice low. "Mu's isolating her. She's exhausted. She won't open up, but I can feel it—he's pulling her into something toxic."

"She's not just tired," he agreed. "She's scared. And Dali's poisoning still doesn't sit right with me."

Her chest tightened. "You think they're connected?"

"It's possible." He ran a hand down her arm. "When I get back from California, we'll talk to her. Together. We'll get to the bottom of this."

Kim nodded and rested her head on his chest. The steady rhythm of his heart anchored her. "She's family," she whispered. "We protect our own."

Ethan held her closer. "Always."

Chapter 54

Unraveled
Jon
Los Angeles, California

Thomas Hsu drew back the brocade drapes, letting the afternoon sun spill into the dim master suite. Jon squinted behind mirrored sunglasses, sprawled across silken sheets.

The TV hummed softly, looping DVDs of Jon's box office hits. Familiar scenes flashed—choreographed fights, gravity-defying stunts, a vibrant version of himself moving with effortless precision.

A ghost now of the man he used to be.

"You probably hear Frank Castle again. He say he sue your Chinese ass. You never work again." Thomas's voice stayed calm, betraying no hint of how serious it was.

Jon's mind was a fog, but Frank Castle's name cut through it. Memories of the set, the rehearsals, the brilliant lights—all seemed distant now.

Thomas poured a cup of tea and held it to Jon's parched lips. He drank as Thomas tilted the cup. Something in Thomas' nod—subtle, assured—suggested approval. "I call Lawyer Tan. He make sure Mr. Castle not come here again. No more harassment."

Jon said nothing, his mind still grappling with Frank

Castle's threat. How had it come to this?

Since returning from San Luis Obispo, Jon had barely moved, barely existed. His body had given up on him. His mind, worse. The mansion, once a testament to his success, was now suffocating—a tomb built for a man who no longer existed.

Through the fog of his days, one thing remained constant. Thomas.

Jon had met him years ago—just a waiter at a favorite restaurant. Somewhere along the way, he'd become more. A caretaker. An unassuming presence keeping the house from crumbling like Jon had.

Jon never asked him to stay. But Thomas was there anyway—boiling herbs, pruning the garden, handling what needed handling. The soft rustling of paper signaled the daily ritual Jon had grown used to.

Thomas began reading the daily mail aloud.

"Dear Li Wei, of all the kung fu experts in the world, you are the greatest. I have seen every one of your movies, and my mother said I can start taking kung fu lessons on my twelfth birthday, which is only three weeks away. What I would like most for my birthday is a personally autographed poster of you."

Thomas set the letter down. "Yes, we definitely send Randy Baker autographed poster."

Jon closed his eyes. The innocence in the boy's words—so pure, so full of joy—stood in painful contrast to the void inside him.

Thomas continued, methodically opening envelopes—solicitations, talk show requests, appeals for donations. Then, among them, another invitation. Jon barely listened. These letters, once his lifeblood, now seemed written to someone else entirely.

A burst of light from the screen caught his eye. The past refused to fade.

And then, the latest copy of the Golden Masters Tournament invitation. The third time they'd sent it.

Thomas hesitated before he began reading aloud.

A Global Tournament Celebrating Martial Arts Excellence

Event Highlights: Global Sparring Extravaganza, Kata Kaleidoscope, Weaponry Wonders, and a Special Tribute to

Li Wei

legendary martial artist and film celebrity, for his unparalleled impact on elevating martial arts in film and entertainment

Date: Saturday, November 15, 1997

Venue: Los Angeles Memorial Sports Arena

Time: Noon to 10:00 P.M.

His voice carried something close to excitement as he folded the invitation and tucked it into his pocket. "Li, you are invited to be honored. This event could be a new beginning for you. People honor you. Have you been listening to the letters I read each day? They want you back. They love you."

Jon turned his head away. "What do they love, Thomas? The image they've created? The celebrity? The martial artist?"

Thomas' hand rested gently on his arm. "They love what you represent. Strength. Honor. Discipline. You can find yourself again."

Jon's throat tightened. "I don't know who I am anymore."

Thomas's eyes were kind. "We will find it, Li. Together."

But Jon wasn't sure there was anything left to find.

The doorbell's chime pulled Jon from his haze. He barely noticed Thomas stepping away to answer it, his attention drifting back to the flickering images on the TV screen—a younger, stronger version of himself frozen in time.

Moments later, a man entered the room—tall, with a sharply trimmed beard and a contained intensity in his gaze. He carried a leather briefcase, his suit crisp and professional.

Thomas, standing beside him, folded his arms. "This Dr. Xavier," he said. "Sunset Pictures send him."

Jon didn't respond.

Dr. Xavier offered a polite nod before pulling a chair beside the bed. "Mr. Li Wei, I'm here to assess your well-being on behalf of the studio. They're concerned about you—and, of course, the completion of *Shadow Fist Chronicles*."

Jon ignored the outstretched hand.

If the doctor was bothered, he didn't show it. "Before we begin, I'd like you to remove your sunglasses."

Jon hesitated.

"I need to check your pupils." The doctor shined a small flashlight.

After a long moment, Jon exhaled slowly and slid the glasses off. The light flicked across his eyes, and he flinched at the intrusion, his vision adjusting sluggishly.

Dr. Xavier switched off the flashlight, studying him. "Can you hear me, Mr. Li Wei?"

Before Jon could answer, Thomas scoffed. "Of course, he hear you. You waste time."

Dr. Xavier ignored him. "What are you feeling?"

299

His voice was calm. "Whatever you say remains confidential."

Jon remained silent, watching himself on screen—his younger self, executing flawless techniques, movements sharp, controlled.

A man he no longer recognized.

Dr. Xavier followed his gaze. "How does it feel to watch yourself on film?"

"I am not Li Wei," Jon said, his voice hollow as he turned to him for the first time. "Li Wei is dead."

Dr. Xavier's expression remained neutral. "How did Li Wei die?"

"He was buried in a mine collapse in northern China."

A beat of silence.

Dr. Xavier leaned forward slightly. "Perhaps we can rescue him."

Jon's lips barely parted. "No, I tried."

The final moments of *Iron Palm* played on the screen—his greatest fight scene, one he considered the best he had ever filmed. His gaze remained locked on it. He was lost in the past and hardly noticed Thomas rising to his feet or the muted exchange between the two men. He only vaguely registered the sound of footsteps retreating, the closing of a door.

Because Li Wei was dead.

And Jon had yet to figure out who remained.

****

Six months had slipped by since Jon's visit to Master Hin, the passage of time nothing more than a dull undercurrent. The days ran together—until something on the television screen cut through the haze.

Thomas had been about to slide in another one of

Jon's movies when the news flashed to a scene in Hong Kong. The Pillar of Shame sculpture filled the screen—its twenty-six-foot depiction of piled bodies standing as a stark reminder of the Tiananmen Square massacre. The date was June 4th.

Jon's breath hitched. A sharp, visceral reaction ran through him.

"Tai spoke truth when all were silent," Master Shen had gazed at him with sadness. "And he had the talent to have been my successor one day. His life was precious…and lost to those who value only power and wealth. Now he feeds worms and maggots."

Jon sat up. The motion foreign, his muscles stiff from neglect, but the sudden clarity commanded movement. He pulled off his sunglasses and stretched, rolling his shoulders. The fire that had gone dormant inside him flared to life.

He needed to move.

Thomas, hovering nearby, hesitated. Surprise flashed across his face before shifting into something else—something closer to recognition. And Thomas didn't stop him.

That very day, Jon began training. At first, his body rebelled. Years of pushing himself to his limit had been undone in mere months of stillness. His strength had withered, his endurance drained. But he refused to stop. He ran until his lungs burned. Lifted weights until his arms trembled. Practiced five hundred kicks and strikes a day, sweat pooling beneath him, muscles aching from the relentless assault. He consumed the food Thomas prepared not with hunger, but with raw desperation—devouring every bite as if his survival depended on it. His body gave out more than once, collapsing under exhaustion. But even then, when his limbs failed and vision blurred, he refused to stay down.

He rose. Again. And again.

The mirrored walls of the training hall reflected back a man who could not rest. Because rest meant vulnerability. Rest meant the past could catch up to him. And he could not afford that.

The world noticed. Reporters called incessantly, hungry for a scoop on the fallen martial arts legend. Thomas, ever protective, answered them in Mandarin, pretending not to understand English. Then came the headlines.

Li Wei's Psychotic Break—Psychiatrist Declares Him Mentally Imbalanced. Jon saw the words but barely registered them. His training consumed him. Every fiber of his being was focused on regaining what he had lost.

One morning, between sets, his breath still uneven from training, he turned to Thomas and finally spoke about what had haunted him since San Luis Obispo.

"You told me Master Hin put a curse on me," he said, breathing hard. "But the truth is, it was me."

He rolled his neck, then folded forward in a deep stretch, his hands grazing his toes, his body finally responding to the relentless regimen. Soon he moved his training from the bedroom to the studio.

He worked up to one hundred one-handed push-ups, left and right. Ran six miles daily. Lifted until the clang of iron weights became a metronome of determination. The sweat dripped. The muscles bulged. The transformation took hold.

But the question that continued to haunt him, the mystery that drove him to the brink of madness, remained unanswered.

Who was he? What had he lost? And what would it take to find himself again?

Jon exhaled, savoring the cool drink on his lips after an unrelenting workout. The TV droned in the background—news and DVDs echoing past glories. His body still thrummed from exertion, his mind half-focused—until he heard Thomas announce a name he had not expected.

Frank Castle.

Jon blinked. The moment Frank stepped into the room, Jon could see it—this wasn't just a courtesy visit.

Frank extended a handshake. Jon met it with a firm grip.

They exchanged small talk at first—pleasant but superficial. Jon sensed Frank wasn't here for pleasantries.

Finally, the conversation shifted.

"Li," Frank said, "I know the committee of international masters has reached out to you multiple times about the Golden Masters Tournament, but you haven't responded. I'm here today as a friend—to encourage you to accept. The world misses you. Your fans miss you. And I'm not going to lie—it would bring huge attention to *Shadow Fist Chronicles* before its release."

Jon's focus drifted as the news broadcast shifted back to Hong Kong. The Pillar of Shame again filled the screen. The protestors. The defiance. The growing rumors that the police would seize the sculpture—erase history, dismantle memory. And then—Master Shen's voice. "We don't study martial arts to become martyrs. Tai had the potential to make a greater impact in life than in this death."

Jon drew a sharp breath, then turned back to Frank. His spine straightened with resolve.

"I'll do it," he said. "I'll be the honored master at the Golden Masters Tournament."

Chapter 55

Person of Interest
Kim
Grand Rapids, Michigan

Kim glanced at the clock in the kwoon, moving through her warm-up stretches. With Ethan and Logan landing in California earlier that day, she relished a rare girls' night with Yan. As she stretched, a warm sense of gratitude for their deepening bond settled over her.

A sound from the entrance drew her attention. Thinking it was Yan, she didn't turn. "You're early—ready to get a good sweat going?"

The answer came in a rush of movement.

Mu.

His face was hard with fury and intent. Before she could react, he was on her.

Her instincts flared too late. The world tilted—then went black.

When Kim came to, she was tied to a chair, head pounding, vision swaying. Panic surged, but she forced herself to breathe.

Focus.

Mu loomed in front of her, a cruel smile on his lips. Cold steel traced her throat, then down her chest. In a swift motion, he sliced open her uniform.

She clenched her jaw. "What do you want from

me?"

"It's you I want," he said, voice low, controlled.

She glared.

"But first," he continued, "where is Jon?"

There it was.

"What is this?" she snapped. "What did my brother do to you?"

Mu's mouth twisted. "He stole something. Something precious to my sifu in New York. I'm here to get it back."

Her mind raced. *Jon, what the hell have you gotten into?* "Help you?" she spat. "Why the hell would I do that?"

A breeze from a door.

Yan.

Hope surged—then Mu leaned in again.

"Unless you want to end up like Master Dali…"

She froze. "You…" she whispered. "You killed him."

Mu's knife hovered at her chest. With a flick of his wrist, the blade cut through her bra. "Tell me where Jon is…or suffer."

"Mu, leave her alone!" Yan shouted, her voice fire and steel. Her eyes burned.

Mu turned, his stance angling toward Yan—just the opening Kim needed. But his attention didn't return to her. His grip tightened on the knife, breath shallow, weight shifting between his feet. He didn't lower the blade—he didn't move or even look her way.

Yan lunged. "Was any of it real?" she cried, shoving him hard.

Mu stumbled back, barely keeping his footing. The knife slipped from his hand and clattered to the floor.

Kim didn't hesitate.

She rocked the chair with violent force—it toppled onto its side. The frame splintered on impact, just enough. Twisting hard, she wrenched herself free and crawled forward. She grabbed the knife and cut the ropes.

But Mu was moving toward her again. With a grunt, he kicked the blade from her hand and snatched it midair.

He had the knife again.

Kim rose fast, lunged, and drove her thumb toward his eye. He screamed, stumbling back, his free hand clutching his face. Mu snarled, blood dripping from his eye. He raised the knife to attack.

Kim spun, delivering a sharp hook kick to his forearm. The blow knocked his arm sideways, the blade deflected back toward his center.

In the same instant, Yan stepped in—channeling all her fury into a driving front kick aimed squarely at the knife. Impact. The blade drove into Mu's chest.

He staggered, a shocked gasp escaping him. He looked down, eyes wide, the blade of the knife driven straight into his heart.

A beat of silence.

He was dead.

Kim scanned the lifeless body. "I guess this means the engagement is off."

Yan stood frozen, tears streaking her face. "I was so naive."

Kim pulled her into a fierce hug. "Hey, none of this is on you," she said. "Family isn't just blood. It's who stands by you when everything else falls apart." They stood like that, bodies trembling, the adrenaline finally crashing.

307

Then Kim stepped back, wiped a smear of blood from her cheek, and reached for the phone on the front desk. Her fingers shook slightly as she punched in 911.

When she hung up, Yan was still staring at Mu's body, unmoving.

Kim walked back to her, crouched slightly. "It's over. Help is coming."

They sat against the far wall, backs pressed to the mats, breathing slowly as the world outside began to stir again.

The sirens came first—a chorus rising through the dark, pulsing louder by the second. Red and blue lights washed across broken glass and a blood-streaked floor. Police entered, followed by paramedics. A detective examined the scene and took photos. Two EMTs moved swiftly but respectfully, checking Mu's vitals. One shook his head. A gurney was rolled in, and within minutes, Mu's lifeless body was zipped into a black bag and wheeled out.

Later, as officers combed through the wreckage of the center, one approached Kim and Yan. "We found something in the dumpster," he said, holding up a sealed plastic bag.

Kim narrowed her eyes. "What is it?"

The officer opened it. Inside were shredded knockoff Beanie Buddies—Yan's discards from weeks ago. The seams had split open—but it wasn't stuffing inside.

A fine white powder coated the plush remains.

Yan gasped. "What…what is that?"

The officer's face darkened. "Heroin."

Kim's stomach dropped. "That's what they were moving."

"We've been tracking Zheng Mu for some time," the officer continued. "Daniel Wu—private investigator and ex-NYPD—tipped us off. Mu had ties to the Flying Dragons."

Chapter 56

Golden Masters
Jon
Los Angeles, California

Nothing could have prepared Jon for the sight that
awaited him.

As the limousine snaked its way along Da Vinci
Parkway toward the coliseum, he stared out the window
at the sea of people. Thousands had gathered outside the
gates—sleeping bags, beach chairs, even portable stoves.
A pop-up village, humming with anticipation.

A knot formed in his chest.

"Why are all these people in line?" he asked,
bewildered.

Across from him, Frank Castle glanced up from his
documents, then followed Jon's gaze with a smile.
"They're here for you, Li. Fans from all over the world.
They've been waiting a long time."

Jon swallowed hard. *All these people...for me?*

Inside the coliseum, the energy was electric.
Banners from every continent stretched across the
rafters. Contestants buzzed around registration tables
and warm-up rings. It was a global convergence—
martial artists of every discipline and language, all drawn
here by shared discipline and reverence.

The moment Jon stepped into the arena, a hush

rippled outward. Heads turned. Conversations faltered. Then—applause. First scattered, then rolling, then rising like thunder.

Then came the chant.

"Li Wei, Li Wei."

The rhythmic clapping pulsed like a heartbeat, synchronized with the syllables of his name.

Jon stood still. Emotion surged up his throat.

Frank's hand settled on Jon's shoulder. "They never stopped believing in you, Li. Neither did I."

Cameras swarmed. Reporters surged forward.

"Li Wei, what's it like to be back in the spotlight?"

"Can you tell us about your time away?"

"Is it true that you trained with Master Hin?"

Then—the question that hung in the air, weighted with expectation.

"Will you be returning to film?"

Before Jon could respond, Frank Castle stepped in with his signature charm and raised a hand. "Li Wei will take questions and sign autographs after the closing ceremony. But I *can* confirm he'll be returning to the screen—look for *Shadow Fist Chronicles*, hitting theaters this spring."

Flashbulbs fired as Frank ushered Jon away toward the VIP lounge.

Jon stood at the panoramic glass wall, surveying the tournament floor. He spotted Ethan quickly, surrounded by a cluster of students. Among them was a young fighter whose stance made Jon pause—something fierce, familiar in the way he moved. Then Ethan's proud, beaming reaction clicked it into place.

The boy from the photograph—now a grown man. His nephew. Ethan's son.

Jon exhaled, emotion tightening his chest. The legacy hadn't ended—it had evolved. He pressed a hand to the glass, steadying himself. This wasn't just a comeback. This was a bridge to the family he thought he'd lost.

As the day shifted toward evening, the lights of the coliseum grew brighter. The main exhibition floor had been cleared, and the grandstands filled.

Ethan stepped into the spotlight first, carrying a gleaming broadsword. A red silk scarf trailed from the hilt, fluttering like flame with every movement. His form was precise, fluid, powerful—each strike a fusion of control and artistry.

Jon watched in awe. He had trained with Ethan as boys, had sparred and laughed and bled with him—but this was mastery. Not just of the weapon, but of himself.

When Ethan finished, the crowd erupted in cheers.

Then Jon stepped forward.

He carried a Chinese spear—a polished bamboo shaft capped with a sharp steel blade. A tuft of red horsehair flared where wood met steel, catching the light like fire. He took his place at center stage with the spear at his side like a Chinese soldier.

And then—he moved.

He kicked the spear into motion—it arced overhead, spinning through his fingers like liquid. He thrust, pulled back, blocked, and leapt. The red horsehair trailed behind him like a comet's tail. This wasn't performance. It was remembrance. Every technique was an echo of the masters who shaped him. Every breath was a homecoming.

The final flourish brought the blade to a still point above his heart. The crowd thundered. Jon stood, breathing deep, the red plume fluttering in the stillness.

Across the floor, he met Ethan's gaze. Jon's fingers flexed against the spear. Would Ethan even recognize him? Years had reshaped Jon, both inside and out. His face was different. His path had twisted through shadows Ethan had never walked. He wasn't just returning to the spotlight—he was stepping back into a life where the people he once called family might see him as a stranger.

Then, from the center stage, another figure emerged—his satin and gold uniform shimmering under the lights. Master Hin. The crowd hushed in an instant, reverence rippling through the air. A microphone descended from the rigging and stopped just before his lips.

"Ladies and gentlemen," he began, his voice echoing through the vast space. "Tonight, we present an unprecedented sparring match between the renowned celebrity, Li Wei, and the highly respected martial artist, Master Ethan Wolf."

The jumbotron flashed to Ethan, capturing the widening of his eyes, the flicker of surprise tightening his jaw. Jon's pulse pounded. The two took their places.

The crowd buzzed with anticipation, but for Jon, the world narrowed to the man standing before him. The match began. Each movement was a clash of precision and well-honed reflexes, their attacks fluid, measured, deadly in their control. The exchange unfolded like a dance—choreographed yet raw, fierce yet intimate. It became a conversation—of years past, secrets shared, lessons learned.

And then something inside Jon shifted. Something passed between them. Recognition. Not of faces. Not of names. But of warriors who had walked different paths—and found themselves here, standing in the same place once more.

Jon stepped back, hands lowered at his sides.

"This match is a draw." His voice rang clear. Then he bowed—deep, humble, final.

The arena erupted.

Because the real victory wasn't reclaiming a title. It was in remembering who he was—and where he belonged.

****

The crowd's roar had long since faded, the journalists had departed, and the dazzling lights had dimmed. The coliseum stood empty, its silence a stark contrast to the storm of energy that had filled it hours before.

Jon sat alone in his dressing room, staring into the mirror. The face looking back at him was Li Wei, the martial arts legend. But the eyes belonged to someone else. Someone he hadn't faced in a long time. Someone he wasn't sure he still knew.

A creak at the door. Jon didn't turn.

A moment passed.

"Jon…is that you?" Ethan's voice broke the silence—gentle, hesitant, carrying the weight of a question that had waited years to be spoken.

A tremor ran through him. Not from the fight. Not from exhaustion. But from the moment he had never let himself imagine. Past and present collided like a storm, leaving him adrift. His pulse pounded in his ears, loud and unrelenting.

Jon gripped the edge of the vanity, grounding himself against the swirl of emotion rising inside him. He forced himself to look up again, to meet his own gaze in the mirror. "Yes, old friend," he said. The words caught in his throat—brittle, uncertain. A plea.

He turned then, searching Ethan's face, watching for any flicker of recognition—something to bridge the chasm of time and loss. Ethan didn't look away.

Jon's breath came unevenly, the walls of the room seeming to press in. The past was clawing its way back. Memories surfaced unbidden—laughter, dreams, shared pain. It was all still there, buried beneath years of silence.

"Are my parents alive?" He swallowed hard, his voice breaking under the weight of what he needed to know. The words tore from him. Not just a question. A lifeline.

Ethan met his gaze, steady and sure. "Yes, Jon. They're alive."

The answer landed like a pulse of light in a tunnel Jon had wandered through for too long. The air in his lungs changed. Something deep inside him shifted, cracked open, let go. He hadn't realized how tightly he had held on to the fear that the past had left him with nothing to return to.

The wall around his heart—one he had built out of necessity, out of survival—was breaking. Ethan moved closer, placing a firm, steady hand on Jon's shoulder. "I know exactly who you are."

Jon let out a slow breath, the words settling inside him like an anchor. The mirror before them was no longer just a reflection of a face he barely recognized. It was a window to something real, something remembered. His chest tightened, his grip clenching around an instinct he had spent years suppressing. Then, without thinking, his hand moved to his pocket.

His fingers found the small, tarnished key—the

metal cool, solid, grounding. He turned it over in his palm, tracing the worn edges—past and the future converging in its weight. It wasn't just a key. It was Fourth of July parades, red and blue crepe paper twisting through bicycle spokes. It was his father's steady hands fixing a broken toy. It was Kim's laughter, ringing through the house. It was home.

His hand tightened around it as he lifted his gaze to Ethan. "I'm ready to come home."

Ethan smiled, warmth flickering in his eyes. "Welcome back, Jon."

The words settled deep. Jon exhaled, the tension he hadn't realized he was carrying finally releasing. As Ethan pulled him into an embrace, the weight of the years begin to lift. He was not just Li Wei, the legend. Not just the warrior who had fought his way back. He was Jon Fenton.

And for the first time in a long time, that was enough.

www.ingramcontent.com/pod-product-compliance
Lightning Source LLC
Chambersburg PA
CBHW072100020726
47501CB00003B/657